THE HUNTED HARE

Also by Fay Sampson

For adults:

The Land of Angels
The Flight of the Sparrow
A Casket of Earth
The Island Pilgrimage
The Silent Fort
Star Dancer

The Suzie Fewings series:

In the Blood
A Malignant House
Those in Peril
Father Unknown

The Morgan le Fay series:

Wise Woman's Telling
Nun's Telling
Blacksmith's Telling
Taliesin's Telling
Herself
Daughter of Tintagel (Omnibus edition)

For children:

The Sorcerer's Trap
The Sorcerer's Daughter
Them
Hard Rock

The Pangur Ban series:

Pangur Ban
Finnglas of the Horses
Finnglas and the Stones of Choosing
Shape Shifter
The Serpent of Senargad
The White Horse is Running

Non-fiction:

Visions and Voyages: The Story of Celtic Spirituality
Runes on the Cross: The Story of our Anglo-Saxon Heritage

The Hunted Hare

Fay Sampson

The first volume in The Aidan Mysteries

MONARCH
BOOKS

Oxford, UK & Grand Rapids, Michigan, USA

Copyright © 2012 by Fay Sampson

The right of Fay Sampson to be identified as author of this work has been asserted by her in accordance with the Copyright, Designs and Patents Act 1988.

All rights reserved. No part of this publication may be reproduced or transmitted in any form or by any means, electronic or mechanical, including photocopy, recording or any information storage and retrieval system, without permission in writing from the publisher.

First published in the UK in 2012 by Monarch Books
(a publishing imprint of Lion Hudson plc)
Wilkinson House, Jordan Hill Road, Oxford OX2 8DR, England
Tel: +44 (0)1865 302750 Fax: +44 (0)1865 302757
Email: monarch@lionhudson.com
www.lionhudson.com

ISBN 978 0 85721 204 7 (print)
ISBN 978 0 85721 339 6 (Kindle)
ISBN 978 0 85721 340 2 (epub)

Distributed by:
UK: Marston Book Services, PO Box 269, Abingdon, Oxon, OX14 4YN
USA: Kregel Publications, PO Box 2607, Grand Rapids, Michigan 49501

The text paper used in this book has been made from wood independently certified as having come from sustainable forests.

British Library Cataloguing Data
A catalogue record for this book is available from the British Library.

Printed and bound in the UK by MPG Books.

With thanks to Pollinger Limited, Authors' Agents, www.pollingerltd.com

To Jack

Author's Note

All the characters in this novel are fictitious, and bear no resemblance to any real person, living or dead.

The shrine church at Pennant Melangell and the St Melangell Centre are real, and well worth a visit. For the purposes of this novel I have added the fictional House of the Hare and Capel-y-Cwm. My apologies to local landowners, some of whose land I have appropriated for this.

I have also invented Caradoc Lewis's museum in Llanfyllin.

My thanks to the priest and congregation of St Melangell's Church and the St Melangell Centre for their welcome. The site has a special aura of holiness. My apologies for the fictional damage I have inflicted on their historic church in the course of the novel.

I am grateful to Sergeant Darren Brown for advice on local policing.

To Joyce Perry for her careful critique.

And to my husband, Jack, for allowing me to drag him over steep and thorny Welsh hillsides.

Chapter One

THE BERWYN MOUNTAINS closed in around the narrow lane. Bluebells gleamed in the hedge banks. Aidan wondered whether his camera could capture the subtle blend of young green ferns and violet-blue flowers.

The sign ahead warned them that there was no through road. They drove on.

Two walkers with backpacks flattened themselves against the hedge. The fair young man was almost dwarfed by his rucksack, while the darker-skinned girl carried a lighter load. Aidan steered round them.

In the rear-view mirror, he caught his daughter's small intent face, under its mop of light-brown curls. He grinned at her.

"When your mother and I came, that's what we did. Walked all the way from the village. It's the best way for pilgrims to come to Pennant Melangell. In a little while, there's a footpath you can take over the side of the hill to the church."

"I'm sorry. I'm going to be holding you two back." Jenny's quiet voice came from beside him.

Aidan glanced at her, guilt-stricken. The pink-and-purple scarf hid her bald head, which chemotherapy had robbed of its own unruly curls.

"I didn't mean…"

"I know you didn't." She laid a hand on his knee. Too thin a hand. "Don't worry. Once we're at the House of the

Hare, you two can set off wherever you like. You have to take Melangell to the waterfall."

"Did you call me Melangell because I was conceived here?" The child's voice came from the back seat.

The car swerved as Aidan started.

"Don't look so shocked, Daddy. Michael Jackson called his daughter Paris because that was where she began. Everybody knows that."

Aidan caught Jenny's eye. "Did you know that sort of thing when you were seven?"

She smiled. "Melangell knows a surprising number of things we didn't."

She leaned over the back of the seat. "We stayed in that pub back in Llangynog last time. The one where we had lunch. There was no accommodation at Pennant Melangell then."

"I'm glad there is now. The House of the Hare. I like the sound of that."

"Yes, the hare was St Melangell's animal. Even before that, it was an ancient symbol of new life. But, really, we called you Melangell because we just fell in love with the place, as soon as we got there."

"It's one of those 'thin places'," said Aidan. "Like Iona. Where heaven and earth come close together. You can feel it."

"Aidan!" Jenny cried.

He braked sharply. A large car came hurtling down the narrow lane towards them. There was no room for two vehicles to pass. At intervals along the way he had seen passing places. There was none in sight here. The black Jaguar screeched to a halt, only feet from their bumper. The horn blasted. Two faces were hardly discernible from behind the tinted windscreen.

Aidan felt a surge of anger. Idiots!

He took a deep breath. He must not lose control of his

temper. There were two precious lives, as well as his own, to consider.

He reversed the car back down the road until he reached one of the indentations. He pulled over. The Jaguar shot past. Through the side window Aidan had a glimpse of pale shirt fronts and darker suits. The driver did not raise his hand in acknowledgment.

He waited several seconds more, while his blood pressure steadied.

"So much for the spiritual atmosphere."

"They didn't look like your average pilgrim," Jenny said.

He pulled out on to the road again.

"I can see it! I can see it!" Melangell bounced on the back seat.

The low tower of the ancient chapel emerged from between the budding branches. It rose hardly taller than the slate roof, and was capped with a small latticed bell turret. Around it lay a scatter of whitewashed cottages, with their own slate roofs.

Aidan turned off the road and drew up by the churchyard. The car had hardly come to a halt before Melangell jumped out. She was running for the gate when she stopped dead. She stared up. Her mouth fell open in awe.

"It's gi-normous! And that one! And those two!"

Aidan glanced at Jenny and met her smile.

Around the church grew five gigantic yew trees. Centuries had swelled their girth to a size Aidan could not recall having seen anywhere else. These were not the disciplined churchyard yews he was used to, clipped into neat cylinders. Their canopies were vast. Two of them had split their trunks, so that you could see the sky between the two halves. The one nearest the gate had a hollow tall and deep enough to stand inside. Melangell ran and did just that. Her elfin face peeped out at them from a doorway of hoary bark.

Aidan swung the Nikon from his shoulder and caught the moment. The frame of his photograph held the frame of the yew tree, with his daughter captured inside both.

"I'm the hare. I'm Melangell's hare, hiding from the hunters under her skirt. You're the hounds, and you can't get me."

She jumped out, too excited to stay still for long. "Can we see the carvings in the church?"

"All in good time,' Aidan said. "Let's find the House of the Hare first. I expect your mother could do with a rest, before we start exploring."

"I could murder a cup of tea," Jenny laughed. She turned slowly, taking in the remembered circular churchyard, the long, low shrine church, the whitewashed buildings beyond.

"The St Melangell Centre's down that lane, isn't it? It was the Cancer Help Centre then. Funny." Her smile faded. "When we came here before, it never occurred to us that I…"

He gripped her hand. "There's a lot we didn't know then."

She reached up her free hand to stroke the bark of the yew. "I seem to remember the women recovering from cancer saw these trees as part of their therapy. And it's true. You get taxol from yews. It's one of the best treatments for ovarian cancer. The only trouble is, if you strip too much of the bark, the tree dies."

Aidan was silent. They both knew that Jenny's condition was worsening. The drugs had not done what they hoped. Jenny had been given only months to live.

He turned his head towards the church. His heart filled

with longing. If any place could work miracles, surely this was it. There was an aura of holiness about Pennant Melangell, these quiet meadows at the head of the valley, where the road ran out. Already, standing in the shadow of these yews, he could feel the stillness reaching to his heart. If they prayed here, if they really believed, could the power of this place reverse the conclusion of the oncologists?

Jenny was looking about her, more confused now. "I can't see anything that looks like the House of the Hare. There's no new building. Just the cottages and the Centre, as there used to be."

"There are gates over there." Melangell pointed.

A little way along the road, before it ended at the foot of the mountains, there were indeed two stone gateposts, with circular globes on them which must be lit at night.

Aidan got back into the car. "Come on. Let's try it."

Melangell was right. A decoratively carved slab of slate bore the inscription: "The House of the Hare". They turned into the drive. Trees screened the way ahead.

"It's certainly well hidden," Jenny said. "They've done their best not to let it ruin the place."

"There must have been a house here before. These are mature trees."

The drive curved. Melangell gasped.

The house soared in front of them. Timber-sided, with huge, floor-to-ceiling windows. The roof of blue Welsh slate tilted at steep and unexpected angles. Aidan's eye delighted in the complex planes of sunshine and shadow.

"Wow!" he said, reaching for his camera. "I guess the planning committee took some convincing, but I bet this design knocked them sideways. It's stunningly modern, yet everything belongs in this locality."

"The views from the top windows should be fantastic," Jenny said. "I can't wait. I'm so glad we booked here, and not back at the pub as we did before."

Aidan started towards the glass doors. The foyer was empty. He rang the bell on the reception desk. But as he did so, there were voices on the stairs. Down the wide sunlit flight came two people.

The first was a large man in expensive-looking cream linen slacks and a crisp short-sleeved shirt. The white of the fabric set off the sandy brown of his skin. Close black curls topped his wide face. Dark eyes surveyed them. Then he broke into a dazzling smile.

Behind him came an equally striking young woman in a pale green dress and a darker cardigan. Her heart-shaped face was almost white. Jet black waves of hair fell around her shoulders. Her eyes were a startling blue.

The man reached the bottom step and held out a broad hand to them.

"Thaddaeus Brown. Welcome to the House of the Hare." He released Aidan's hand and waved at the foyer around them. "I hope you'll find everything to your liking."

"It looks amazing," Jenny said. "We're the Davisons. We've booked to stay for a week."

"Ah, yes… *Sian!*' His voice boomed along the resonating wooden walls. "Guests!"

It was not the young woman behind him he was summoning. She still stood on the lowest stair, clutching her cardigan around her, unsmiling.

Thaddaeus Brown turned back to them.

"I can't tell you how excited I am. This is the fulfilment of a dream. Well, Lorna's dream, actually." He threw the girl behind him an affectionate smile. "People in need, able to stay here at Pennant Melangell, in the House of the Hare. We built this just for someone like you, Jenny."

He turned his deep brown eyes on her. The woman he had called Sian came hurrying along the corridor into the foyer, but he did not turn to her.

He had not introduced the girl in the green dress he called Lorna. Aidan looked her way, and saw her standing a little apart, biting her lip. He could not be sure whether the pallor of her lovely face was natural, or whether she looked frightened.

Chapter Two

IT WAS LONG MOMENTS BEFORE Thaddaeus Brown's dark eyes released Jenny's. Only when he moved on towards the door did she realize that she had been holding her breath.

The girl followed him out into the sunlight. Jenny hardly noticed her.

She was suddenly immensely tired. She leaned against the reception desk for support.

"Mrs Davison? Are you all right?"

Sian the receptionist came hurrying forward. Jenny looked up with a forced smile.

"I'm all right, thanks. Just a bit tired from the journey."

Aidan, always watchful, was steering a chair towards her. She sank into it thankfully. His ginger-bearded face leaned anxiously over her.

"Sorry. I was doing fine until just now."

"Can I get you something? A cup of tea?" The woman's voice had a warm Welsh lilt.

Now that her attention steadied on Sian, Jenny thought she looked more like a park ranger than a hotel receptionist. She wore a khaki short-sleeved shirt, khaki denim trousers and canvas boots. Her full round face was framed by fair hair. She had the kind of plumpness that bounced with health.

Jenny was conscious anew of her own wasted frame. She looked down at her hand on her knee. Too thin, too transparent.

She drank the offered tea and felt the glow spread through her body.

"Who was the girl?" Aidan asked.

"With Mr Brown? That's Lorna, his niece."

"Do they live in the house?"

"Oh, no. But this is the beginning of our first season. Thaddaeus… Mr Brown… wanted to be here to make sure it was a success. He's so excited about it. We all are." Her wide smile turned to include Jenny. "This is just what we hoped for. A place where people like you could come and stay. Pennant Melangell was always a healing place."

Jenny caught Aidan's eye and saw the flicker of apprehension. This was dangerous ground. After the last round of chemotherapy there had been a long discussion between her oncologist and the two of them. Jenny had made her decision. No more treatment. She would conserve her energy to live the last months of her life to the full, not shuttling between home and hospital for sessions that left her weaker than before.

But they had long known the reputation of this place. Medieval pilgrims had come to the saint's shrine just for this. More recently, the Help Centre had offered support to women with cancer, before it extended its remit to others in need. There was still a weekly service with the laying on of hands. It lay unspoken between Jenny and Aidan, the possibility that beyond the power of medicine there might be something more.

But could this hope itself gnaw away at the serenity she sought for these last precious months?

"Can you show us our rooms?" she asked.

"Of course. There's a lift."

Sian seized a pair of keys from the rack behind the desk and led the way.

Jenny gasped as Sian flung open the door. Light flooded across the centre of the room. A tall window gave on to a balcony. Beyond, above the darker woods, the purple ridge of the Berwyn Mountains was bathed in afternoon sunshine. The sky over the hills was the singing blue of springtime.

She sank down on the folkweave bedspread. Everything about the room spoke of this locality. The timber walls, the framed watercolours of Welsh landscapes, the slate top of the dressing table. There was a vase of wild flowers on the chest of drawers.

"It's lovely."

Sian beamed. "It is, isn't it? I'll say that for Thaddaeus, he's got taste."

Melangell ran to the balcony. Aidan followed her.

"There's a swimming pool!"

"It's got a cover over it."

"It'll be a bit cold yet," Sian laughed, crossing to join them. "If the house does well, Thaddaeus wants to heat it. He's thinking of solar panels, though the sun goes down early below the hills."

Jenny made an effort to rise from the comfortable bed and join them. Behind the house, the trees that, at the front, screened it from the road had been cleared. There was not just the swimming pool to the right, but a tennis court, and to the left... she craned further to look...

"Are those archery butts?"

Sian nodded. Her broad smile tightened. "Thaddaeus has big ideas. He had a big fight to get planning permission. There was a lot of local opposition. Still is. He told them he wanted facilities that guests could enjoy even if they're... not on top form." She glanced anxiously at Jenny. "Swimming's good for that, isn't it?" Jenny nodded. "I was all for that. I

gave up my job as a PE teacher to be the warden here. But…
I don't know. Today he's been talking about waterfall walking
and rock-climbing."

"You'd have to count me out."

"That's what I mean. I thought I heard them say
something about extending the clientèle with team-bonding
for executives. I hope he's not losing the plot. Maybe Caradoc
Lewis had a point… He's the leader of the anti-brigade…"
She frowned, staring down at the wide gardens of the house.
In a low, bitter voice she said, "If he did anything to change
the character of this valley, it would break Lorna's heart. I
think I'd kill him."

Jenny saw her go suddenly rigid. When she looked
down, following Sian's eyes, she saw Thaddaeus and Lorna
walking round the corner of the house. An expression, almost
of fear, twisted Sian's face. She backed away from the balcony,
as Thaddaeus lifted his hand to wave to them.

Next moment, she snapped back into her professional
smile. "Sorry. I shouldn't be talking out of turn. Don't tell
him I said that. I don't want to lose my job!"

But Jenny sensed it was not a laughing matter.

Aidan smiled. "Don't worry. We'll be discreet."

"Mummy's good at archery," Melangell said from the
balcony.

"Was." Jenny gave a difficult smile.

"Really? That's great!" Sian's laugh was back. "We must
get you out there."

Jenny's tired arms remembered the strength it had needed
to bend the stave and draw the bowstring back to its fullest
extent.

As if she read Jenny's thoughts, Sian reassured her.
"Don't worry. You can do archery sitting down, if it helps.
Did you know that? They have it in the Paralympics. We've
got a wheelchair you can borrow. Really, you'll be fine."

Jenny felt herself brighten in the warmth of the young woman's enthusiasm. "That sounds great. I might give it a try. I'm not sure I could handle a full-strength bow, though."

"No problem. I'll help you choose a suitable one." Sian turned for the door. "I've put Melangell across the corridor. Is that all right? Give me a shout if there's anything you need. Supper from half past six."

She left them. Jenny heard her steps bouncing down the wooden stairs.

Melangell grabbed the second key and darted across to the room opposite, faster than they could follow her. When they caught up with her, she was laughing with joy.

"Look! I can just see my yew trees, and the tower of the church."

This room was smaller and had no balcony. Through the screening branches outside there was indeed a sidelong glimpse of the churchyard with its massive dark trees, of the little church of St Melangell and the cottages around it.

"Can we go and see the church now? Can we? And the carvings?"

"But you already know what they look like. They're in your book. Daddy's photographs."

"I *know*. But I want to see them *really*."

So do I, Jenny thought.

She felt Aidan's eyes on her. He knew how much this meant to her. Bringing Melangell to the place where her story began. Showing her the church with the carvings of St Melangell's legend. Reliving their first discovery of it, when it had been just herself and Aidan. Jenny researching for another of her books on Celtic saints. Aidan taking the photographs to illustrate it. Both of them falling in love with this place.

"When your mother's rested," Aidan said, "we'll all go."

Jenny lay back on the bed, letting her body relax. "I can see the mountains without even getting up. Bliss."

Aidan came over and kissed her. "I'm glad it's worked out as you wanted. It's a lovely place. And we always said we must bring Melangell here."

"'One day', we said. 'One day, we'll take her.' As if we had forever." She rolled over and drew his sandy-haired head back down to hers. She placed her finger on his lips, feeling the brush of his beard. "No regrets. Remember? We have today. We're here. Let's make the most of it."

"You're amazing," he murmured. "And you're right. As always."

She watched him struggle to hold his smile in place.

He sat down on the bed and caressed her hand.

"This Thaddaeus is an amazing guy, isn't he?" she asked. "To do all this." Her hand gestured at the room and the tall window. "I bet there was a lot of opposition to building here. But he's done it so sensitively. It... *fits*. As though it grew here."

"Let's hope it stays that way, then. Sian seemed worried about it. I think she's scared of him."

She sat up. "Scared of Thaddaeus? I thought he seemed a lovely man."

She did have a momentary recall of the sudden change in Sian's face when she thought Thaddaeus might have overheard her. But her memory went back more vividly to their meeting in the foyer. The dark brown eyes that had held hers for such long moments. Her face softened, remembering that look.

"And the girl. Lorna? She looked nervous too." Aidan's face was sober.

Jenny turned a wondering face to him. "Did she? I didn't notice." She lay back on the pillows and settled herself comfortably. "You're imagining things."

Chapter Three

MELANGELL RAN TO ONE of the yew trees as though it was an old friend. She tried to throw her arms around the trunk, but could not encircle even a quarter of it.

"It must be hundreds of years old!" she laughed. "Hundreds and hundreds."

"Two thousand, they reckon, the oldest," Aidan said.

Melangell dropped her arms and turned to face him, frowning. She flicked her fingers as she calculated.

"That's silly," she pronounced. "Isn't it? Jesus was born 2,000 years ago, so there couldn't have been a church here then."

She was not, Aidan thought, the daughter of a church historian for nothing.

It was Jenny who answered. "Do you notice anything funny about the shape of the churchyard?"

Melangell's eyes flashed as she accepted the challenge. She looked around her, carefully. It did not take her many moments to make the discovery.

"It's round. Most of them have corners and straight walls."

"Good girl. This is a *llan*. The traditional shape of a Celtic monastery or hermitage site. The church is on a raised circular mound. But this one is older than that. A *llan* can mean any sacred enclosure. The yews show this must have been a holy place long before the Christians got here. Perhaps that's why St Melangell chose it."

Aidan smiled. Jenny had lost none of her enthusiasm for Celtic history.

Melangell's eyes encompassed the setting with new awe. "That's kind of shivery, isn't it? A holy place just waiting for her to find it."

They walked past the guardian yews. Aidan let his fingers brush over the deeply grained bark. Automatically, his hand reached for his camera case, but he let it fall.

"They sometimes say that yews were planted in churchyards to supply the bows for medieval archers. But that can't be the reason for these."

"No," Jenny said. "These trees were sacred too."

They stepped inside the church, and Aidan was surprised all over again by its proportions. Where the nave of other churches occupied most of the space, leaving only the eastern end for the choir and sanctuary, here the chancel with the shrine of the saint formed half the building.

Jenny sat down in one of the pews near the back and bowed her head in prayer. Was she putting off approaching the shrine of St Melangell because it was so important to her?

But the saint's little namesake ran forward. Melangell was not yet looking at the stone-canopied tomb that rose behind the altar in the chancel. All her eager attention was on the woodwork frieze above the screen that separated the two halves of the church.

She looked up at the carvings and her brilliant smile greeted them like old friends.

"That's Brochwel!" She pointed to the figure on horseback on the left.

"Brochwel Ysgithrog, Prince of Powys," Aidan agreed.

"And there's that funny man kneeling down. He looks as if he's got a telescope, but really it's a horn."

"Brochwel's huntsman, trying to blow his horn to urge

the hounds to the kill."

"Only he can't, can he?" She bounced with joy. "And that's Melangell, sitting in the middle."

"She's got her crozier in her hand, to show she's Abbess of a monastery." Jenny had joined them. "Though that came afterwards."

"And the hare is running towards her. The hounds are howling and howling, and the prince is shouting, 'Get it, hounds, get it!' but they can't catch the hare, can they, because she's protecting it? God won't let the hunt kill either of them."

"So he asks her to marry him." Jenny took up the story. "And she won't. She's an Irish princess who's run away to Wales because she didn't want to marry the man her father chose. And Brochwel is so impressed by her courage and compassion that he gives her land for a monastery. And he says he'll never hunt hares again in this valley. So she sets up a house and a church for her nuns, right here."

"Right here, where we're standing?" Melangell looked down at her small sandalled feet in wonder.

"Yes. Right here."

There was wonder in Jenny's voice too.

Aidan watched as they moved on up the step to the chancel. St Melangell's shrine reared its gabled canopy of pinkish sandstone. Leaf sculptures sprouted from the slopes of its eaves like the raised wings of birds. It was covered in pink-and-green brocade. Low, decorated pillars supported the roof over a stone slab.

He winced. The ancient shrine, which had been the site of medieval pilgrimage, was evidently still the focus of prayer. A profusion of cards lay heaped on the slab. Pink, blue, turquoise, white. Some decorated with pictures. Something in him, a lifetime of plain Methodism, shied away from these pious tokens. Superstition, he wondered? Like the coloured rags people hung above holy wells?

Jenny was examining the cards. "These are the names of people someone lit a candle for, or entered in the Book of Remembrance. So much prayer." Her voice fell quiet. "For both the living and the dead."

Something wrenched his heart. Aidan was caught between his nonconformist aversion to the veneration of saints and the possibility that he was overlooking something of real importance. He studied Jenny's face. Calm, serious. What was she thinking? What was she hoping?

Would it make a difference to her if he left a token of his own faith here?

He watched her move on, towards the archway behind the altar. It led through to the apse where the saint's original grave had been found. The apse was a place for private prayer. He saw her halt in disappointment. Someone else was already there.

"Look!" cried Melangell. "Here she is!"

The moment passed.

The effigy of St Melangell his daughter had discovered was not on the stone slab under the canopy, like the tombs of bishops and knights in a cathedral. She lay to one side of it. Her hands were clasped serenely in prayer. His fingers caressed the stone.

"Look," he said to his own Melangell, "you can just see two hares peeping out from under her."

As he studied the sculpture, his hand itched for his camera. It was silly, really. Jenny's book on St Melangell had been published years ago, with Aidan's photographs to accompany her story. He did not need more.

But cameras had moved on since then. Would his Nikon D5100 capture more subtleties? The grain of wood in the carvings? The play of light and shadow which threw the figure of St Melangell into relief? Perhaps he would come back tomorrow with his tripod and try a longer exposure, using more of the natural light.

"You found her, then?"

He looked up, startled. A dumpy, middle-aged woman stood between the choir stalls. Her wide shoulders and short stature made her body almost square. The elastic of her black skirt strained at her waist. Her light blue shirt was parted at the neck to show a glimpse of a clerical collar. Above her black-rimmed spectacles, her greyish hair was dragged back over her skull so tightly that it might have been hidden under a veil.

Melangell evidently thought so.

"Are you a nun?"

The glasses flashed in the light of the east window.

"No. But I am a priest. Not the Priest-Guardian of the shrine. She's away this week on holiday. I'm just minding the shop."

Melangell looked uncertainly towards the room at the base of the tower, where racks of greetings cards showed through the glass partition.

"That shop?"

"Well, yes, that too. But I meant I was minding things in general. I'm here some days, or at the Centre, for people in need."

She looked directly at Aidan. He was disconcerted. It was Jenny who was dying of cancer. But the penetrating grey eyes were on him. She held out a business card.

The Reverend Joan Banfield

Spiritual counselling and psychotherapy

"Some people call me Mother Joan," she added, with a faint smile. "You know where to find me. My number's on the card." She turned to Jenny and held out her hands. "May I?"

Slowly, Jenny extended her own hands and the priest enfolded them in her own. They stood in silence for long moments.

Aidan felt a flash of disquiet that was almost fear. What was she doing? What did Jenny believe she was doing?

Melangell's clear voice rang from the other end of the nave. She was standing in the tower gift shop.

"Mummy! They've got your book here."

Jenny dropped her hands from the other woman's. With an apologetic smile she hurried down the aisle to join her daughter. Aidan followed.

Melangell was waving the book with Aidan's photograph of St Melangell's effigy on the cover. He heard the gasp behind him.

"Jenny Davison? You're *the* Jenny Davison?"

Jenny blushed. "If you mean did I write that, yes. The photos are Aidan's."

"My dear! So you won't need me to tell you about the shrine, and what a very sacred place this is."

"No, we knew that. This little brat is called Melangell."

The glasses glinted again as Mother Joan turned her gaze on the child.

"Lucky girl. It's a very special name."

There were voices on the path outside. A group of some fifteen people came crowding into the chapel, talking eagerly. In the stone-flagged shadows, and the muted colours from the windows, they fell silent. Some crossed themselves and went to sit, as Jenny had done, in the pews. Aidan, watching them, felt that prayer was palpable in the nave.

Then they were off, heading towards the screen with its carvings and the sandstone shrine itself. Voices rose again.

"A minibus party," Mother Joan said. "They can't get a full-sized coach up the road, thank God." The grey eyes darkened behind the lenses. "Yet."

Chapter Four

JENNY CAST HER EYES ROUND the almost empty dining room. In the far corner were the two young walkers they had passed on the road. They looked barely in their twenties. Relieved of his large rucksack, the fair young man's body looked even slighter. His companion was more generously built. As she leaned towards him, her curtain of straightened black hair hid her face. They were tucking into large platefuls of home-cooked food with enthusiasm.

A little way behind Jenny were an older couple they had not seen before.

Evening sunshine threw fingers of light across the lawns between the trees. But the shadows of the hills were closing in.

Sian came bustling from the kitchen with three loaded plates.

Jenny smiled at her. "You're warden, receptionist, sports coach and waitress too? They keep you busy."

"We had Mair from the village helping out over Easter. Comes from Llangynog on her bicycle. Her mother helps with the cleaning. But Mair's only free in the college vacs. Besides…" Sian set down their meals and ran her fingers through her blonde hair. 'We're not so busy now."

"You don't have to do the cooking as well, I hope."

"Oh, no. We've got Josef, from Poland. He's brilliant. Well, you'll taste for yourself. And all our food is local. This is new season Welsh lamb. And the vegetables are grown within five miles from here."

Aidan looked around the spacious dining room, at the blue linen napkins, the pottery bowls for butter, the fresh spring flowers, the floor-length folkweave curtains. He was obviously making the same calculations Jenny had.

"This place must have cost a mint to build. And you've furnished it to the highest standard. The menu looks great. But how are you paying for it?"

Sian's face tightened in a defensive mask. "We were almost full at Easter. It's early days yet. But youngsters like Harry and Debbie are worried that we charge too much." Her eyes shot a look of alarm at the door.

Jenny sensed his presence behind her before she saw him. The large, confident figure of Thaddaeus Brown strode into view, followed by the lesser shadow of his niece.

"Hello, there." He paused by their table with a broad smile. "Have you settled in? Is everything to your liking?" Again, those wide brown eyes found out Jenny's.

"Yes, wonderful," she smiled back.

"Great food," Aidan agreed. "These lamb chops are out of this world."

"Josef's a star, isn't he? I want only the best for the House of the Hare."

He moved on. "Hi, Harry, Debbie. How was your walk?" to the young hikers.

"I see you've been exploring the neighbourhood," to the older couple.

The Browns, uncle and niece, settled themselves at the table reserved for them by the window. Lorna had her back to the Davisons.

Jenny watched her, thoughtfully. Aidan had had some idea that the girl looked frightened of her uncle. It was true that her body language was a little tense. She spoke too quietly for Jenny to hear, though Thaddaeus's voice rang cheerfully across the room as he discussed tomorrow's weather forecast, for anyone who wanted to listen.

Just teenage gaucheness, Jenny decided. Awkwardness in front of an older man who was so much in charge of the situation. Perhaps she didn't know him very well. Was this the first time they had been away alone together?

She put down her knife. Maybe there *was* something odd in their relationship. Did Thaddaeus have a wife? How many other girls as young as Lorna would go away with an uncle, without an older woman or a companion of her own age?

She shook her head slightly. It was none of her business. Thaddaeus was obviously thrilled with his new House of the Hare. He had poured into it not only a lot of money, but loving attention to detail. No doubt he would want to keep it in the family. If he had no children of his own, he was probably schooling Lorna to take a share in the business.

"Mummy, you're not eating. I've finished all of mine," Melangell said.

Jenny smiled quickly. "Sorry, love. It's delicious, but I don't have much appetite these days. I hope Josef won't think I'm insulting his cooking. He knows his job. That combination of garlic and rosemary… I can still savour it after I've eaten it."

"The wine's not bad, either," Aidan said. "I think I'm going to enjoy it here."

Jenny's eyes strayed back to the hunched shoulders of Lorna, and the beaming smile of Thaddaeus opposite her. Would it work? Could this diffident teenager ever step into the shoes of her extrovert uncle?

But maybe she wouldn't need to. Sian was the warden of the house. And she had all the warmth and energy needed for the job. Lorna might just need to handle the money side.

She turned to Melangell. "Have you seen the desserts?"

"What's caramel fudge torte?"

"It's sweet and brown and sticky."

"Yup. That's the one."

Jenny toyed with a lime sorbet. She raised her eyes to Aidan. "Thaddaeus says the weather will be fine tomorrow. A bit cooler than today, but not much chance of rain. I think you should take Melangell to the waterfall while it holds."

"Pistyll Blaen-y-cwm? Are you sure? It's our first full day here, and we'd be gone for several hours."

She read the concern in his green-flecked eyes. She knew that, even now, he was counting the precious hours left to them.

"It's what we agreed. Life doesn't have to come to a stop because I can't do all the things I used to. You go. I might take Sian up on her offer of archery. And that's something I didn't think I'd be able to do again."

"You'd use a wheelchair?"

Jenny made a face. "Other people have to. It would be less tiring than standing up." She made herself smile for Aidan's worried face. "And you can show me your new photos of the waterfall when you get back."

They took their coffee in the lounge. Melangell gave a cry of delight when she discovered a stack of jigsaws.

"Mount Snowdon, 2,000 pieces. Great!"

In a moment, she was lying on her stomach, with pieces strewn across the beechwood floorboards.

The older man and woman stopped beside Jenny and Aidan.

"Do you mind if we join you?" The man's loud voice had the confidence that did not consider the answer "no".

"Of course not. Please do."

They lowered themselves into the deep leather settee opposite. The man's frame seemed to take up twice as much space as his smaller wife's. Jenny judged them to be in their sixties. They had the unseasonable tan of people who had sought winter sunshine on a foreign holiday. But the woman's pinched face spoke of chronic pain. She had trouble settling her body even in the comfortable leather seat.

The man held out his hand.

"Colin Ewart. And this is my wife, Rachel."

Introductions made, they paused while the ubiquitous Sian set jugs of coffee down in front of them.

"Have you been here long?" Aidan asked.

"This is our second day." Rachel Ewart managed a self-deprecating smile. "I've got a bit of a back problem, so I can't walk as far as I used to. But we've been enjoying ourselves, visiting the shrine, and pottering round the neighbourhood."

Jenny knew a flash of fellow-feeling. She hesitated. Would it be too much of a conversation-stopper to say, "I've got terminal cancer"?

Instead, she smiled back and settled for, "I know. I've been ill myself. I'll be taking it easy too."

"Ran into some of the locals," said Colin. "A lot of Welsh-speakers around here. Load of nonsense, if you ask me."

Beside Jenny, Aidan bristled with indignation. "It's a funny thing. Lots of English people can manage a few words of French or German or Spanish. But Welsh is the national language of this island, or was once. And most people can't even say 'Good morning' or 'Thank you'."

"No need for them to have a chip on the shoulder," Colin snorted. "We came across one of them who chewed our ears off – Caradoc Lewis. You met him yet?"

They shook their heads.

"Wait a minute," Aidan exclaimed. "Didn't Sian say something about him? 'Maybe Caradoc Lewis had a point.'"

He looked round suddenly, but the warden was nowhere in sight.

"Spitting fire and brimstone, he was, about this House of the Hare. Said Brown should never have been given planning permission. He led the antis, by all accounts," Colin said.

"We told him we thought it was a lovely place," Rachel put in. "And so close to the healing shrine, for people like me." She shot a sympathetic look at Jenny. "But he wouldn't listen."

"I think if he had his way he'd put a bomb under this place," her husband agreed.

A flare of indignation surprised Jenny. It wasn't fair. If her oncologist was right, she had about five months left. She had so much wanted to bring Melangell here. This was meant to be such a special week. A bittersweet goodbye for her. A time of healing, spiritually, if not physically. A golden time for Aidan and Melangell to remember. The last thing she wanted was for the atmosphere of this place to be made ugly by antagonism. It was a place she had fallen in love with for its aura of peace.

She looked over her shoulder. Thaddaeus Brown and Lorna were still in the dining room behind her.

"That's wrong. Mr Brown seems to have done everything to make this place blend in. And he's using local materials and local produce as much as he can. You'd think the people who live here would be glad of that. A boost to the economy."

"But even Sian has her doubts," Aidan reminded her. "Extreme sports? City types on away days?"

"I can't imagine he means that," Jenny argued. "Pennant Melangell's just not that sort of place. It's for people like us."

"Got it!" Melangell cried from the floor. "That's the whole of the bottom edge in place. Look, Daddy."

***

"You can't wait to get into shorts, can you?" Jenny laughed.

Aidan's bearded face grinned as he laced up his walking boots. "Never mind May Day. Summer's officially a-cummin' on the day I pack away my long trousers"

Melangell came running into their room in jeans and trainers. "Come on, Mummy. Sian said she'd help you choose a bow before we start."

"You don't have to wait for me if you want to go. It's a long way to the waterfall."

"Only two miles, Daddy said."

"And two miles back."

"Pooh. That's nothing. And I want to see the bows and arrows."

Aidan raised his sandy eyebrows at Jenny above Melangell's head.

Sian led them to a wooden hut at the start of the archery range. A remembered joy sprang to Jenny's heart as she saw the targets at the far end. The familiar circles of gold, red, blue, black and white. She measured the distance with her eye. Could she still draw a bow at 70 metres and send her arrow speeding across that space into the bullseye? In the freshness of the morning, after a fairly good night's sleep, she felt a surge of hope that she could.

She heard Melangell's scornful voice behind her. "Is that what you call a bow?"

She turned, and felt her eyebrows rise. They were not playing at archery here, in a Robin Hood theme-park sort of way. This was a serious competition bow Sian was holding out to her. Not wood, but a recurve design in carbon fibre and aluminium alloy. It had a red central riser, with back-curving upper and lower limbs. Circular holes in the metal made for lightness as well as strength.

Sian's usually cheerful face looked a little put out at Melangell's disparagement. "These are the top Olympic design. Thaddaeus only buys the best."

Jenny took the bow and tested it tentatively. A moment before, she had felt strong and confident. Now, her weakened arms told her she would not be able to exert this strain for long.

"I'm sure it's top-class kit," she said. "But I'm not sure I'm in top-class form."

Sian flushed. "I didn't want to insult you. I mean, if you were a good shot, before… But if you'd rather, I can find you one with a lower draw strength. We have an assortment of bows we give to first-timers and children."

From the back of the shed, Melangell gave a cry of delight. "This one!"

She emerged with the sort of bow that might have come straight out of the pages of a history book. The golden wood of the stave glowed. The shape was clean: a single curve that would bend along its whole length, without the complicated joints of the three-part recurve. The string, Jenny saw, was natural fibre too. Flax, perhaps, not a modern polymer.

Aidan took it from Melangell. His hands caressed the polished wood.

"Yew." The sandy brows rose again as his eyes met Jenny's.

"Let me." Her arms were reaching out. She had fallen in love at first sight. Her hands ached to hold it. She was suddenly sure she could find the strength to draw this one. Already she could feel the lie of the arrow along her cheek, see the point aimed at the target, gauge the tension in her elbow before she let fly.

"That's funny," Sian said. "That's the one Lorna likes to use."

Chapter Five

AIDAN HANDED HER THE WEAPON. She had been an archer before he met her. It had not been a hobby they shared.

He watched her string the bow and test it. A shaky laugh escaped her, as she showed it to Melangell.

"If this was a full-size medieval longbow, you'd need to be one of the strongest men in the village to draw it. You had to train from when you were a young boy. Everybody looked up to an archer. English longbow men were the most feared of any soldiers on the battlefield. If the enemy captured you, they'd cut off your fingers so you'd never shoot again."

"You'll be able to manage this," Sian assured her. "I gave it to a couple of kids last week, to get them started. Really, you don't need to be that strong."

Jenny gave her an understanding smile. "I know that. It's right for me. And I don't underestimate it. It's still a lethal weapon. Can we start?"

She faced the target.

Aidan's fists tightened as he watched. Could she still do it?

The first arrow fell some ten metres short. He shot an anxious glance at her face, but she looked calmly determined. He saw that knowledge was returning to her hands and eyes.

The next arrow rose higher. It thwacked into the target, hitting the red inner circle, close to the yellow bullseye.

"Yes!" Jenny's laugh rang across the clearing.

Aidan and Melangell applauded.

"I'll get you that wheelchair," said Sian. "So you don't get tired too quickly. Is that all right?"

Aidan saw the knowledge of her mortality return to Jenny's face. He felt it in the pit of his own stomach. For a heady moment, they had forgotten it. But Sian was right. Jenny must husband her strength, spin out these moments of enjoyment. Make each day count.

He felt a wave of longing. He should not be leaving her, even for a few hours. They had so little time left. But she had made him promise.

Jenny turned to him and Melangell. Her face shone now with genuine happiness. "I'm going to enjoy myself."

Still he hesitated.

"If you're sure." He leaned forward and kissed her forehead.

She caught his hand. "Enjoy the waterfall. Bring me some photos."

He heard the thud of another arrow as they rounded the corner of the house.

In spite of himself, he felt his spirits lift, and he and Melangell swung out along the lane. It felt adventurous to be setting off on foot along the last strip of tarmac past Pennant Melangell. A sign warned motorists that there was no turning place beyond. At the head of the valley, the road ended.

Before they reached it, they came to a sign saying "WATERFALL". It pointed them off the road and up the hillside.

"Sorry, kid. You used to be able to walk straight up the valley. Looks like we have to make a detour now. This road runs out at a farm, so we have to go up and round it. We can't just walk to the foot of the fall."

The path angled them away from the road, up through fields where sheep grazed. The steep gradient slowed even Melangell's eager feet.

They came out on to the bracken-covered crest. The footpath sign pointed forward, away from the river's source.

Aidan consulted the map. "The bad news is that there's no public footpath marked the way we want to go. The good news is that I can see a track on the ground that does lead towards the head of the falls. Do you want to give it a go?"

The pointed face with its dusting of freckles had a determination that mirrored his own. "Of *course*."

The path through the bracken followed the lip of the valley. Far below them, miniature cows grazed the meadows at its foot. A ribbon of trees marked the course of the young river.

"Is that it?" Melangell pointed ahead.

Scarves of white came cascading down from the skyline, leaping sideways as they hit the rocks.

"Pistyll Blaen-y-cwm. The Waterfall at the Head of the Valley."

"Why are we going to the top and not the bottom?"

"Because there's no public path down there. I expect we'll be able to scramble down to the foot once we're past the farm."

It was like walking with a puppy. Melangell was forever darting off to one side of the narrow path or another. Early bilberries caught her eye, their jewelled fruit just beginning to turn from green to purple. She found the bleached skull of a dead sheep. She tipped back her head to search for a skylark, whose song was pouring from overhead.

Suddenly she stopped. Aidan almost bumped into her.

They were on the edge of an almost-dry stream bed. In the winter, this little tributary would come rushing past to hurl itself down the almost vertical slope.

Melangell looked at its stony course. "Couldn't we get down this way? It's a sort of path."

"If you're lost on the hills, the first rule is never to follow a stream. You could find yourself on the edge of precipice."

"*Are* we lost?"

"Well, put it this way. I know where we are. But I'm not sure how to get where we want to be. Down there."

They went on. Walls of gorse were growing higher on either side. The thorny branches were dark. They had yet to break into golden flower.

Aidan paused. He was beginning to have doubts. The route was proving more difficult than he expected. But a streak of obstinacy would not let him admit defeat.

"Sorry, kid. It doesn't look as though too many people come here. We'll just have to make our way down to the river as best we can."

"I don't care," Melangell said. "It's a real expedition, isn't it? Like David Livingstone finding Victoria Falls in the middle of Africa."

"Mosi-oa-Tunya. The Smoke that Thunders."

"Will it be like that?"

"Wait and see."

They broke out into open sunshine. A rare patch of grass was speared with the bright green fronds of young bracken still uncurling.

"Look!" cried Melangell. "There's someone down there."

The steeply plunging slope hid the nearer foot of the valley, but across the stream Aidan made out two small figures making their way along what looked like a green path towards the waterfall. The white top of one shone out like the flash of a gull's wing.

He felt his hand reaching for the camera slung round his

neck. The zoom lens would show them more clearly. But he let it drop back.

"There *is* a path down there!" It was a burst of indignation. "It's not on the map. But if *they* can use it, we're going to take that way home. Come on."

Recklessly now, he struck off the path that followed the high contour. He went angling down the slope. He was aware of scree slipping under his boots between the bracken stems. He looked back. Melangell seemed to be managing all right.

They hit the gorse again. There were bigger rocks hidden among its thickets.

"Ow! Daddy, I'm getting scratched. Are you *sure* this is the way?"

"I'm pretty sure it's not, but I can't see anything better."

He knew he was taking foolish risks. He was glad Jenny was not here to see it. But he had set himself to take Melangell to the foot of Pistyll Blaen-y-cwm and he was determined to do it.

He fought his way down to a lone oak that overhung another of those minor waterfalls. There was a sheer drop of twice his height, with water trickling over the edge. Below, he could at last see his way clear over tumbled stones to the foot of the hill. He felt a rush of triumph. Determination had paid off. They would get there, after all.

He stowed his camera in his rucksack for safety and scrambled down the side of the fall. He held up his arms to Melangell.

"You said we shouldn't follow a stream."

"I know, but I can see there are no more precipices below us."

The litter of rocks down the watercourse was still steeper and the boulders bigger than they had looked from above. But they made it to the bottom, Aidan with only a grazed knee and a boot full of water. He turned to share his delight with Melangell. Her arms were bloodied from scratches and there were bits of gorse in her hair. Her freckled face looked tired.

"Sorry, love. That wasn't one of my best-planned expeditions. But the waterfall's just along there. Then it's picnic time."

They turned to face the high cascade. One, two, and then three torrents came leaping down from the rim. They could hear the pounding of the falls. This was the force that gave birth to the placid river they had seen gliding through the pastures around the church.

Aidan led the way across a tiny field to a gap in a stone wall.

He came face to face with a running figure. Her ragged panting was close to sobs. The tumbling black hair could not hide the fact that the heart-shaped face was streaked with tears. Brilliant blue eyes went from father to daughter.

Aidan was staring into the distraught face of Lorna Brown.

"Sorry!" she gasped. She tried to hurry past.

Aidan put out a hand to stop her. "It's Lorna, isn't it? Mr Brown's niece. What's wrong?"

She flinched away from his touch. Fear flared in her eyes.

She shook her black curls vigorously. Her lips were pressed tight. Then she gasped. "No! No, nothing's wrong. I… I mean I… Sorry!"

She backed away from him, then turned and fled. She was not running up the hillside, but along the stream towards Pennant Melangell.

Aidan watched her go, uneasily. Belatedly, without the beauty of her ravaged face to distract him, he noticed that her white shirt hung unevenly off one shoulder. His memory showed him the image of a button torn from the fine cloth.

He looked up the last stretch of path to the waterfall. No one seemed to be following her. Yet they had seen two figures from above. He listened, but could hear no sound above the rushing falls. What, or whom, was Lorna running away from? What had happened in this secluded spot?

He wondered if it was right to take Melangell on. But he could not define what he was afraid of meeting.

He looked round for her. She had slithered down to squat at the foot of the wall and rest her legs. Her face was serious.

"She's not a very good liar, is she? She was crying."

"Yes. But it's not our business. Her uncle will look after her."

He held out his hand and pulled her up. Her body felt small and light. He sensed a sudden urge to protect her from whatever it was that had brought that look of shock and fear to Lorna Brown's exquisite face.

For a while, he kept her hand in his as they went on further along the stony stream. They came at last to where the falls crashed between overarching trees into a black pool at their feet.

There was no one else there.

For a while, Aidan let the sound of pounding water wash away the long, foolish scramble down the hill, and that strange, disturbing encounter with Lorna Brown.

He retrieved his camera bag from his rucksack. His mind was calculating how best to convey the whirling dance of the falls in a single, still photograph.

Melangell had climbed up on to the dark, wet rocks beside the cataract. She seemed to have forgotten her aching limbs.

41

"Be careful!" he called, instinctively.

She pulled a face at him and began to dance. He struggled to follow her movements in his viewfinder. She flitted across the screen, flickering in and out of the frame, like a moth. It was the movement itself which was the joy. How could he capture it?

"Hold still," he ordered.

But she stretched her mouth to her ears in a grimace and waggled her fingers at him. She was refusing to be his model.

He ached to capture that naturalness, the uninhibited grace of her dancing, before she had known she was being watched.

"At least let me have one decent photo to show your mother."

She halted instantly in full flight. Her weight was poised on the toes of one foot. Her arms spread wing-like before and behind her. The noonday sun turned her nondescript curls into a halo.

One second. Just long enough for him to click the shutter and capture it. Then her grin shot back and she was off again.

She scrambled down the rocks, slipped off her trainers, and tried to see if she could find a way behind the waterfall.

Aidan turned his attention to the higher view. The white leaps and bounds carved their cleft out of the almost-black rock. Softer white clouds drifted across the lofty skyline.

Melangell's voice sounded suddenly beside his elbow.

"Why did you say her uncle would look after her? Yesterday, I thought she was scared of him."

They found a slab of rock in the sunshine and ate their sandwiches. Melangell demolished Aidan's chocolate bar as well as her own.

Aidan slipped his rucksack on and stood up.

Melangell was paddling her way along the young river, as it tumbled among the stones.

"Can we walk back beside the stream? We don't have to climb up there again, do we?" Her eyes followed the high, precipitous slope down which they had come.

"I sincerely hope not. You could clearly see a path from up above. That's how Lorna came here, and whoever she was with."

Melangell climbed out of the water. She pulled on her trainers and picked up her own small knapsack. "Come on, then."

The path showed as a green ribbon among the rough grass. It angled away from the river.

"Mind you," Aidan warned her. "It's not marked on the map, so we could end up in someone's farmyard, or run into a notice that says 'Private'."

"My legs say they're too tired to care. And if there's a farm, there'll be a road, won't there?"

They walked in silence for a while. Aidan was desperately hoping she was right. If they were turned back now, it would make a long, tough walk even harder.

Ahead of them was a stone wall, with a belt of trees behind it.

Beside him, Melangell crowed triumphantly. "See? There *is* a farm."

Aidan checked the map. "There shouldn't be, yet. There are farms either side of the river, but they're further down the valley. All it's got here is a bit of Gothic lettering that says *Chapel (ruins)*."

"If it's a ruin, there won't be anyone there to stop us, will there?"

She headed with determination towards the stone wall. Aidan caught a glimpse of a grey building between the trees.

"It *is* a house, Daddy. I'd like to live here, between Pennant Melangell and the waterfall."

There was a gate. To Aidan's relief, there was no sign forbidding entry.

He put out his hand to open it, and stopped. Against his expectations, there were voices on the other side of the trees. Loud voices.

Between the trunks, Aidan could make out two figures. Both men. One he recognized, even from behind. The burly figure of Thaddaeus Brown with his distinctive black head. The other was even taller, but cadaverous. He stooped over the large bulk of Thaddaeus. His Welsh accent rose sharply on the breeze.

"I'll never let you do it… Vandal!… Hang-gliding in this valley of the hare? It would be sacrilege!"

The lower boom of Thaddaeus's voice was harder to make out. Whatever he said, it caused the other to lunge towards him. There was a brief struggle, before Thaddaeus broke free.

Aidan was suddenly reminded of Lorna's torn shirt.

As Thaddaeus strode away, he turned his head. His words sounded clearly now.

"I've told you. You'll regret this."

The Welshman shouted after him, "I warned you. I'll do what I like with what's mine."

Thaddaeus marched past the small grey house and was swallowed up among the trees. They heard the sound of a car.

Aidan and Melangell looked at each other, like guilty conspirators.

Then a grin transformed Melangell's face. "See? I was right. If Mr Brown came by car, there's got to be a road."

"There's just a small problem," Aidan reminded her. "It could be a private drive. He'd come to see the man who lives here. We haven't."

But Melangell scrambled lightly over the gate. She walked out from the trees on to the open grass before the house. The tall man turned to stare at her as she emerged. The skin of his face was stretched tightly over sharp cheekbones. Thin black hair, streaked with white, swept back from his brow like the crest of a heron. Black eyes snapped at her.

"What are you doing on my land?"

"Hello. Do you live here?"

Girl and man spoke simultaneously.

Aidan strode to catch up with his daughter. He tried what he hoped was a disarming smile.

"Excuse me. We've got a bit lost. We walked over the hill from Pennant Melangell to the waterfall and we were looking for an easier way back. We didn't realize anyone lived out here."

The stranger ignored him. Some of the anger drained out of his face as he stared down at Melangell.

"Caradoc Lewis," he said, to her not Aidan. "Yes. I rescued it. It was a ruin when I found it. But I sold my museum in Llanfyllin to buy this land." He gestured at the small stone building. "Capel-y-Cwm. The chapel in the valley. Nobody's cared about it for centuries. Never even asked how it got its name. Some say it was an old Methodist chapel." He gave a scornful laugh. Then he bent low over Melangell. "But I know better. Shall I tell you a secret? Forget about that old church in Pennant Melangell. This is older by far. Long before Christianity, this was a sacred place of worship. The girl with the hare is thousands of years old."

Melangell gazed up at him wide-eyed. "Was *her* name

Melangell too? Like the saint? Mine is."

He gave a start of surprise. "Oh, she's veiled in the mists of time. The Anglo-Saxons called her Eostre, who gave us Easter, long before Christ's resurrection. She will have had an ancient Welsh name earlier still. But yes, Melangell is the one that lives on. You have been given a powerful name."

Aidan stepped forward and held out his hand. "Aidan Davison." He was aware of wanting to break the intimacy between man and girl. "I'm afraid we're staying at the House of the Hare. I hear you were spearheading the opposition to it."

"That man!" Caradoc Lewis almost spat. "Not an ounce of sensitivity in his body to the things of the soul."

"Oh? I'm surprised. We thought the new building blended beautifully with its surroundings."

"And the people he wants to bring to it? I don't mean you. You must have some feeling for the place to call your daughter by that name. But in the future…"

"I shouldn't think he'd get planning permission for the things you were talking about, would he? Hang-gliding? I can't imagine that here."

The black eyes darkened further still. "Thaddaeus Brown is a man who is used to getting what he wants. *Ask his niece!*" There was venom in his last three words.

It brought Aidan up short. His mind flew back to the figure of Lorna Brown, tearful and dishevelled, rushing along the path from the falls. What had happened to her? And which of these two men had been with her?

"Was she at the waterfall? Lorna? With him?" He heard the urgency in his own voice.

Caradoc Lewis's expression changed. It became wary, calculating. Then he smiled thinly.

"I rather think that's a private matter… Now, you were looking for a way back to Pennant Melangell." He smiled at the girl. "I don't usually allow holidaymakers to use my garden as a right of way. But for a young lady called Melangell, I would have to make an exception. Go past the house, through those pine trees, and you'll find a track that will bring you out on the road." He stood aside and made a welcoming gesture that invited them to proceed.

Aidan paused beside the house. He turned to look at it curiously. It was a patchwork of old grey masonry. The gable end showed a round-arched window that could well have been part of a Methodist chapel. But that door post… He felt a flash of both excitement and anger. Surely that was a standing stone older than Christianity? Who had put that there? There were carved heads over the low door that looked medieval.

"May I?" His hands reached for his camera.

"Be my guest. The world should know more about the ancient past of this valley. There are secrets still to be revealed."

Aidan's fingers were busy with lens and shutter. Images of ancient masonry against a backdrop of mountains streaked with the cataract clicked into the camera's memory and his.

"Thank you," he grinned. "I don't know why I hadn't heard of this place before."

"You will," said Caradoc Lewis, vehemently. "The whole world will."

Chapter Six

IT TOOK A FEW ATTEMPTS for Jenny to get used to firing from a wheelchair. She was glad no one was watching now. But soon she settled into a rhythm. Seated comfortably, she could harness all her energy into the draw of arms and chest.

The yew bow felt good in her hands. She loved the wood, golden on the outside of the curve, paler on the inside. It was a beautiful thing. It was odd to think it was designed as an instrument of death.

It was the thought that she held a weapon in her hands that made her suddenly conscious of her surroundings. How safe was this range? Over to her left, a row of outbuildings faced the butts. They, like the mature trees, must have been left over from an earlier house. She was sure they were a safe distance away. But what about the dense shrubbery on her right? She got up from her wheelchair and paced the distance between the firing area and the nearest bushes. Twenty strides. A little over the minimum safety margin. Relieved, she took her seat and picked up the bow again.

The next shot zipped into the bullseye. She was beginning to enjoy herself.

When she had exhausted all her arrows, she started to propel the chair across the grass to collect them from the target. Did she need the chair for this? Couldn't she just get up and walk?

She was just standing up when a young man emerged

from the rhododendron bushes flanking the butts. Jenny felt a flash of alarm. What if he had walked out while she was shooting?

"Stay where you are," he called. "I'll get them."

Jenny paused. She had thought herself alone, but someone had been watching her.

He retrieved the arrows and brought them towards her. He was not someone she had seen in the house, as guest or staff. He looked no more than a teenager in a checked flannel shirt. Over a pair of rather muddy jeans he wore a leather belt with pouches for tools.

"Euan Jones," he said. He held out the red-and-white flighted arrows. "I do the gardens." His voice had the strong music of mid-Wales.

"Jenny Davison," she said, smiling her thanks. "That's very kind of you."

"You like it, do you? This archery stuff?"

"Yes. I've done it for years. At least, before I fell ill. But Sian said I might still be able to do it sitting down. She was right."

"Lorna's good at it." Was that a challenge in his voice?

"Yes, Sian told me she was an archer."

"That's her bow."

Jenny looked at the wooden weapon she was holding. "Sian said I could use it."

"She won't mind. She's not here this morning. Out with *him*." There was fierceness in that last word. Immediately Euan looked round in alarm, as though Thaddaeus might, after all, be listening.

Is everyone here afraid of him? Jenny thought. That nice man with the warm brown eyes?

"I shouldn't think I'll keep it up for very long. I'll probably be finished before she's back."

"It's all right. They're for the guests, really. It's just that this is the one she likes."

"She's got good taste. So do I."

"Well, then. I'd better get back to work. Shout if you need me."

He disappeared into the shrubbery. She had a glimpse of a wheelbarrow before the branches closed behind him.

When she had fired all her arrows again, she waited for a moment. But Euan did not appear from the bushes. She did not want to call him. He had work to do. And she was not going to act the part of an invalid before she had to. There might be so little time left.

This time she got out of the chair and walked the length of the grass to pull the arrows out of the target herself. Eight red bullseyes, and four in the inner circle of yellow. She might have been more accurate standing up.

By the time she got back to the chair, she was more tired than she expected. But she would not give in. She made herself keep going until she had been at the butts for an hour.

Time for coffee.

The house seemed empty. But as Jenny made her way across the hall, Sian appeared from her office.

"How was it? Did you find the chair a help?"

"Yes and no. It took some getting used to, drawing the bow sitting down. But it meant I could keep going for longer than if I'd been on my feet the whole time. I could do with a sit-down now, though. Any chance of a cup of coffee?"

"Coming up. Make yourself at home in the lounge. I'm sorry there's no one else about. The youngsters are off hill-walking. I think the Ewarts have gone back to the church. Mrs Ewart is having a lot of pain in her back. They really hope St Melangell can cure her."

"Do you think she can? I mean, does that sort of thing really happen?"

"Miracles? Like Lourdes? It's hard for me to say. But people believe it does."

Jenny stood, considering this. Was that where she should be? Praying in the church for a miracle?

Did you have to be here, in Pennant Melangell, to pray for help? She knew that at home and across the country, friends were praying for her. And still the oncologist had told her that there was little more they could do. Five months, perhaps. She tried not to be afraid of the shadow that was coming. To meet it bravely, even joyfully. To believe in what lay beyond. The words of the requiem echoed in her mind. *May light perpetual shine upon her.*

She grieved for Aidan and Melangell. She grieved for her own bereavement of their future.

The leather armchair enfolded her kindly. The coffee was rich and strong. She would go to her room presently and rest.

The dining room was even emptier than last night. Only the Ewarts had come back for lunch. Jenny hesitated.

"Would you mind if I joined you? It seems a bit stand-offish to be eating on my own."

"Of course. Our pleasure." Colin Ewart motioned to a chair.

Rachel, she noticed, did not smile. She looked drawn with pain.

"Is your back bad today?" Jenny asked.

Colin's large hand smashed down on the table. "There was all that stuff in the brochure about this place. How people had come here for centuries to get healed. It's a con."

"Colin." Rachel put out her hand to his in embarrassment.

"It's early days yet. They say there's a healing service on Thursday. You've got to be patient."

Is this what it's like, Jenny thought, if you set your faith on a miracle cure and nothing happens? Does it destroy the peace you might otherwise weave for yourself? Or do I just not have enough faith?

"I'm telling you," Colin went on. "If nothing's happened by the end of this week… If Rachel's not better, I'm telling that Mr Brown straight. He's no business putting that on his website. Just to get people here."

Jenny was beginning to wish she had opted to lunch alone.

The meal passed awkwardly. Jenny enjoyed her spicy chicken salad. Archery seemed to have revived her flagging appetite. But Rachel ate little, and her husband glowered through the meal.

Should we have come back here? Jenny wondered. Or kept our precious memory of this place intact?

After lunch, she headed towards the lift. There were voices in the foyer. She was just in time to see Thaddaeus disappearing down the corridor to the right marked "PRIVATE". Sian shot Jenny a small, embarrassed smile. She looked untypically flustered.

On the landing, the sound of tyres on gravel made Jenny pause. Through the front-facing window she saw the Ewarts driving off. And slewing sharply to stop in front of the house, the black Jaguar of yesterday. Two men got out. One small, rotund, with dark-rimmed glasses and grey-black hair curled closely against his scalp. The other taller, square-shouldered, blond. Their closely tailored suits looked oddly out of place in a spot usually frequented by holidaymakers and hikers.

She crossed to her bedroom, picked up the book from her bedside table and lay down. The archery had tired her more than she expected. She had turned two pages before the book began to fall from her limp hand...

She was drifting away when she heard the sound of raised voices below. Men's voices. A twitch of curiosity wondered whose they could be.

Then the house fell quiet again. Sleep claimed her.

She struggled to remember where she was. What time of day. Her hand groped for the watch on the bedside table and did not find it. She opened her reluctant eyes and sat up. The watch was still on her wrist. It showed twenty to three. It was still afternoon. Aidan and Melangell should be back soon.

She got out of bed feeling refreshed. There was an ache in her arms. It took her a moment to remember using the bow that morning. This was a good pain. Wholesome.

She splashed water on her face and retied the pink-and-purple scarf over her bald head.

Before she went downstairs with her book, she walked out on to the balcony. She drank in again the view of mountains and woodland. There were splashes of colour in the grounds. Rhododendrons and azaleas.

She searched the garden below for any sign of Euan in his red checked shirt. Had he worked all morning in the shrubbery by the archery range, or moved on to the flowerbeds or vegetable plot?

These were extensive grounds. One more expense for the House of the Hare. How could Thaddaeus make it pay, with so few guests?

There was no one in sight.

Then she stiffened. There was a high cry by the row of outbuildings beyond the archery range. A slender figure in a black skirt and grey sweater came running into view from the side of the house. Lorna Brown.

"Euan!" Jenny heard the wail distinctly.

And here he was, running out of one of the sheds to meet her.

Lorna fell into his arms. Her black hair cascaded over his shoulder. They were too far away for Jenny to hear what she was saying. But from her heaving body, she was sure that Lorna was pouring out a story to him.

Euan gripped her fiercely, then let her go. His head went up to look at the house. Jenny withdrew swiftly behind the long folkweave curtains.

She sat down on the bed and found she was trembling. Even at that distance, the emotion of that meeting had shaken her. Something had happened to Lorna. Something that had made Euan Jones blaze with anger.

Troubled, Jenny took her book downstairs to one of the wicker chairs on the patio and tried to lose herself in a world of fiction.

Chapter Seven

MELANGELL WAS QUIETER on the way back. She no longer skipped to the sides of the road, examining every unfamiliar flower or newborn lamb.

"Tired?" Aidan asked.

"Quite a bit. But the waterfall was nice."

The low tower of the church came as a welcome sign of familiarity. Aidan marvelled again at how well hidden the House of the Hare was among its trees. Only when they turned in between its gateposts did its angled planes and clear windows rise up in front of them.

The afternoon peace was shattered by the roar of a car engine unnecessarily revved. A black Jaguar shot from the car park in a spray of gravel and zoomed towards the gate. Aidan and Melangell leapt out of the way.

"Them again!" Aidan watched the aggressive spin that slewed the car on to the road. "What's the point in buying an expensive, whisper-quiet car like that, and then driving it like boy racers?"

"They didn't *look* like boy racers," Melangell said. "They're wearing posh suits and ties. They look all wrong for the country. Not like you." Aidan looked down ruefully at his peat-stained shorts and his jumper stuck with bits of gorse.

"I suppose they have business with Mr Brown."

"*I* wouldn't do business with them."

"No. But you're not a million or so pounds in debt. I guess he may be. Seven of us guests are hardly going to pay for all this… Boots off," he ordered at the door.

Melangell removed her trainers. They padded in their socks across the wooden floor.

Sian appeared from her office behind the reception desk.

"She's out on the terrace, enjoying the afternoon sun."

"Did the archery go well?"

"I think so."

Jenny was leaning back in a cane chair among flowered cushions. Aidan could not see her face from behind, but he sensed the relaxation of her pose and was grateful. He tiptoed up and dropped a kiss on her forehead.

She opened lazy eyes and put up a hand to clasp his. "How was the waterfall?"

"Tremendous! It comes down and down and down out of the sky." Melangell slipped round to stand in front of her. "And we heard two men arguing and it was Mr Brown and a very Welsh man called Caradoc Lewis. And before that we saw Lorna Brown and she was crying. And Mr Lewis let us walk back through his garden so we didn't have climb up the hill again."

Jenny looked bewildered at Aidan. He made a wry face.

"It's true, but not necessarily in that order. We met Lorna first, coming away from the waterfall. She really did look distressed. I've been kicking myself ever since that I didn't do more to make her tell us what was wrong. But then we came across Thaddaeus at Caradoc Lewis's. If something had happened to Lorna, you'd think her uncle would be the one she'd go to. Instead, she was rushing back to Pennant Melangell on her own."

"Unless she was running away *from* him," Melangell said.

"Her shirt was torn. I thought at first it might be a boyfriend… Something got out of hand. But the only people who were near were the two men."

Jenny looked up at him, her eyes dark. "She was still in tears when she came back here. She went straight to those outbuildings over there. To Euan Jones. He's the boy that does the gardens."

"You think he... Thaddaeus...?" He cast a warning glance at Melangell.

Jenny shrugged. "You were there. I wasn't. I find it hard to believe that. But it's been worrying me all afternoon. At least... Well, it was rather nice out here in the sun. I think I dozed off again."

He stroked her scarfed head. "I'm not sure this is something we can get involved in. I tried to help, but she just ran past me."

He settled himself into a chair beside her. Melangell had begun to make a daisy chain. The peace of the garden was broken only by the murmur of wood pigeons.

Then out of the shrubbery that separated the house from the archery range someone came running. It was Harry Townsend, one of the young walkers staying at the house. His rucksack bounced on his thin shoulders as he sprinted towards them. Moments later, his dark-haired partner Debbie broke into view. She was looking back over her shoulder as she ran.

Fear rose in Aidan's throat. He leapt to his feet. He should not have let Lorna Brown pass him when something was so obviously wrong. Had something worse been done to her?

Harry reached the terrace. His young face was distraught. "Where's Sian? Something terrible's happened. Back there," he panted. "In the bushes. We took a short cut down from the mountain and he's... he's dead."

"*Who?*"

"Thaddaeus. Mr Brown."

"You go!" Jenny cried, rising from her chair. "Harry! Get Sian to ring 999."

Aidan tore across the lawn. Thoughts were somersaulting through his head. Thaddaeus? Not Lorna?

He was aware of Melangell running beside him.

"Go back!" he ordered.

When he looked round, she was standing where he had left her, a little figure in the middle of the lawn.

He tried to remember where Harry and Debbie had broken out of the trees. A path led through the rhododendrons. Red blossoms shattered as he rushed past.

The path ended in grass. The big man's body was not where Aidan had expected to come upon it, hidden among the screening bushes. Instead, it came into view at the end of the shrubbery, at the side of the archery range, quite near the butts.

Thaddaeus lay on his back. A red-and-white feathered arrow skewered one eye socket.

Aidan stopped dead. Then he moved closer and bent over the body. There was no need to feel for a pulse. The owner of the House of the Hare was undeniably dead. The other eye was open, staring unseeing at the spring sky.

He could not help it. He had done his share of selling news photographs. His first instinct was to reach for his camera. He had left it standing with his rucksack beside his chair, back there across the lawn. Yet his eye still composed the picture in front of him.

The way the red quill matched the scarlet of the blood. The slight iridescence of the fluid escaping from the ruined eye. The mouth stretched in the rictus of shock.

One part of his mind was appalled that he could think like this. Yet he recognized that this was what he did. Took photographs. And the instinct of professionalism saved him from the true horror in front of him. The imaginary lens and viewfinder sheltered him from the full blast of reality.

It was only when he took his eyes away that he felt sick.

Harry and Debbie had followed him back, more slowly. They stood a little way off. Debbie was crying. Harry had his arm around her shoulders.

From far behind he heard Melangell's high voice. "No, Mummy. You're to go back. Daddy said so."

It was not strictly true, but he blessed her for it.

It was a relief when Sian came running, not directly from the house but from the other end of the archery range. She was pale, but struggling to take control of the situation. Her khaki slacks and shirt gave the comforting impression of a uniform.

"I rang the ambulance first. Then the kids told me it was no use. I've called the police. They have to come from Llanfyllin, so it will take them a while."

"There's no need for you to stay," Aidan told the young couple. "There's nothing you can do. Go and get yourselves a hot drink." To Sian: "I can stay with him, if you like. You'll have things you need to see to."

None of them saw her coming. Lorna's high shriek shocked Aidan, almost more than the sight of the dead man had. She had her hand to her mouth, biting her fingers. He noticed she had changed out of the torn shirt and stained jeans. She wore a grey, tight-fitting sweater and a black skirt. Eerily funereal. Beside her, a boy her age in a tartan shirt had his arm round her. He must be Euan, the gardener Jenny had told him about. Beyond the butts were the sheds where she had said the young pair had met.

Sian went to Lorna. "You shouldn't be here, love. Let me take you back to the house. This is a dreadful business. Dreadful."

"What…? Who did it?" The girl's voice was shaking.

"Goodness knows. That will be for the police to find out."

Sian's arm was firm round the girl, steering her away.

The little crowd was dispersing, leaving Aidan with the macabre remains. Only Euan stayed. He glared down at the prostrate form of his employer, with the arrow of death still upright in his skull.

"He deserved it," he muttered.

Chapter Eight

THE POLICEWOMAN CAME more quickly than Aidan had expected. He heard her talking to Sian as they came through the bushes.

"I was in the area, 'making enquiries', as we say. Mine was the nearest car, so I got landed with it."

They came out on to the grass. She was a small dark woman.

"Dear God!" She recovered her professionalism. "Well, you don't need a degree in forensics to tell he's dead, do you?" She held out her hand, then changed her mind and showed him her warrant card. "PC Watkins. Was it you who found the body?"

"No. It was a couple of teenagers who are staying at the house."

"Harry Townsend and Debbie French," Sian put in. "They were coming back from a walk on the hills and took a short cut through the grounds. A nice pair, but they're a bit shaken up by this."

"I'm not surprised. Like King Harold at the Battle of Hastings, isn't it?"

"I said I'd stay around until you came," Aidan explained.

"Good of you. Who do you think shot him?" PC Watkins turned to Sian. "Could it have been an accident? Someone missed the target and was too frightened to say?"

Sian shook her head. "I've no idea. As far as I know, no

one was shooting this afternoon. Nobody asked me for the key to the games shed."

"That would be where?"

Sian pointed to the wooden building where Jenny had chosen her bow that morning. "I keep the key at reception. I suppose someone could have helped themselves."

Constable Watkins seemed to shake herself out of her train of thought. "I'm running ahead of myself. Whatever happened, he certainly didn't die of natural causes. In fact, they might as well have put it straight through to CID as soon as they heard about it."

She drew out her radio.

"I don't know if you'll get a signal," Sian said. "We have trouble with mobile phones, because we're pretty hemmed in by mountains. You can use the land line back in the house if you need to."

"Don't worry. I've got a hook-up to the system through my car radio set. And there are a couple of things I need from the car."

The policewoman looked at Aidan a little unhappily. "I'm sorry to land you with this again, sir. Would you mind staying with the body a little longer? I'll be right back." She disappeared with Sian.

But it was not Watkins who relieved him of his macabre responsibility. Two uniformed policemen came striding up the archery range. A burly sergeant with pepper-and-salt hair and a lanky constable.

"Sergeant Morris and PC Roberts. We'll take over now, if you don't mind."

"Are you the CID? I wasn't expecting you so soon." He looked at their uniforms in surprise.

"She's called them in, has she?" snorted the sergeant. "At least she's done something right. But you'd think she'd have the gumption to mark off the crime scene. Roberts, get some tape."

As the constable headed off, PC Watkins came hurrying back from the house, alone this time. She carried her own coil of tape in her hand.

She checked when she saw the man with Aidan. "What are you doing here… if you'll forgive me asking, Sergeant? I was the one Newtown sent. It's my shout."

"We were nearly as close, *Constable*. And this looks like more than a girl can handle on her own."

The small policewoman drew herself up to her full height. "For your information, I'm twenty-nine, Sergeant. And I've been through the same training as you." The dark eyes took on a metallic glint. "I know the drill for being the first on a murder scene. If it *is* murder, and not an accident. But you wouldn't want to miss out on your bit of excitement, would you?"

"I suggest you get back to whatever you were doing before that call, Constable. Let the big boys handle this one."

"I've called in CID. I'll be here when they come."

Roberts came loping back across the range with a coil of police tape.

"Right. Fence off this area, will you?"

Watkins watched them. "You don't suppose he was shot in the eye from point blank range, do you? Shouldn't you be preserving evidence back there?" She nodded towards the other end of the range, where Jenny had positioned herself this morning.

This recollection jolted Aidan out of the stupor he had felt since the police arrived and took matters out of his hands. Jenny, so happy with that golden yew bow, recovering some of the joy she had felt in the sport when she was well. And someone else who must have been standing there not long after her, drawing back another bow, loosing it at the unsuspecting figure of Thaddaeus Brown.

Meanwhile, over his head, the uniformed police manoeuvred for professional advantage.

He was startled when a hand tapped his shoulder. "It's all right, sir. You can go back to the house now. We'll handle this." Constable Watkins's eyes were more sympathetic for him.

Aidan rose stiffly to his feet. He had not realized how long he had been kneeling beside the body. He felt a little unsteady now.

"You all right, sir? Shall I walk you back?"

"No, thanks." He managed a shaky smile. "I guess I could do with the obligatory hot cup of tea."

"Don't leave the house, sir," Sergeant Morris ordered. "We'll want to question you."

"I was going to take statements from everyone," muttered Watkins as she steered him away.

"I'm not going anywhere. We're staying at the house."

A darker shadow fell over his mind. He had been sustained by that self-righteous feeling that he was doing his citizen's duty. Guarding the body until the police arrived. Shielding young Harry and Debbie from staying longer with this sight. Now he had moved into a different category. A witness to be questioned. Even, judging from the sergeant's severe tone, a possible suspect.

As he walked back across the lawn, he was belatedly aware that he was still in his hiking socks. His boots were back on the patio with his rucksack.

More alarming facts were slowly sinking in. Pennant Melangell was a small and remote place. There were only a handful of people here who could have shot Thaddaeus Brown.

Suddenly he was jolted out of his thoughts. Seemingly out of nowhere, there was a camera in front of his face. Even in that moment of shock, Aidan recognized its professional quality. The large lens was trained on his face. His image snapped.

"Who the...?" Aidan shouted, overcome with anger.

The camera dropped from a round, almost boyish face. Fair, wavy hair was combed up above his innocent blue eyes.

The younger man held out a hand. "Marcus Coutts. I gather we're in the same line of business." His voice had a nasal twang.

Aidan's outraged eyes took in the high-end Leica camera, the tan leather jacket, beige trousers and floral shirt.

"What the hell are you doing here?"

"Come now. I should have thought that was obvious. Don't tell me you haven't got a shot in first. Over there, is he? The body? They tell me this is a juicy one. Arrow in the eye. Like it! You'll need to be quick off the mark to beat me to the dailies. They're going to love this."

With a wink at Aidan, he went almost running across the grass to the path that led to Thaddaeus's corpse. Aidan heard the shout of fury from Sergeant Morris.

Still shaking with anger, Aidan picked up his own camera case from the terrace. It did not help that he had imagined himself taking photographs of that grisly scene.

He went through to the lounge to meet the shocked and silent faces of Jenny and Melangell.

Aidan looked round at the sober gathering in the lounge. Like him, they were all waiting to be questioned.

The uniformed police had already taken brief statements of their whereabouts that afternoon. Aidan was aware that his own replies to Sergeant Morris had been terser than they would have been to PC Watkins.

Now the investigation had switched to a higher gear,

with the arrival of the CID. Chief Inspector Denbigh and his sergeant, Lincoln. They had been followed shortly by a forensics team. Out there, on the edge of the archery range, expert minds, gloved hands, protective-suited bodies, would be examining Thaddaeus's corpse. Meanwhile, the inspector had taken over Sian's office as an interviewing room.

It seemed incongruous that the sun was still shining out there on the lawns. That they were all sitting here in their leather armchairs, in this pleasing room Thaddaeus had designed for their comfort and enjoyment. What would happen to the House of the Hare now?

His eyes went to Lorna. Oddly, she seemed less upset now than she had been when he saw her before her uncle's death. Her small figure, in sober black and grey, was half lost in the deep armchair. She looked pale but composed, unlike the distraught figure in torn shirt and jeans they had encountered near the waterfall. Euan looked the more nervous of the two. His shaggy dark hair fell over his downcast eyes. He sat on the very edge of his seat, as though he felt he did not deserve the greater comfort of the cushions behind him. Clearly, he was longing to be out of doors, more at ease with his tools and wheelbarrow.

The Ewarts looked bewildered. They had arrived back at the house after Aidan and Melangell. They seemed like two innocents caught up in a horror for which they could not possibly be responsible. Aidan could not imagine Rachel, small and pain-wracked, even attempting to draw a bow. And the precision required to send that arrow through Thaddaeus's eye seemed out of place with Colin's blustering.

Harry and Debbie were still clearly frightened by their experience. Harry's white-knuckled hand was gripping Debbie's.

Josef, the chef, Aidan had barely glimpsed before. Just a figure in a long white apron and black-and-white checked trousers, busy in the kitchen preparing mouth-watering food. Now he sat, still and tense, awaiting his turn with the rest of them. Had he other things to be nervous of? Was he really from Poland? If not, did he have the necessary work permit?

Sian herself seemed the calmest of them all. Aidan guessed that it must help that she was in charge now. Her head must be full of all the practical things that needed to be done in the wake of her employer's death. It was like the busyness of a family before a funeral, for whom the full impact of the loss would only hit home after the necessities of death certificates and funeral teas were dealt with.

Did Thaddaeus have any family besides Lorna?

His questing eyes and questioning mind had passed over the only other two people in the room. Jenny, still and pale. Melangell, who was lying on her stomach behind the sofa, intent on her jigsaw.

The door opened. The lanky form of Constable Roberts appeared. He was visibly swelling with the importance of being involved in a murder enquiry.

"Mr Townsend, please."

With a startled look at Debbie, Harry rose from his seat and made his way across the rugs, watched by all those other pairs of eyes.

Chapter Nine

ETECTIVE CHIEF INSPECTOR Denbigh had the world-weary air of an elderly schoolmaster, who has seen all the tricks adolescent boys can play and is impressed by none of them. Aidan was aware of the balding DS Lincoln in the corner of Sian's office, watching him over his notepad with sharp black eyes.

The office surprised Aidan. The computer desk might have been cleared to assist the police, but the shelves of colour-coded, neatly labelled files were meticulously tidy. The bushranger outfit Sian habitually wore had led him to think she might be an outdoor type who spent as little time as possible on the minutiae of office work. But perhaps he was wrong. PE teachers would be particular about playing by the rules. And the House of the Hare showed every sign of being a well-run establishment.

The inspector's voice called him back to the serious task in hand. "Now, Mr Davison, if you'd like to give us an account of your movements, leading up to the time when Mr Townsend told you he had found the body."

"I'd come back from a walk, about three o'clock."

"A walk, Mr Davison? Could you be more precise?"

Aidan hesitated, then launched into an account of their ill-advised expedition to reach the foot of the waterfall. He passed over their fleeting encounter with Lorna Brown without mentioning it. There had been something too disturbing, too unexplained. He was not sure he had the right words for it.

But it clearly mattered that he tell the inspector where he had last seen Thaddaeus Brown.

"I was sure I'd seen a short cut back, so we set off down the valley, and then we heard these voices."

The heavy grey eyebrows rose, waiting.

"It was Thaddaeus Brown and a man I hadn't met before. Caradoc Lewis. They were arguing about something."

"*Something*, Mr Davison?"

"I heard the word 'hang-gliding'." Aidan felt the colour in his cheeks. How much was it right to pass on hearsay? "I've heard that sort of thing before. People expressing fears that the House of the Hare might not be just for those who want to come on pilgrimage to St Melangell's shrine, or enjoy the peace of the mountains. That he might want to make it more of an extreme sports centre, to make it pay."

"*People*. Now that's not very precise, is it?"

"Sian," he murmured, feeling guilty now. "She used to teach PE, so she's keen on sport for keeping people fit. Like archery…"

He saw the sergeant's balding head jerk up.

Aidan rushed on. "I mean, I don't know whether she shoots herself. But you've seen the butts. It's for guests. That's the sort of thing Sian's promoting. Not waterfall walking or bungee jumping."

The inspector's voice pressed relentlessly on. "What time was it when you saw Mr Brown?"

"About two, I think. We'd had our lunch. He drove away towards Pennant Melangell. We talked to Caradoc Lewis after he'd gone, and then walked back along the road to here."

The steady grey eyes regarded him. "You're a photographer, I hear. A man whose sharp eyes notice things. What else have you seen or heard while you've been here that would give you the feeling that there was animosity towards Thaddaeus Brown?"

Aidan was growing increasingly uncomfortable. It was one thing to give an account of his own movements. Another to implicate other people. It seemed unlikely that the eccentric Caradoc Lewis could have followed them to Pennant Melangell unnoticed, in time to shoot Thaddaeus. But he felt guilty that he might have cast suspicion on him. And Sian.

It seemed better to cast the net wider.

"Mother Joan at the church didn't seem to want Pennant Melangell to be overrun. But I don't remember her saying anything personal against Thaddaeus. Harry and Debbie were worried that the House of the Hare is a bit too expensive for people like them, but that's hardly a motive for murder. Colin Ewart was upset because the place doesn't seem to be doing anything to help his wife's back. He blamed Thaddaeus for misleading advertising. But the Ewarts got back after we found the body."

"Anyone else?"

Conscience hammered at Aidan's sense of honesty.

He lowered his head, addressing the hiking socks, where leaf mould from the shrubbery still clung. "We were nearly at the foot of Pistyll Blaen-y-cwm," he muttered. "Someone appeared from the direction of the falls. Lorna Brown. She was... crying. Her shirt was torn. She wouldn't say what was the matter."

The sergeant's voice came from the corner. "And that was how long before you saw Mr Brown with Mr Lewis?"

"About an hour, maybe less. We stopped for a picnic and a rest."

"How far would it be from this waterfall to Caradoc Lewis's place?"

"Capel-y-Cwm? A quarter of a mile, I should think."

"Was she heading that way?" the inspector asked.

"She was walking beside the stream when we met her.

Almost running. But on the left side. The path we took veers off to the right. I don't think she took it, but I'm not sure. But we'd seen her earlier on that path, coming from there towards the falls with someone else."

"Who?"

"It was too far away to see. We were up on the hill. But I saw Lorna's white shirt."

"Now I wonder whether Miss Brown knows how to use a bow."

Aidan felt his heart sink lower. "Sian said she does."

There was a long silence. Aidan raised his eyes. There was a shaving cut on the inspector's chin. He looked like a man who used an old-fashioned razor.

"Thank you, Mr Davison. You've been very helpful."

Aidan's panicked eyes met the inspector's. He rose. "If it *was* Thaddaeus who upset Lorna, ask Euan Jones."

The inspector's brows lifted again. "Really, now? I think I shall."

Aidan turned at the door. "Could I ask a favour? Would you see my wife next? She's unwell, and this is very distressing. She needs to rest."

Inspector Denbigh glanced down at the list on the desk. "Jennifer Davison. Writer. Suffers from cancer."

Aidan's heart felt more hollow. Was nothing secret? He supposed Sian had supplied details of the guests and staff.

The inspector's eyes softened a little. "Tell your wife she can go upstairs and rest. We'll see her later." He gave a weary smile. "I don't expect she's letting fly with arrows these days, is she?"

Someone was rocking her shoulder. Aidan's voice said gently, "Jenny, love? It's time to wake up. The police want to talk to you."

She sat up slowly, fighting off the grogginess of sleep and drugs.

Aidan's bearded face looked anxious. "Are you OK? If not, I'll tell the inspector. They can see you some other time."

"No." She made an effort to swing her feet to the floor. "I've got to do this. A man is dead. Let's get it over with."

He helped her find her shoes. She rearranged her headscarf. The face that looked back at her in the mirror was paler than she would have liked, the eyes darkly hollowed. She looked more ill than she wanted to admit yet. For a moment, she thought of accepting Aidan's suggestion and going back to bed.

Instead, she stood, unsteadily, and let Aidan take her arm.

She smiled at him ruefully. "Thanks. Perhaps the people who told us 'Don't go back' were right. We could have kept our memories intact."

Entering Sian's office, her senses came more keenly alert. Chief Inspector Denbigh rose to greet her with old-fashioned courtesy. He held out his hand.

"I'm sorry to disturb you, Mrs Davison. We'll try not to keep you long."

"That's all right. I understand. Mr Brown is dead. If I can help in any way, I will."

"That's very understanding of you. Please. Take a seat."

The smile withdrew. The look was steadier now. "If you could just take us through your movements this afternoon…"

"There's not much to say. I had lunch with the Ewarts. Then I went back to bed. I'm afraid I spend a good deal of the time resting these days. Then I took a book down to the patio. I was sitting reading when Aidan and Melangell got back."

"What time would that be?" asked the plain-clothes sergeant with the notepad.

She turned a confused face to him. "I didn't notice. Around three, I think. We'd only been talking for a few minutes when Harry came running across the lawn shouting that they'd found a body."

Inspector Denbigh tapped the desk with a fingernail. "I understand your room is at the back of the house."

"Yes."

"Did you, by any chance, see anything, anyone at all, in the grounds before you came downstairs, or after?"

Jenny frowned. Aidan had shared with her the guilt he felt that he had told the police about his meeting with the distraught Lorna at the waterfall.

"*I didn't want to give them the impression that she had something against Thaddaeus,*" he had said.

Now she felt the same sense of betrayal.

"I saw Lorna come back," she said, reluctantly.

"Alone? Or with Mr Brown?"

"I don't know how she got here. I might have heard a car. No, that was earlier. The Ewarts going out after lunch. And two men coming in. I didn't know them."

The sergeant consulted his notes. "Mr Secker and Mr McCarthy. We know about them. They left around three."

"It was earlier than that when I saw Lorna. About twenty to three. She was on foot then. I don't know how she got back."

"Would you mind telling me where you saw her?"

"There's a sort of stable-block. Old outbuildings, beyond the archery butts. She came running past that side of the house. And met Euan Jones."

"The gardener."

"That's right."

"How did she seem? I know it's a long way from your window, but was there anything you noticed?"

"Yes,' she said, unhappily. "She seemed... distressed. She

ran straight to Euan. He put his arms round her."

There was a long pause.

"Thank you, Mrs Davison. That's very helpful."

She raised her eyes. "Can I go now?"

"Just one thing. I hear you were at the archery butts this morning."

Jenny tensed. "Yes," she said, tersely.

"Don't misunderstand me," he smiled. "We realize you are hardly in a fit state to fire an arrow in anger, even if you had a reason. Miss Jenkins tells me you used a wheelchair."

It took a moment for Jenny to remember that Miss Jenkins was Sian.

"It's perfectly possible to do archery sitting down," she said, crisply. "It's a sport in the Paralympics. I can still shoot standing up, but Sian suggested it would be less tiring in a chair."

"Of course," he said, soothingly. "I'm sure a little light exercise is good for you." His tone changed. "I understand Miss Brown is also something of an archer."

"I haven't seen her shoot," Jenny answered. "But when Euan Jones brought me back the arrows I'd shot he said she was good. We have the same tastes, apparently. It seems we both think the natural yew bow I was using is nicer than the new high-tech alloy ones. It feels right, somehow."

"Like the longbow men at Agincourt."

She felt her face register surprise.

"Some of us know our history books, Mrs Davison. The yew longbow was a deadly weapon. Not that I'm comparing that to your own hobby."

The sergeant's voice cut across them. "Can ballistics tell which bow fired an arrow? Like with a gun?"

The inspector turned a weary face to him. "Now how would they do that, boy?" He turned back to Jenny. "Thank you. You've been most helpful. I'm sorry we had to disturb your rest."

She rose with the strangely disorientated feeling that she was not certain just how much she had said or how he had interpreted it.

On her way out, his voice arrested her.

I believe you have your daughter with you."

At once, alarm bells rang. "Melangell? Yes."

"How old is she?"

"Seven."

"I wonder if you would mind if we asked her a few questions? You or your husband would be present, of course."

"She didn't see anything. She'd only just got back from the walk."

"I assure you, we won't say anything to upset her."

Melangell sat, self-importantly upright, in front of the chief inspector. Sergeant Lincoln had been replaced by PC Watkins. The constable was glowing with satisfaction that she had been given this part in the investigation. Aidan stood behind Melangell, while Jenny sat beside her.

"They were arguing," Melangell said in her clear voice. "Mr Brown and Mr Caradoc."

"Mr Lewis," PC Watkins explained. "Caradoc Lewis."

"Yes, him. He's a funny sort of man. But I liked his house. It's got a carving of a hare over his door. And he shouted at Mr Brown that he could do what he liked with what was his own."

"Mr Brown could? Or Mr Lewis?"

"The Welsh one. Mr Lewis."

"And what did he mean by 'his own'?"

"I don't know. Before they saw us, Mr Brown went away. We heard his car. Then Mr Lewis shouted at us, but in the end he was nice and let us go through his garden to the road."

"Well done, Miss Melangell. You've got sharp ears and eyes." He raised his eyes to Aidan. "I don't think you told us all of that, Mr Davison."

"I'm not sure I remember all the details of their argument myself. But I think she's got it right."

Jenny felt relief sliding over her. Whatever was wrong between Lorna and her uncle, someone else had reason to hate him, by the sound of it.

Melangell's voice cut across her thoughts. "There was something else I forgot to say. We were just coming back to the house when this car came zooming past us. We've seen it before, when we were on our way here. The car had dark windows, but you could just see two men inside it. In the wrong sort of clothes for here." She reached up an affectionate hand to fondle Aidan's Fair Isle jumper. "Suits and ties." Then she clapped her hand to her mouth, blushing, as the inspector looked down at his own. "They were driving much too fast," she added, defiantly.

The inspector's gaze was enigmatic. Jenny turned a questioning glance up at Aidan. Why had the men in the Jaguar come back to the House of the Hare so soon before Thaddaeus's death?

"Thank you, Melangell. You can go now. Don't have bad dreams. We'll catch whoever did this. You're quite safe."

Jenny ushered Melangell out of the crowded office. The quality of silence in the House of the Hare was no longer peaceful, but tense.

Chapter Ten

"**P**OOR JOSEF**,"** Jenny said. "I hope they let him get back to his kitchen in time to prepare the evening meal."

"I'm not sure anyone's going to have much appetite." Aidan had carried his walking boots upstairs. He peeled off his sweater. "Gorse," he explained, as Jenny watched him removing the spines from the wool.

Out in the grounds, the scene-of-crime officers were still at work. Jenny tried not to think about it.

"Mummy! Daddy! Quick!" Melangell's cry came from across the corridor.

They rushed to her room. She was at her window, bouncing with impatience. "Look! Look! And there's that man taking photographs."

Jenny was just in time to see Lorna Brown's black hair bowing beneath the hand of Sergeant Lincoln, who was guiding her into the back of a car. He went around to the other side and got in beside her. Detective Chief Inspector Denbigh took the wheel. The car circled in front of the house and drove off.

From Aidan's description, Jenny recognized Marcus Coutts dashing forward to snap the occupants, while a uniformed constable tried in vain to hold him back. She had a glimpse of more photographers outside the gate.

Jenny sat down suddenly on Melangell's bed. She felt herself go pale.

"What are they doing?" Melangell asked. "Why are they taking her away? Has she done something wrong?"

Aidan's guilt-stricken face ignored his daughter's alarm. "I could kick myself for telling them about what happened at the waterfall," he said, savagely. "I should never have jumped to conclusions as to what that was all about. She could have been jilted by a boyfriend. Her pet cat might have died. It didn't have to be anything to do with Thaddaeus."

"You had to tell him." Jenny laid her hand on his bare arm. She felt the tickle of sandy hairs under her palm. "So did I. I had to say I'd seen her come back, in distress. About her meeting Euan. I couldn't *not* tell him."

"It's all right." She turned gently to Melangell, whose eyes were darting from one to the other. "They've just taken Lorna to the police station to ask her some more questions. They're trying to find out how Mr Brown died."

"Do they think she did it?"

"I don't know."

"*I* don't think she did. She's nice."

"Neither do I. Now get washed. I don't know where your father took you. You've still got blood all over your arms. It'll be time for supper soon."

Hungry or not, the guests of the House of the Hare were gathered in the lounge, waiting for the dining room doors to open. The Davisons passed the sofa where Colin and Rachel Ewart sat staring morosely out at the lawn.

Colin erupted into life as they came within earshot.

"It's a disgrace! '*Peace and tranquillity*' he promised us. '*You can sense the healing in the air*'. And what do we let ourselves in for? A murder enquiry! Some sort of peace, this is."

"Hush, now." His wife placed a nervous hand over his.

"I don't think poor old Thaddaeus could have foreseen this when he wrote the brochure," Aidan said, in an attempt to mollify him.

Jenny had a sudden vision of the revised text. "*Guests are advised to avoid 24 April, because I shall be murdered that day.*" She had difficulty restraining herself from bursting into hysterical laughter.

Colin Ewart's glinting eyes found hers. "You find this funny?"

"No, no. We're all upset, I think. It certainly wasn't what we imagined when we booked a week here. Like you, we came for the peace... and the healing." Her voice dropped. She met Aidan's eyes. Spiritual healing? Physical? They had never fully discussed the delicate subject of why they were here. Was it just to remember the golden days of their first love? To show Melangell?

Melangell said, "What do you think's for supper?"

As if on cue, the doors of the dining room swung open. It was not Sian in charge this evening. They were met by a teenager with bouncing dark curls. She wore a red apron over black shirt and trousers. Behind the heavy make-up, her brown eyes flashed with excitement.

Three tables had been laid. The one in the window, where Thaddaeus and Lorna had dined last night, stood bare.

Jenny studied the menu. "I'll have the sausage and mash with onion gravy," she told the girl. "But could you make that a small helping?" She looked up at the teenager's face. "You must be Mair, from the next village. I thought Sian said you'd gone back to college."

"I've got my course work to hand in next week. Business Studies. But you have to help out, don't you, when it's a friend? Sian's been good to me."

Jenny looked around the room. "She's not eating here tonight?"

"She's in her office. Crying her eyes out. Something to do with a bow. Says she wishes she'd never told the police how good Lorna was with it." Mair gave an exaggerated shudder. "Gives you the heebie-jeebies, doesn't it? She's no older than me. Lorna Brown, I mean. And to think of her shooting her uncle in the eye. Must have been a horrible sight."

Jenny shot a warning look at Melangell. Mair took the hint, too late.

"Oh, sorry! Big mouth, me. I'll give Josef your orders. Poor sod. He hardly knows whether he's coming or going. And Sian's asked him to do sandwiches for them out there." She nodded towards the shrubbery that hid the archery butts from the ground floor rooms.

She swept away, ignoring the peremptory beckoning of Colin Ewart.

A subdued group sipped coffee in the lounge. In the evening shadows, the SOCO team packed up and walked round the house to their vehicles. Harry and Debbie got up abruptly and left the room.

"We thought we might drive over to Lake Vyrnwy tomorrow," Rachel Ewart said, timidly. "Get away from it all."

"I'd pack up and go," her husband snorted. "But that police inspector as good as ordered us to stay."

"I suppose they may have more questions to ask us," Jenny suggested, "when they've looked at the evidence they've found today."

"Obvious, isn't it? The man was shot with an arrow. And

who shoots around here? His niece. Probably did it for the money."

"Is there any?" Aidan asked. The pointed beard gave his head a gnome-like air as he cocked it towards the Ewarts. "I'd have thought he was up to his ears in debt, now he's built all this, and the tourists are hardly streaming through the doors."

"Oh, he'll have been rolling in it. I know the sort. This will just have been a little sideline of his. Something to set against tax. He's in the money, all right. Look at those two characters who showed up this afternoon in a Jaguar XF. Dark glasses. Savile Row suits. You mark my words. There'll be all sorts of shady dealing you and I know nothing about. Nor HM Revenue and Customs either, I shouldn't wonder. The House of the Hare. *Peace and healing.* Do me a favour! More likely links with the Mafia, if you ask me."

Jenny felt wearied by his outrage.

"I think I'll have an early night. It's been a bad day. You all right with your jigsaw, honey?"

Melangell twisted her mop of curls from where she lay on her stomach. "Night, Mummy. I'm fine. Just this bit of mountain and the sky to do. There's too much blue."

Jenny bent and kissed her. "Sleep well, love. Sweet dreams."

What would her own dreams bring her? she wondered.

Aidan kissed her, too. "I'll be up later."

In the hall she met Sian. The manager's face was tear-streaked. Her fair hair stood out wildly, as though she had pulled her fingers through it.

"Oh, Mrs Davison. You're calling it a day? I don't blame you."

Jenny hesitated. "I'm sorry to hear about Lorna. This is a dreadful business. But I can't really believe that it was her, can you? To shoot her uncle in cold blood?"

Sian's plump face was anguished. "I told them about her using the archery butts."

"Don't blame yourself. So did I. Euan told me she did. He said she liked that yew bow, too. I've wondered since. Was it the yew bow that killed him, or one of the modern ones?"

"Does it matter? They'll know it has to be someone who's a good shot."

Sian turned away. Jenny watched her go. That morning on the archery range seemed so long ago now. Sian had discussed the equipment with her so knowledgeably. It had never occurred to Jenny to ask if Sian practised archery herself.

Chapter Eleven

A IDAN WOKE WITH A SENSE of horror. He was sitting bolt upright in the darkness, sweat cold on his skin. He struggled to put a name to the terror of his nightmare.

It came flooding back. Jenny. He had to watch, immobile, as she raised the yew bow from the unfamiliar stance of a wheelchair. Drawing back the string to full stretch. And at the fatal moment, Thaddaeus Brown emerged from the shrubbery on to the range.

A start of her arm. Too late to abort the shot. Unable to move a limb to stop it, he saw their host felled by that cruelly deflected arrow.

As he had in reality, he looked down into that ruined face.

Even as he relived the horror of it, his rational mind told him it was nonsense. He and Melangell had left Jenny practising archery in the morning, hours before Thaddaeus's death. They had come back to find her drowsing serenely on the patio. Even if she had returned to the butts, it was inconceivable that Jenny, who was facing her own death so bravely, would not have confessed to such a ghastly accident.

But the sense of helpless horror remained.

He turned towards her. In the dark, he sensed rather than saw that she was sleeping peacefully.

He was appalled at himself. He must never, ever, let her know what his unconscious had accused her of.

An air of waiting hung over the valley next morning. The police had taken over a workshop on the far side of the archery range. Melangell watched avidly as a van drew into the drive and unloaded some computers and whiteboards. From Jenny and Aidan's balcony they could see officers carrying this equipment along the path. Sergeant Morris was uncoiling a cable to the house.

There was still police tape around the place where Thaddaeus's body had been found and the games hut at the nearer end of the range.

"They'll find my footprints on the grass," Jenny said. "My fingerprints on the arrows and the bow. But the inspector is gallantly convinced that I'm too frail to have fired a shot with lethal effect."

She saw an expression of alarm widen Aidan's eyes. Then he rallied. "He should see you in action. How many bullseyes did you hit?"

"Two out of three. The wheelchair took a bit of getting used to."

"How do you feel today? Any after-effects?"

"It's better if different bits of me hurt. And better still when I don't think too much about it."

"We could take a drive, if you like. It doesn't look as though they're in any hurry to question us again. The Ewarts have gone to Lake Vyrnwy. We can tell the police what time we're coming back."

Jenny thought for a moment. "Perhaps later. I'd like to go over to the church, if that's all right."

"Of course. Do you want us to come with you?"

"That's up to you. We ought to take Melangell's mind off things, I suppose."

"What I'd really like to do is to take more photos of

those yews. They're astonishing. I'm fascinated by the way the trunks are knotted and coiled, as though a giant had seized them in his fist and twisted them. Melangell's fallen in love with them. She'll be off in some fairy tale adventures about them."

There was a policeman on the hotel gate, but most of the reporters had gone. They walked the short distance down the lane to the little church. Outside a cottage, a man in a tan leather jacket was talking to the owner. A camera hung ready round his neck.

"That's him," growled Aidan. "That press photographer who stuck a Leica in my face."

"He's horrible." Jenny shuddered. "Thaddaeus's blood was hardly dry when he got into the house. He was taking photos of all of us. Asking all sorts of questions."

"Did you tell him anything?"

"Of course not. I didn't *know* anything. But I saw the Ewarts talking to him when they got back. I think they were flattered by the attention. Colin must have fancied seeing himself in the national newspapers."

The noticeboard in front of the church announced it open. There was a welcome in Welsh and English.

They went through the lychgate, overshadowed by the first of the yews. Others spread to left and right inside the low circular wall.

"That's the one with the hiding place," Melangell cried. She ran round to the side of the gigantic trunk facing the church.

Aidan marvelled at it. "That hollow in the trunk's so vast, you wonder there's enough wood left to hold the tree up."

It was the perfect place for make-believe. Melangell was already away from them, lost in a world of her own making.

Aidan was getting out his camera, choosing lenses.

Jenny touched the convoluted bark. It felt rough against

her fingertip, not the smooth polished wood of the bow stave. Yew. Guardians of so many churchyards, and of a sacred meeting place here long before that. Wood for the longbow men of England and Wales, feared across the Continent. A healing drug for cancer.

The berries were poisonous, she remembered.

She walked on, into the cool of the church. She sat on one of the embroidered hassocks in a pew and bowed her head in prayer. She had not really formulated why she had wanted to come today, or what she dared to pray for.

She emptied her mind and let the peace steal in.

What came was not what she expected, though a reproving voice told her she should have thought of it. Not a prayer for herself, for the disease invading her body, for courage in the months to come, for Aidan and Melangell. To the forefront of her mind sprang the image of Lorna. The lovely black-haired girl with the astonishing blue eyes. Alone in a police cell, her uncle horribly dead. What other family did she have? Jenny felt guilty that she hadn't asked Sian. It was Lorna who needed peace and courage.

She got up and walked to the chancel. This time, she paused only briefly at the stone-canopied shrine behind the altar, with its drift of prayer cards.

She stepped through into the cobbled apse beyond. A simple space, almost devoid of furnishings. To the right, an irregular slab of natural rock, set in the floor. Coffin-shaped. Leaning against the wall behind it was a banner embroidered with the figure of a young woman with a hare at her feet. Jenny gazed down with a strange quickening of her heart. Under that slab had lain the bones later interred in the shrine. A woman's bones. Almost certainly St Melangell's.

Jenny didn't really believe in praying to the saints to intercede for you. What was wrong with talking straight to God? But the sanctity of centuries reached out and enfolded her. Prayers, like a multitude of snowflakes drifting down out of the vast sky. She added her own.

"Please, if you can intercede for Lorna, help her now. Hold her safe as you did the hare."

She tried to push away the thought that Lorna might actually be guilty. She had looked frightened. A victim, not a murderer. Where would the girl who had come fleeing to Euan have found the steadiness and resolve to aim an arrow so precisely at her uncle's eye? Whatever Thaddaeus had done to her.

If not Lorna, then who?

The answer came with startling clarity. Who had been there to hear her story? Whose arms had gone round the girl to shield her? Surely the police could see that a far more likely suspect was Euan Jones?

Then she sighed. She remembered Euan collecting her arrows from the butts. The possessive way he had told her that she was using Lorna's bow. There was nothing to suggest that the young gardener had ever fired an arrow himself.

Whoever killed Thaddaeus must have been an expert archer.

Aidan's viewfinder scanned the walls of the church. It picked out a block of pink sandstone among the grey. Almost certainly a fragment of St Melangell's shrine, incorporated after its destruction in the sixteenth century.

The lychgate banged loudly behind him. He turned.

The tall, stooped figure striding up the path was instantly recognizable, even after a single meeting. Caradoc Lewis, of Capel-y-Cwm near the waterfall, and leader of the opposition to Thaddaeus Brown's plans. Lank black hair fell forward over his forehead. Dark eyes snapped. He had the air of a predatory heron.

Aidan felt a stiffening of unexplained alarm.

"Hello," he said. "We meet again."

Caradoc Lewis stopped with a jerk. His eyes travelled swiftly over Aidan. "Do I know you? Ah, yes. The Englishman with the significantly named little girl. Where is she?"

Melangell's pointed face was peeping out from her hiding-place in the yew, like a hare about to bolt.

"Behind you."

Caradoc's cadaverous face mellowed. He waved to her, somewhat awkwardly. "Hello, Melangell."

"Hello," she said, smiling uncertainly. She did not come out of the hollow tree.

"Bad business." Lewis addressed Aidan again. "I gather I have you to thank for the fact that I've had to waste half a morning with the police."

"Me?"

"It was you who told them you'd seen me talking to that rogue Brown, while you were trespassing on my land."

"Well, yes." Aidan felt indignation stirring. "We all had to account for our movements yesterday. I couldn't not tell them that that was the last time I saw Thaddaeus."

"Hmmph! Well, I dare say they'd have roped me in, anyway. It's no secret I couldn't stand the man. Oh, he played his cards cleverly to get planning permission. Said all the right things. A place to stay for those who want the healing of the shrine. A sort of pilgrim's hospice. But we all know he had worse plans that that. Or he did until I scotched them."

Aidan's eyebrows went up. What did he mean by that?

But Caradoc swept on. "The man hadn't a grain of sensitivity in his body to the spiritual significance of this valley. And I don't mean the Priest-Guardian, as they call her, and the godly St Melangell's Centre. There are far older powers at work here."

Aidan looked appreciatively at the massive yews. "I know those trees are 2,000 years old. And where this church stands is thought to be a Bronze Age sacred site."

"I don't need an archaeologist to tell me that. Not when I can feel it in every bone of my body. And the hare! Since when was that a Christian symbol? Did you know the Catholics show the Virgin Mary with a white hare under her feet, to symbolize her crushing of lust? The old ones knew better. The hare is rebirth, new life. Have you ever seen hares boxing in the moonlight?"

"No."

"It's a magical sight. And it's no coincidence that the hare was found hiding under Melangell's skirt."

Aidan glanced past him at his own Melangell, listening avidly. He thought it time to turn the conversation in another direction.

"You're in the clear, though, aren't you? The police may have thought you had a motive for getting rid of Mr Brown. But whoever did it shot an arrow through his eye. That must narrow down the list of suspects. Did you know they've arrested his niece, Lorna?"

The skull-like face registered shock. "Silly asses! Does she look to you the sort of girl who'd have the nerve to do a thing like that? Wouldn't say boo to a goose, as the saying is."

Aidan shrugged, with feigned indifference. "I've hardly met her. I've no idea what went on between them." He would keep his worst suspicions to himself.

A new thought struck him. Had Thaddaeus really been that second figure with Lorna, on the path to the waterfall? Could it possibly have been Caradoc? What *had* reduced her to tears?

The tall Welshman's avian eyes studied Aidan intently. As if he knew what he was thinking, he asked suddenly, "Did you meet Lorna yesterday on your walk?"

"Yes. Briefly. She passed us." He did not think it necessary to tell this man the details of his encounter with the frightened girl.

"Did she, now?"

The silence was strained with tension. Was Caradoc Lewis waiting for him to say something more? But Aidan kept the vivid image of Lorna's tear-stained face and torn shirt to himself.

Aidan was just putting his camera away when someone else came through the lychgate. He recognized the dumpy figure of Mother Joan.

She gave him a beaming smile as she approached. "All well?"

It was on the tip of his tongue to give the conventional answer, "Yes, fine, thank you," when the truth hit him. His eyebrows lifted.

"You haven't heard?"

"Heard what?"

"Thaddaeus Brown has been killed."

She halted. He took her blank expression to mean incomprehension.

"The owner of the House of the Hare," he explained. "Probably murdered."

The priest's body was rigid now. "How?"

"Shot through the eye with his own bow and arrow. From the games shed. They've arrested his niece."

The rigor of shock softened into an expression of concern. "How dreadful! I didn't know the man, of course. I'm new around here. Just filling in for a week. Still... I wonder... Is there anything I can do? That poor girl."

Aidan shrugged. "Everyone's pretty much in shock at the

house. You might have a word with Sian. She's the manager. She seems the hardest hit."

"I wonder. One doesn't like to intrude. But I could offer. Even non-believers suddenly feel themselves vulnerable to God in the face of mortality. Thank you for telling me."

She walked on into the church, where Caradoc Lewis had disappeared a few minutes before.

He heard her subdued greeting as Jenny emerged.

Chapter Twelve

"**A**RE YOU SURE YOU'RE up to an outing?" Aidan looked at Jenny with concern.

She gave a brave smile. "All I have to do is sit in the car and let you drive me. You're right. We need a change of scenery."

"I suppose I ought to let the police know where we're going. So they don't think we've done a runner."

"The Ewarts went. I bet they didn't ask for permission."

Aidan strolled across the grounds. He noted that the tape had been removed from the spot where he had knelt beside Thaddaeus's body. The games equipment shed was still out of bounds.

The workshop the police had taken over seemed strangely quiet for a murder incident room. There were few officers about. The rest were probably out following up leads elsewhere, Aidan thought.

What leads? It was frustrating to have been so close physically to the murdered man, yet to know so little about him. Those two men in the black Jaguar, for instance. There had been an almost stereotypical air of menace about them, a startling intrusion on the peaceful rural landscape. Business partners of Thaddaeus? Impatient creditors? It was impossible to guess the extent of Thaddaeus Brown's business ventures, but Aidan felt sure that the House of the Hare must be only one of a multitude of enterprises.

Who would inherit them now? If Mair was right,

and it was the teenaged Lorna, could she cope with the responsibility? How could she possibly stand up to those two men with the sharp suits and the aggressive driving?

He could not help but see Lorna as a victim, not a murderer. It was ridiculous that the police should hold her in a cell overnight, just because she was one of the few people in the neighbourhood who could fire a bow.

Did he know that was the sole reason? Might they have other evidence?'

He tapped on the half-open door.

"Come in," called a woman's voice.

PC Watkins looked up from her computer. She smiled when she saw him. "What can we do for you?"

There were two male officers in the room. One was the lanky uniformed Constable Roberts, who had been the second to arrive in answer to Sian's phone call. The other wore a sports jacket and fawn trousers. CID, Aidan guessed. The two men's eyes were on him, with interest. It was irrational the way the mere presence of police officers could make you feel guilty, he thought.

He looked round the almost empty space. On one cobwebbed wall, ancient horse harness hung. A rusted hay rake was propped in the corner. There was a startling modernity about the two grey telephones on the folding table. The whiteboard with a sketch map of the murder site. Two computers.

"I thought it would be busier than this."

The policewoman's merry brown eyes laughed. "It's only temporary, this. If we plugged in all the computers we need for this enquiry to the electricity supply here, we'd short-circuit half the Tanat Valley. The real incident room's back in Newtown. But that's twenty miles away. So you're stuck with me. What can I do for you?"

"I was hoping to see DCI Denbigh. I just wondered if

it was OK if I took my wife and daughter for a drive over to Lake Vyrnwy this afternoon. We'll only be gone for two or three hours. He doesn't need us for anything, does he?"

"No, he's over at Welshpool this morning. Suspicious death. A woman died in a house fire. Probably the husband, if you ask me." Watkins glanced anxiously at the CID man, in case she had said too much. The officer coughed warningly.

"Well, it usually is, isn't it, with a murder?" She recovered herself defiantly. "Someone in the family. Or a lover."

"Unless it's for money," Constable Roberts added.

"But I thought Chief Inspector Denbigh was in charge of *this* case."

Watkins' eyes widened.

The detective threw back his head and laughed uproariously. "You didn't think we can afford a Senior Investigating Officer for every suspicious death, do you? We'd need a police budget the length of the Severn. Denbigh's probably got a half a dozen cases on the go. No, sir. Our investigations are, shall we say, ongoing. We'd be grateful if you didn't leave the area just yet, but there's no harm in your seeing the sights while you wait. Better get going, though. There's rain in the wind."

Aidan watched Jenny take her medication. She was paler than he would have liked. But they would all be glad to be on the other side of the mountain for a while.

"Looks like we have to head for Penybontfawr and head up the next valley."

Aidan negotiated the gateposts warily. He half-expected to find the lane beyond still packed with journalists and photographers. There was no one.

Though the day was dull, Aidan felt a shadow fall behind

him as he drove along the valley of the Tanat down the narrow lane. Slate and granite quarries scarred the hillsides ahead, evidence of great industrial activity in the past. A few yellow diggers were still at work in one.

They turned west again, following another clear stream bubbling over stones. Another hillside dark with conifer plantations. The turreted wall of the dam came into view. A sign pointed across it – "LAKESIDE DRIVE". The sky was patchy with shower clouds. The water was slate grey.

They pulled into a small car park. "Ice cream?" asked Aidan, twisting round to Melangell.

"Of *course*." She was out of the car instantly.

Another couple were coming away from the shop. The Ewarts.

Colin stopped abruptly when he saw them. "You! I thought we'd got away from it all for a few hours."

"Sorry." Aidan grinned unsympathetically. He was finding it hard to like Colin Ewart. "We thought we needed a change of scene, same as you."

"I've a mind to get in that car and drive away for good, no matter what that officious police inspector says. What right has he got to tell me where I can and can't stay when I'm on holiday? It's supposed to be a free country, isn't it?"

"They'd just like us on hand in case some more questions come up. And you're booked till the end of the week, aren't you? Like us. It's Harry and Debbie who are the problem. They're supposed to be leaving."

"I can't imagine they have anything to do with this," Jenny said. "They were really shocked when they found the body. Debbie looked quite ill."

"And what's that supposed to mean?" Colin Ewart snapped. "That we don't look innocent? I suppose you think Rachel here got a bow out of that sports shed when no one was looking and shot a man bang through the eye?"

"Colin!" Rachel protested.

"Well, I'm fed up with being treated as if we were all suspects."

"Not suspects," Aidan protested. The man's loud protestations were irritating him. "Potential witnesses. None of us knows what we might have seen that's relevant."

"I know what I saw. Damn all."

He got into his car and banged the door. Rachel took the passenger seat more quietly. She turned her head and smiled apologetically. "I hope you have a lovely afternoon. Between the showers."

Drops spattered the car park. The Davisons hastened into the shop.

Aidan drove slowly. The road hugged the lake shore, so that they constantly glimpsed the water through a frame of trees. Showers beaded the windscreen.

At the head of the lake, Aidan turned off on to a parking place. They walked down through the trees to the open shore. The sun gleamed out between the clouds. It lit the woods around the lake. Their varied spring foliage shone almost as colourfully as autumn. Far down the suddenly blue water, the sun caught a group of scarlet canoes. But for once, Aidan did not feel the urge to go back to the car for his camera. They stood in silence.

Presently Aidan turned quizzically to Melangell. "You're quiet today, poppet."

"Yes, I am."

He and Jenny looked down at her. What did all this mean to a seven-year-old?

Melangell wandered down to the water's edge and began skimming scraps of slate.

"I wonder if they're still holding Lorna," Jenny said in a low voice. "Do you think they'll charge her?"

Aidan shrugged. "I can't imagine she did it. But look at it from the police's point of view. Who else could have shot him?"

"Sian?"

Aidan stared down the ruffled waters of the lake. He tried to picture the well-muscled figure in the ranger-like clothes. Was it plausible? "Why? Her job depends on him."

"To protect Lorna from him? She was in tears yesterday when they arrested Lorna."

"And if Lorna inherits the House of the Hare, she'll keep Sian on. Yes... I see what you mean. You really think I was right? That Thaddaeus was abusing Lorna?"

"I didn't want to believe it at first, but the evidence is pointing that way. Something upset her." There was the set of determination in Jenny's thin face.

Aidan joined Melangell skimming stones.

"Seven!" Melangell cried. "Did you see that?"

Aidan flicked his wrist. "Eleven!"

"But you're twenty-five years older than me, so I get twenty-five extra points. That makes thirty-two."

"That's not fair. I'll never get to win."

He was relieved to hear her laugh.

The chief inspector's car was parked outside the house again. A dark blue Rover from the turn of the century. The leather upholstery looked somewhat worn, not unlike the inspector himself.

Aidan felt the tension as they entered the foyer. He glimpsed Sian in her office behind the desk. His gaze steadied on her. He remembered Jenny's speculation by the lakeside.

Was it possible?

"I see the chief inspector's back," he called. "Is there any news of Lorna?"

Sian looked up, her plump face serious. "No. He's not saying anything. They've taken the tape away from the sports hut, but no one's much in the mood for games."

"Ridiculous," snapped Jenny. "I know she didn't do it."

Aidan wondered at her vehemence.

Upstairs, Jenny stretched herself out on the bed for a rest. He looked down with concern. It had been a long excursion for her.

"Are you all right?"

"I will be."

He took Melangell downstairs. They found a room at the end of the corridor with a ping-pong table. Melangell proved surprisingly good. It was not difficult to let her beat him. Once, at least.

When he returned to the bedroom an hour later, he was surprised to find Jenny standing by the window, looking sideways across the grounds.

"The inspector's still here," she said.

"He'll be checking up on whatever his team here have discovered today. And all the others he's got out on the case."

She turned with sudden decision. "I think I'd like another go at the butts. I was beginning to get the feel of it again, last time."

He stared at her in astonishment. "You're not serious? After what's happened?"

He saw the set of her jaw. "You heard Inspector Denbigh. He thinks because I've got terminal cancer I'm too frail to draw a bow in any serious way. I'm going to show him."

"Jenny! You've got nothing to prove. What does it matter what he thinks?"

"It matters to me."

Jenny borrowed the key from Sian, ignoring the manager's shocked expression. The three of them made their way in strained silence to the now accessible shed. Jenny went straight for the corner where the yew bow stood. She held it for a while, stroking the polished wood. Then she straightened herself. She gave Melangell six red-and-white flighted arrows to carry. She walked outside.

"Do you want the wheelchair?" Aidan asked.

"No."

He saw how she glanced sideways at the police room before she drew the bowstring back. If the inspector was there, he would have a clear sight of what she was doing.

The zing of the arrow startled him. He had not seen her fire.

"Hurray!" Melangell jumped up and down, clapping.

The arrow hung quivering in the bullseye.

Jenny fired again. Another hit. And another.

When Aidan next looked sideways, Chief Inspector Denbigh was standing on the step of the workshop, watching.

What is she doing? The questions were racing through Aidan's mind. Is she just trying to prove a point of feminine pride, that she's an archer to be reckoned with?

Or something more? Could she possibly be wanting the chief inspector to think that it might not have been Lorna Brown who fired the fatal shot? That for some unguessable reason, it might have been Jenny? His mind reeled.

She fired six arrows. Five of them found the bullseye. Melangell ran to retrieve them. She held them out to her mother.

"No. That's enough."

The inspector was walking across the path towards them, tossing his car keys. His bloodhound eyes were thoughtful.

"Very impressive," he said. "I underrated you, Mrs Davison."

Back in the bedroom, Aidan exploded.

"What were you playing at? Did you want him to arrest you? Instead of Lorna?"

"What if he did?" she said, defiantly. "How long does it take to prepare a murder trial? I'd be dead by then."

He stared at her with incredulity. "You'd really do that? To protect her? But what possible motive could he think you had to kill Thaddaeus Brown? You're not thinking straight."

"You just said it yourself. To protect Lorna."

His mouth fell open. He could find no words. He swallowed.

"For a girl you'd only met the day before?"

An expression of worry leaped into her eyes. "Aidan! I wasn't serious. That inspector was so patronising. I just wanted to show him."

"Show him! Oh, yes, you certainly did that. Whatever you may have meant by showing off, you realise that you've just added yourself to a very small list of suspects? Did you stop to think about Melangell? Knowing her mother went to her grave accused of manslaughter?"

"Manslaughter?" He saw Jenny wince. "Denbigh couldn't really believe I killed Thaddaeus?"

He was appalled at himself for shouting at her like this, but he was driven by an irrational fear. The words came tumbling out before he could stop them.

"I had a nightmare last night. You were shooting from the wheelchair when Thaddaeus came out of the bushes onto the butts. You were startled. You let the arrow fly, but it went wide and hit him. What if your chief inspector has the same thought now?"

Her blue-grey eyes widened in shock. "Aidan! You can't have suspected that? That I'd kill a man by accident and say nothing about it?"

It was too late to call the words back. "I told you. It was a nightmare. I never for a moment thought it was true."

Her cheeks had paled. "But you've been carrying the thought around with you all day. That's why you lost your temper with me."

She turned away and disappeared into the bathroom.

Chapter Thirteen

A IDAN WAS VERY QUIET over the evening meal. Jenny felt stricken with guilt. She should not have indulged in such reckless showmanship.

She tried to keep up a bright conversation with Melangell, about the possibility of Lake Vyrnwy housing a monster like Loch Ness.

"But Loch Ness is a natural lake. Millions of years old. Lake Vyrnwy's just a reservoir. They made it in the 1880s."

"But a baby monster from Loch Ness could have walked there, Mummy. When it got big enough to leave home."

Pangs of physical pain came at intervals. Jenny tried not to show it, but she knew Aidan would notice the tightening of her face.

But tonight he hardly looked at her. He was supping his watery soup without enthusiasm. Soup should be comfort food, Jenny thought. But it was not up to Josef's usual standard. Just when they needed comforting.

"Something's burning." Melangell's clear grey gaze was accusing, almost as if she blamed Jenny.

She was right. There was an acrid smell. Jenny looked up, over her daughter's head. There was a haze of smoke through the hatch to the kitchen.

Sian jumped up from the table where she was dining alone. She sped into the kitchen. The diners could hear the sounds of argument with the cook. Then Sian's voice rose higher.

"*I'm* upset! But I've got a job to do. So have you."

Mair raised her eyebrows as she cleared the soup plates. "Sorry, folks. I think the ragout is on hold. Does anyone mind the vegetarian option?"

For a long time after that, Aidan sat silent, staring down at the tablecloth. There were no jokes with Melangell about their missing supper, no comments to Jenny about the strain the staff must be under.

"Are you all right?" she asked him.

"Of course," he answered, curtly.

It was some twenty minutes later when Mair appeared with plates of a rather pedestrian cheese pasta.

"I'm demanding a discount," Colin Ewart announced to the whole dining room, "or there'll be trouble."

Harry and Debbie had their heads bent close together over the table. They were talking in low voices. Occasionally they darted nervous glances at Sian.

Jenny suddenly noticed a happy smile spreading over Melangell's face. It seemed incongruous among so much sadness and tension. She turned her head to follow her daughter's eyes.

In the doorway of the dining room stood the slight figure of Lorna Brown.

Sian leapt to her feet with a strangled cry. She bounded across the room and hugged Lorna.

"You're back! They let you go?"

Lorna's quiet voice came across the intently listening dining room. "Insufficient evidence. They couldn't charge me."

"I should think not, indeed! I don't know how they could even think of suspecting you."

Lorna pushed the waves of black hair from her pale face. "Someone did it, Sian. They have to find him. Or her."

A troubled glance passed between the two women.

Jenny turned back to the table to find Aidan's gaze

directed, not at the two in the doorway, but at her. She dared not interpret the look of anguish in his eyes.

Lorna was alone in the dining room, finishing her meal.

Sian came through the lounge with a distracted air, but with a lighter spring to her step. Jenny put out a hand to stop her as she passed them.

"What will happen to Lorna now? Does she have a family? Where are her parents?"

Sian's face became grave. "Thaddaeus was all she had, poor kid. Her parents broke up when she was small. I get the impression it was a messy divorce. She lost touch with her father years ago. Doesn't know if he's still in the country. Her mother was Thaddaeus's sister. Well, half-sister."

"I thought he and Lorna didn't look much alike."

"No. She's a real Welsh beauty, isn't she? That black hair and delicate skin. But Thaddaeus was handsome in his own way. His mother was from Antigua."

"Where's Lorna's mother now?"

Sian sighed. "She died, three years ago. Appointed Thaddaeus as Lorna's guardian. Since then, he's been training her to join him in his business."

"So what will happen now? She doesn't look much more than sixteen."

"She's eighteen."

"Still, I imagine this isn't his only business interest. How can a teenager handle all that?"

The manager shrugged. "She'll manage, I hope. If only because my future depends on her making a success of this. There was something about a trust fund. Anyway, now that Lorna's back, we can get on to Thaddaeus's solicitor and read the will. Excuse me, will you? You've no idea how much there is to do, with all this happening. I don't know how I'd have managed if Mair hadn't come back to help."

"Yes, of course. I'm sorry. I shouldn't have stopped you."

"That's all right. I'm only sorry it's spoilt your holiday."

"And that's an understatement," said Colin Ewart, loudly. "'Ruined' would be more like it."

" I've said I'm sorry, Mr Ewart. What more can I do?"

The colour was high in Sian's cheeks as she left the room.

Jenny looked across at Aidan, who was playing Snap with Melangell. Just for a moment, it might have been any normal holiday scene. But the eyes he raised to hers were still troubled.

"I think I'll go and have a word with Lorna. She looks awfully small and lonely there."

She went back into the almost empty dining room. The kitchen door was closed, but she could make out Mair's voice, still irrepressibly cheerful. She wished she could hear what Josef was saying.

Lorna sat at the table by the window, a slight figure against the backdrop of mountains beyond the lawns. She was peeling an apple, her heart-shaped face intent upon the trivial task.

"Is it OK if I join you?"

The girl's intense blue eyes were wary as she looked up. But she smiled politely. "Help yourself."

Jenny was not quite sure whether that referred to the wooden fruit bowl on the table, or the chair opposite the girl. She eased herself into it. The pain in her abdomen was worse this evening. But talking to Lorna was better than retiring to bed and being alone with her thoughts and her invaded body.

"I'm terribly sorry about what happened. It would have

been awful, anyway, but to be arrested yourself on top of that, when you're completely on your own..."

"They found me a solicitor."

It occurred to Jenny that Thaddaeus had been the kind of man who would have hired the best lawyer for her, not left her to the care of a duty solicitor. But even if Lorna was his heir, she couldn't get her hands on that money yet.

If there was money. Aidan had seemed sure that this venture of the House of the Hare must have left Thaddaeus hugely in debt. Yet how did they know what other enterprises he might have had, which could still have left Lorna a rich woman?

She tore her thoughts away from money to the vulnerable human being across the table from her.

"Sian said you'd lost your parents. I'm sorry. It must be hard to face this without family."

The girl's face showed little emotion. "I've got used to it. I haven't seen my father since I was five. Mum died three years ago. Cancer."

Jenny's tongue was stilled.

An expression of consternation animated Lorna's eyes then. "Oh, I'm sorry! I shouldn't have said that. That's why you're here, isn't it?"

Jenny managed a small smile. "Partly. There used to be a cancer centre for women here. Something to do with the shrine and the yews. But Aidan and I fell in love with the whole ambience of the place. We wrote a book about it. Well, I wrote the words and Aidan did the photographs. They're selling it in the church shop."

"That's great," Lorna said, with enthusiasm. The blue eyes deepened their intensity. "That's why I did it. Made Thaddaeus build this place, so that people like you could come and stay here."

"It was *your* idea? Not his? This House of the Hare?"

The girl nodded. "My mum and I came here once. To Pennant Melangell, I mean. The church. This house wasn't built then. It didn't cure her, but I think she found a sort of peace. She always remembered it."

Jenny said softly, "I understand. We wanted to bring Melangell here. To show her what it meant to us. So she'll always remember why we gave her her name." Lorna was looking with concern. Jenny made a crooked smile. "I probably only have months to live."

"And here's me thinking I was the one with problems. I'm terribly sorry."

"No, you're right. In a way, I've solved my problems. God and I have come to an agreement about that. He's going to hold my hand." She smiled, a little shamefacedly. Would she embarrass Lorna by talking about her faith? But the girl's mother had also found peace at the shrine.

"Were you and Thaddaeus close?" She knew she was treading on dangerous ground.

"I lived with him. Since she died." Lorna's head was bent now, her words hard to distinguish.

"He must have loved you a lot, to build this house for you. To make your dreams come true."

Lorna's knuckles tightened on the knife she held.

"Yes," she said, dully. "I suppose he did."

There were many more questions Jenny wanted to ask, but to press Lorna further would be inexcusably intrusive.

Instead, she put out her hand impulsively and clasped the girl's. "I know we've only just met. But if there's anything I can do… If you need someone to talk to, I'm here."

"Thank you. You're very kind. I've got Sian." Her face was closed.

Jenny stood up. "I'll say goodnight, then. I'm glad you're back. I suppose the police will need to start asking more questions now."

"You'd better be careful, then. Sian says you're a very good shot with that bow."

Those startling blue eyes looked clearly at her now. Jenny turned in confusion and made for the lounge.

As she entered, she found Aidan was watching her, too.

Jenny lay in bed, watching Aidan undress.

"I'm sorry," she said, quietly. "It was stupid of me."

Aidan had his back to her. She saw his wiry body still.

"What was?"

"Drawing attention to my archery in front of the inspector."

There was a difficult silence. Then, "What, exactly, were you trying to tell him?"

She wished he would turn and look at her. Smile, even. She picked at the edge of the sheet. The pain was worse tonight.

"I told you. Showing off what I could do. My pride was hurt. And, well, yes, letting him know that Lorna isn't the only one who was capable of firing that arrow."

He turned round slowly. His foxy hair was rumpled, where he had pulled his sweater off. His eyes were penitent.

"It was my fault. I never meant to tell you about that nightmare."

She raised herself on one elbow. "Aidan. Inspector Denbigh wouldn't seriously think I could have killed him, would he?"

He bent to pick up his pyjamas. His voice came muffled. "How do I know what he thinks, when you march out on to the butts in front of him and show him just how far you can fire an arrow? It must have looked as if you wanted him to see something."

The enormity of what he was suggesting sank home to her. She stared at him over the duvet.

"He'd think... It's been more than twenty-four hours, and he'd think that all this time I'd have said nothing?" Her eyes begged him for a denial. "You don't really think he'll arrest me? Aidan, we've got so little time. Melangell..."

He came hurrying round to her side of the bed. "I'm sorry, love. I didn't want to upset you."

There were tears on her cheeks. She could not look at him. She felt his hand on her shoulder. He bent and kissed her, tentatively, as if afraid of her reaction.

The last security of her world dropped away. The folly of her pride came swooping in to overshadow her with dark wings. She had taunted the inspector with the vision, not of a frail individual with only months to live, but of a confident woman still strong enough to draw a bow and find her mark. It had not occurred to her that she might be jeopardising the last few weeks she had with Melangell and Aidan.

"I'm so sorry," she whispered.

"The chief inspector's an intelligent man. We have to trust him."

Aidan got into bed. She kept her eyes closed and her back turned to him, staring into an inner darkness. She felt his arm fold comfortingly over her.

Chapter Fourteen

DCI DENBIGH RETURNED even before the Davisons had finished breakfast. They joined the group reassembling in the lounge.

Jenny watched the detective chief inspector with apprehension. She was momentarily startled to meet Euan Jones again. She had not seen the young gardener since the day of the murder. He took the chair behind Lorna, as if wanting to be close to her, but too shy to sit openly by her side.

Lorna herself looked grave. She did not turn to smile at him. Had Jenny been wrong about the relationship between them?

What hope had Euan? she thought with sympathy. A boy probably earning not much more than the minimum wage, and a young woman who might now be the heiress of a business empire…

Only the ebullient Mair was missing. She would be at college. And anyway, she hadn't been here on the afternoon of the murder.

Who else had?

Her mind flew to the two men in the Jaguar. What part did they play in Thaddaeus's enterprises? Could there possibly be any connection between their visits and the entrepreneur's death?

Sian would have told the police about them. Some officer would have been assigned to track them down and question them. And what were the chances that either of them was an archer competent enough to shoot a man through the eye?

But I am, the cold thought came. She glanced at Aidan, beside her. His morning face betrayed nothing.

The chief inspector cleared his throat. "We seem to have two people missing. Where are the youngsters who found the body? Mr Townsend and Miss French?" The question was addressed to Sian.

She looked uncomfortable. "They've left, I'm afraid. First thing this morning. They only meant to stay two nights. We're rather more expensive than they wanted. I let them stay on one more night. But they gave me this for you." She handed him a slip of paper. "It's the YHA at Dolgellau. They should be there in a couple of days. And they've left a mobile number."

"That's disgraceful," burst out Colin Ewart. "I wanted to leave and was told to stay put."

"Forgive me if I'm wrong, Mr Ewart," came Denbigh's steely voice, "but I understood that you were booked till the end of the week."

"And I'm not allowed to change my mind?"

"I'm conducting a murder investigation. I should expect you to cooperate with the police. Do you have an objection to that? Any reason why you would obstruct the police in their enquiries?"

For once Colin Ewart looked cowed.

Chief Inspector Denbigh addressed them all. "I'm sorry to intrude on you again. I know some of you came here for a holiday. But fresh information has come to light. Two days ago we were looking for an archer who shot Mr Brown. There were very few possibilities."

His eyes swung round, not to Lorna, but to Jenny. She had a cold sensation that her heart was sinking into her feet. She dared not look at Aidan, though she badly needed his support.

"However, late yesterday I received the report of the post-mortem. It appears that the penetration of the arrow was not consistent with the velocity of an expert shot. It could have been a low-powered effort from close range, or…" his eyes roved over the gathering, "he was simply stabbed through the brain with the arrow. It would have required some force, but no expertise in archery. You will appreciate that this widens the scope of our enquiry considerably. We will undoubtedly have more questions to ask."

Jenny felt momentarily dizzy. He had not fallen into the trap she had foolishly set for him. Instead, everyone in the room was now not merely a witness, but a potential suspect.

Everyone except… She looked down at Melangell. The girl sat on the rug at her parents' feet, her thin arms clasped round her knees. She was watching the chief inspector intently.

Aidan felt the difference in the questioning. Two days before, he had been a witness. Someone who had potentially seen Thaddaeus's murderer in the moments before or after the crime. DCI Denbigh had evidently discounted Aidan's own ability to fire the fatal shot. Rightly so: Aidan had never taken up Jenny's sport.

Now the Senior Investigating Officer sat across Sian's desk from him with that relentless air of a schoolmaster who could make his pupils quake in their shoes in his pursuit of the latest culprit. Aidan felt that now. He wasn't guilty, yet Denbigh made him feel that he was. The mournful furrows dragged the chief inspector's cheeks down like a bloodhound's. Yet there was nothing canine about his eyes today. His gaze was steely, impersonal.

Could he see into Aidan's soul? Could he probe the

worst horrors that had haunted him in the small dark hours of the night? That Jenny, *his* Jenny, might have let an arrow fly astray from her expert grasp to kill Thaddaeus.

With a shudder, he tried to shake the nightmare thought away.

"Melangell was with me the whole time. She can vouch for the fact that we came straight up the drive to the front door. I didn't go anywhere near the butts until Harry came dashing across the lawn saying they'd found a body."

"Your daughter. Yes, I'm sure she would vouch for you. She is…" he looked down at his notes, "seven years old?"

"Melangell says what she thinks," Aidan replied, hotly.

Still, something of the chill went from the atmosphere. He was made to recount in elaborate detail what he had seen of the others. Harry had come bursting out of the shrubbery alone. It had been a short while before Debbie followed. She had seemed even more distraught. Before that, Jenny had been alone on the patio outside the lounge, half asleep over a book, when Aidan and Melangell returned. Sian had been nowhere in sight, but Aidan thought he had heard sounds from the kitchen, which he had assumed meant that Josef was at work. He understood that Mair had only returned to the House of the Hare after the murder, to help Sian out in a crisis. No, he hadn't seen the Ewarts, and didn't know where they were that afternoon.

"And Lorna Brown?"

Aidan was aware of his too-long hesitation. He answered brusquely. "I told you. We'd met her at the head of the valley, coming away from the waterfall. She was upset. Melangell and I stopped for a picnic, so she should have been back before us, if she came straight here. In fact, I know she was, because Jenny saw her arrive. But you know all this."

DCI Denbigh steepled his fingers and gazed down at them. "I understand Mr Brown drove to the house of Mr

Caradoc Lewis around midday. That's near this waterfall, I understand."

"Capel-y-Cwm. Yes. It's the last house up the valley."

"And Lorna Brown went with him?"

"I assume so. I didn't see them leave here, but Lorna was with someone on the path from Capel-y-Cwm."

"But you did see Mr Brown later."

"Briefly."

"Having an argument with Mr Lewis."

"Yes."

"About? If your excellent daughter has jogged your memory?"

"I think it had something to do with land. We weren't close enough to hear all of it. Caradoc Lewis said something about hang-gliding. Then he started shouting at Thaddaeus, and there was a bit of a tussle."

"So there were three people in the vicinity. All apparently upset."

"Lorna wasn't with them then. But I suppose she was before we met her. With one of them, at least."

"So, whatever the precise means of Mr Brown's death, Lorna could have been back to play a part in it. All she needed was access to an arrow, not necessarily a bow."

The corollary sounded in Aidan's head before the chief inspector voiced it.

"And the same is true of her friend, young Mr Jones."

"Euan? If we're talking about stabbing him with an arrow, anyone here could have done it. Well, maybe not Rachel Ewart. She's only half his size and has trouble with her back."

"Anyone. Precisely. You told me on Tuesday that you left Caradoc Lewis behind at his house. He couldn't have overtaken you and been at the House of the Hare before you got back?"

"No. If he'd passed us on the road, we would have seen him."

Chief Inspector Denbigh looked down at the map spread out beside him.

"Lincoln?"

The unobtrusive detective sergeant leaned his balding head forward from his notepad. He traced a line of green dashes on the map.

The inspector looked up at Aidan. "Are you aware that there is a footpath across the fields which starts not far from Mr Lewis's house and comes out *here*, close to the House of the Hare?" His finger jabbed the point on the map where the green line met the yellow ribbon of the road.

Aidan felt startled that he had overlooked this. But then, he had had no reason to associate Caradoc Lewis with archery. The net had suddenly been thrown wider.

"Yes. I mean, I've seen the footpath sign. I hadn't worked out just where it went."

"I'll ask you again, Mr Davison. Could Caradoc Lewis have got to the House of the Hare before you and your daughter did?"

Aidan studied the route of the path. It was shorter than the road they had followed. He would have taken it himself if he had realized. He thought of Caradoc Lewis's long legs, the controlled energy of his movements. "Yes," he admitted. "We were pretty tired by then. We'd got a bit lost on the mountain before we found a way to the waterfall. So, yes. If he'd waited till we'd gone and then taken off across the fields at a fast lick, it's possible."

"Thank you." The chief inspector almost purred.

Aidan tried to readjust his thoughts. Did that mean Lorna was no longer a suspect? Almost certainly not. She had the opportunity and a possible motive. Unlike Sian. But Inspector Denbigh had not questioned him closely on that.

How much had Lorna told him about her relationship with her uncle? Was it really what he and Jenny had feared?

Jenny! The thought came like a jolt. A wave of guilt swept over him. He should never have told her about that nightmare. No wonder she had been outraged. How could he possibly have entertained for a moment the idea that she might have fired the arrow, even by accident?

But someone had done it, while Jenny lay asleep on her bed or sat drowsily in her chair.

Cold fingers walked up his spine. What else might Jenny have seen? Or what might the killer think she had seen?

A splinter of memory pierced his anguished thoughts.

"Those men. Driving away from the house as we got back…"

"Ah, yes. Mr Secker and Mr McCarthy. Precisely."

The grey eyes regarded him steadily under a wearily creased brow. They gave nothing more away.

"Thank you, Mr Davison."

Chapter Fifteen

"WHY DID YOU upset Mummy?"

Melangell met Aidan in the foyer with that accusing stare of hers. He realized with a start how like the chief inspector's it was. The same clear grey eyes. The same certainty that they were right. It was unnerving.

"I said something stupid," he temporized. "I had a bad dream. I should never have told her about it. She was right to be mad at me."

"Like she might have shot Mr Brown?" His face must have registered his shock. "Oh, *Daddy*! I'm not surprised she's cross. *I* would be."

"Yes," he said, swallowing. "It was just a nightmare. And she didn't mean to hit him, of course…" He met his daughter's eyes. "Yes, it *was* stupid. Very stupid. But now we know that arrow didn't have to come from a bow, it could have been anyone."

"Like you." She looked up at him gravely.

Aidan's mouth fell open. He stared back at her, trying to gauge how serious she was.

Her elfin face broke into a grin, showing the gaps in her teeth. "See? *That's* what it feels like."

"You little horror!" He rumpled her curls in relief.

All the same, it was an unsettling feeling. Did the inspector have any reason to think it might be him? Had he really believed Aidan's account of coming back to the house through the front door, and not taking a route through the grounds, where he could have met Thaddaeus? Would Melangell's testimony be enough?

Was DCI Denbigh shrewd enough to sense the anger Aidan had felt when he thought of Thaddaeus abusing Lorna? He had an uncomfortable suspicion that he was.

"Where's Mummy now?"

"Talking to Josef."

A start brought Aidan back to the present. "Josef? Why?"

Melangell gave an exaggerated shrug. "I expect she wants to know why he's angry."

"Is he?"

"He *sounded* angry."

A new unease was growing. "Where are they?"

He had no idea of the relationship between the Polish chef and his late employer. He hadn't been able to imagine Josef, in his chequered trousers and black cap, taking a bow and shooting Thaddaeus. But now…

The kitchen was on the opposite side of the house from the archery butts. If Josef had gone from one to the other, he must have passed the back of the house. Most people would have been out of the house then. But not Jenny. She could easily have seen him, from the bedroom or the patio.

But surely she would have said?

On the day of the murder it was at the forefront of everyone's mind that the police were looking for an archer. A glimpse of someone else might have slipped her mind. And Jenny had yet to have her second interview with DCI Denbigh, now that the field of suspicion had been thrown wide open. Meanwhile, she was alone with Josef.

"*Where?*"

Melangell looked frightened by his vehemence. "Round the back of the kitchen. There." She pointed in the opposite direction to Sian's office.

He was off down the corridor with long strides. He burst into the kitchen. There was no one there. An outer door stood half open. It led out into the grounds at the side of the house. Aidan strode through it.

They were sitting on a bench against the wall. Josef, in his chef's uniform, was drawing hungrily on a cigarette. Jenny, her bald head bound in her favourite pink-and-purple scarf, was leaning back against the wall.

She looked up in surprise as Aidan burst upon the scene, followed by a curious Melangell. Was that a flash of alarm on Josef's face?

"Oh, there you are!" Aidan said lamely.

"Yes. Is there a problem?" Jenny looked at him coldly.

"No… I just wondered… I didn't expect to find you here."

"Josef and I were discussing his future. He's naturally worried what will happen to his job now. I told him that the House of the Hare was Lorna's idea, that I'm sure she'll keep it going, once the will is proved."

"Yes. I see."

Melangell had said that Josef had sounded angry. Why? With Jenny?

The young Pole lifted his sallow face. "The police think that Miss Lorna killed her uncle. No?"

"The inspector did. But they couldn't find enough evidence to keep her under arrest. And now they say it could have been anyone."

"But she is still a suspect. She gets the money, so she has a reason to do it."

"I suppose that's true."

"And if they find she kills him, she cannot have the money. Is right?"

"Well, yes. I guess it would be. They can't let a murderer

profit from the crime. But I can't believe she did it."

"No?" Josef gave a sceptical shrug. "And if she did, who gets it then? All this?" He gestured around him. The neat kitchen garden, with rows of young vegetables and clumps of silver-leaved herbs. The fruit trees beyond, leaning long branches over the grass, another survival from the days before the House of the Hare was built. A glimpse of empty tennis courts and the covered pool..

"I don't know. Sian said Lorna was Thaddaeus's only family. I've no idea if his will made provision for anyone else."

"You don't think that other girl… Miss Debbie?"

"*Debbie French?*" Aidan had a vision of the weeping teenager, her helmet of black hair dishevelled, emerging from the rhododendron bushes after Harry.

"I see them talking the evening before. Over there." He pointed towards the tennis courts. "This Debbie and Mr Brown. And she is laughing and holding his arm, like she knows him before. And Mr Brown is seeming like he don't want to be talking to her, and looking round to see if people noticing. They don't see me in the kitchen."

"What are you suggesting?"

"This Debbie. She has a look a bit African. Like him. You see it? And I am thinking, what if she is his daughter? Not by marriage, you understand. A… how do you say this?"

"An illegitimate child?" Jenny suggested.

"Perhaps. I don't know."

"But that's preposterous!" Aidan burst out. "There are millions of people in this country with African blood. That doesn't make them all next of kin. It's a daft idea."

"All the same," Jenny said, thoughtfully, "I always wondered what that pair were doing staying here. Like they said, it's outside their normal price range. Do you think she might have had a reason to come here and see Thaddaeus?"

"Cobblers! They were just on a walking holiday. The House of the Hare is the only place you can stay in Pennant Melangell. That's why Lorna wanted Thaddaeus to build it."

"They could have stayed in one of the pubs in Llangynog down the road, as we did when we came the first time."

"Mmm. Have you told the police this?" Aidan demanded of Josef. "Though it's hardly suspicious for the owner of the house to be talking to one of his guests."

"No. The inspector, he ask me what I do the day Mr Brown is murdered. Who I see. He didn't ask anything about the night before."

Jenny's thoughts were following his. "If there really is a connection between Debbie and Thaddaeus… Well, Lorna would still be the obvious suspect, wouldn't she? And if she was convicted, she'd lose the inheritance. If Debbie could prove that Thaddaeus was her father, and there was no provision in the will for anyone else and no other living relatives, then she might claim to be the beneficiary, mightn't she? Not just the House of the Hare, but everything else Thaddaeus owned."

"I'm not a lawyer. But it's all moonshine. One conversation between Debbie and Thaddaeus. A touch of African descent."

"We won't know, will we? Unless they bring Lorna to trial and convict her." Jenny got up. "Try not to worry about it, Josef. I'm sure it wasn't Lorna. So the House of the Hare is safe with her. And your job."

"I hope so."

They walked away, brushing the lavender and sage bushes and releasing their fragrance. Aidan began to relax. The chef no longer seemed a threat.

"He's a racist," he said, when they were out of earshot of Josef. "I bet all black people look the same to him." He watched her crumble a lavender flower between her fingers. "I'm sorry. About last night. I was a complete idiot."

"Yes, you were!" She laughed and took his arm. "I wasn't exactly a model of sanity myself. On Tuesday's scenario, there were only two, or at the most three, of us who could have done it. I never did find out how handy Sian is with a bow. But I do know she cares a lot about Lorna. Perhaps too much."

"You think she might have...?"

"She strikes me as a very determined lady. And practical. Physically strong, too. There weren't many of us left in the house on Tuesday afternoon. But she was one."

Aidan pictured the plump, healthy face of the manager, in her bushranger's outfit. Yes, if Sian had made up her mind that this was the only way to protect Lorna, it was credible. More than Josef's wild theory about young Debbie French.

Jenny squeezed his arm. "It's Thursday. I nearly forgot. They have a healing Eucharist in the church at twelve. I'd like to go. It's up to you whether you come as well."

Suddenly everything else fell away into insignificance. Thaddaeus's murder. The web of suspicion around the handful of people in Pennant Melangell that day. The police investigation. He was back with that single imperative which had brought them to Pennant Melangell and the House of the Hare. Jenny was dying of cancer.

Chapter Sixteen

JENNY APPROACHED THE lychgate of the church with a strange feeling of homecoming. She had a sudden longing to be within the circling arms of its churchyard wall, to be sheltered under the spreading canopy of its massive yews. The sign outside said:

WELCOME

CROESO

She did feel welcomed.

She led the way into the church. Aidan and Melangell followed quietly. It had only been a short walk down the lane, but Jenny felt that she was stepping into another world. All the shock and violence at the House of the Hare, the police questioning, her suspicion of everyone around her, dropped away. There had been a church here for over a thousand years. Now, in the twenty-first century, there was still a group of faithful people who kept these services going.

She smiled at the man who handed her an order of service and the hymnbook *Mission Praise*. Did he live in one of the few cottages in Pennant Melangell, or further afield?

The three of them slipped into a pew with embroidered hassocks. Jenny's showed St Melangell's hare.

The hare was everywhere. In modern sculptures set

against the wall to her left. In the carving of the story above the screen that separated the nave from the chancel. Even in the little Easter garden of slate and flowers at the back of the church, in what seemed to be the children's corner. In Pennant Melangell, the hare was far more than the Easter Bunny. It was a symbol of the persecuted, the hunted, finding sanctuary under the skirts of the saint. Jenny felt in need of sanctuary now.

She bent her head in prayer.

When she lifted it, she looked more carefully at the small congregation in front of her. That middle-aged couple with walking sticks propped against the side of the pew. Hikers, who had made this part of a pilgrimage. There were others she did not recognize. Locals? Holidaymakers? Wounded souls seeking the healing Pennant Melangell offered?

She gave a tiny shiver. She was approaching delicate ground. This service was designated as a laying on of hands. She was not sure what to expect.

She turned her head to look across the aisle, and gave a start. Colin and Rachel Ewart sat with their heads bowed. She had not entirely left the House of the Hare behind her, after all. But of course they would be here. Rachel's chronically painful back was what had brought them to this place. Hadn't Colin Ewart ranted about the false claims Thaddaeus had seemed to make about its healing powers? And hadn't Rachel begged him to wait until this Thursday service? Her own ambivalent feelings about such healing services dropped away as she prayed for Rachel to receive the relief from pain she needed.

She looked down at her order of service for communion and was delighted to find that it was in both English and Welsh.

Then two things happened simultaneously. Mother Joan appeared in a shining white chasuble over a white cassock. The dumpy woman with the scraped-back hair was transformed into the eucharistic priest. Jenny had felt a faint regret that it was not the regular Priest-Guardian of the shrine this week, but suddenly it did not matter. Mother Joan was one with all the priests who had ministered here for a millennium and more.

And from the corner of her eye she saw a latecomer enter the church and slip into one of the back pews. Lorna.

She chided herself for her instinct of surprise. Why had she assumed that the church would hold no consolation for the teenager? If ever anyone needed healing of the heart, it was Lorna.

They were on their feet now, singing the first hymn.

The service proceeded. Familiar liturgy in English. *Lord have mercy, Christ have mercy, Lord have mercy.* Alternating with the music of the Welsh words. *Gogoniant yn y goruchaf i Dduw.* Glory to God in the highest.

St Melangell would have spoken a form of Welsh.

Her nervousness was growing. They were coming to the part of the service which was not familiar to her, which marked this out as different from any other Eucharist.

Mother Joan stood on the step of the chancel and made her invitation.

"Today we offer the laying on of hands and anointing with oil. If any of you would like to receive this blessing, I invite you to come forward now."

Jenny felt a momentary surprise. She hadn't used the word "healing".

There was a waiting stillness. Then the man who had given her a hymnbook stepped out into the aisle and went forward to kneel before her. Did he do this every week? Was it his role to encourage others? The couple who had come in walking gear were next, determined, as though they had come for this. Two women, from either side of the aisle. And the Ewarts. Jenny found herself on her feet, working her way past Melangell and Aidan. She joined the little procession behind Rachel.

She was not the last. She sensed the quiet steps of Lorna behind her.

She knelt at the rail and bent her head. Mother Joan worked her way along the line, one by one. For each, the threefold blessing and the anointing with oil.

She came to Jenny. Her hands were warm on the scarfed head. "In the name of the Father, and of the Son, and of the Holy Spirit."

"Amen," Jenny answered.

She felt the priest's thumb, dipped in oil, trace the cross upon her forehead.

She was aware of a strange excitement, a sense of standing poised on the brink. Of what? Could the impossible be happening, and the malignant growth of her cancer be stopped? Or was the blessing she had received the serenity and faith to face her death?

Whatever it was, she felt shaken, changed, as she rose to her feet.

Had it made a difference to Rachel, to Lorna?

Her eyes were cast down as she walked back to her seat. It was only as she turned into the pew, where Aidan had risen to make room for her, that she raised her eyes and saw him.

DS Lincoln, the chief inspector's sidekick, sitting quiet and observant in the rearmost corner of the church, by the Easter garden.

Had he slipped out in his lunch break to take the bread and wine of communion which Mother Joan was about to offer, or had he been detailed to follow Lorna wherever she went?

All the fears she thought she had left behind her at the House of the Hare came flooding back. The horrible death of Thaddaeus. The suspicion of everyone around her. The rash defiance that had brought suspicion on herself. She glanced surreptitiously at Aidan. Had he really eliminated that blackest thought of all?

She exchanged the kiss of peace with him before the communion, and shook hands with other people, but she did not feel at peace. She moved forward with the rest of the congregation to receive the bread and wine. This time, Aidan came with her.

She was just rising from her knees at the communion rail when she realized that Sergeant Lincoln was also kneeling two places further along. She was looking down on the bald patch in his black hair.

It was a jolt to her perceptions. Was he not here on police duty, after all?

When the service was over, and Mother Joan pronounced the blessing, Jenny looked cautiously over her shoulder.

DS Lincoln was looking directly at her.

Her heart was thumping uncomfortably. Was it possible that he had not followed Lorna here, but her?

Mother Joan called for the congregation's attention. "I'm actually a visitor here myself this week. A few of us are going back to the St Melangell Centre for a light lunch. If you would like to join us, we should be delighted to see you."

Aidan raised his eyebrows at Jenny. "Do you fancy going?"

"I'd like to see inside the Centre. But I'm not sure if I can take much more of Colin."

She could see the Ewarts at the door, responding cordially to the invitation.

"He looks in a better humour today. Not blaming the rest of the world for his troubles."

"Poor Rachel! As if she didn't have enough to put up with."

Jenny was aware of another voice, close to her elbow. "Mrs Davison! We'd like a word with you this afternoon."

So the police sergeant *had* been watching her. Was that why he had followed her to the church? It seemed extreme. She would be back at the House of the Hare this afternoon.

"I'm sorry." She couldn't help blushing guiltily. "Was I supposed to tell you I was going to church?"

"No, not at all. We know where to find you." The words were blandly polite, but she could not interpret the seriousness in his eyes.

"Do you want me to come back now?"

"I think we can spare you time to have lunch first. Are you going to the St Melangell Centre?"

On an impulse, she answered, "Yes." Why did she feel something threatening in his interest?

She was even more disturbed when he fell into step behind the Davisons on the short walk up the lane. She watched Lorna go on ahead of them, back no doubt to the House of the Hare. But when the others reached the stone and slate cottage, flying a wind vane of the hare, they turned in at the gate. Sergeant Lincoln came, too.

The airy Centre looked welcoming. A large room had been created at the back of the original cottage, with plenty of chairs ranged around the walls. On low tables in the middle, a simple buffet lunch had been laid out. Melangell seized eagerly a slice of pizza and a chocolate cake. But Jenny was gripped with uneasiness about why the detective sergeant should be here.

She was relieved when he moved away from her to talk to a small woman bringing more food from the kitchen. She was perhaps in her sixties, grey-haired, with a Shetland jumper and a light tweed skirt in soft heathery shades of mauve and green. She reminded Jenny a little of her own mother.

Suddenly the truth struck her. Was everyone here a potential murderer? All except, perhaps, the two hikers? These people had been in or near Pennant Melangell on the day of the murder. Thaddaeus's building plans must have impacted on all of them. How many of them had joined Caradoc Lewis's opposition? Any one of these gentle, hospitable people might have had a motive. *Someone* had killed him.

To her surprise, Colin Ewart was smiling benignly and handing round plates of cheese sandwiches and chicken drumsticks. Jenny helped herself absentmindedly before she realized that she was not hungry.

She heard the woman in the tweed skirt say, smiling up at the detective, "Freda Rawlinson. I'm afraid I shan't be able to tell you very much. I only moved into the Tanat Valley a year ago."

Mother Joan came and sat beside Jenny. "We met before, my dear. In the church on Monday. And then yesterday I saw your husband in the churchyard and he gave me the terrible news of Mr Brown's death. Shocking."

"Do you know Caradoc Lewis? Did the church back his bid to stop Thaddaeus's plans? I saw him come into St Melangell's yesterday. I thought he might be in the congregation today."

The man on the other side of Mother Joan broke into a roar of laughter. "Not him! Old Caradoc is a pagan, and proud of it. He'd take over the church and turn it into a goddess-worshipping temple if he could."

"Quite so," Mother Joan agreed. "I don't know the man, but I had a run-in with him myself. He's published this book which he wants to put in the shop in the tower room. His alternative version of the St Melangell story. According to him, she wasn't a Christian saint at all. And far from sheltering the hare when the prince was hunting it, she was the one who was being hunted. When the prince got close enough to seize her, she turned into a hare. He thinks the hare and the girl are one. The girl is a goddess, and the hare is sacred. It's the goddess in animal form."

"Well, yes," Jenny said, remembering the research for her own book. "There are quite a few old myths which go like that. I'd say there was something in it. That the hare *was* a sacred animal in pagan Celtic times. And then along came the real-life Christian Melangell, and the hare story got transferred to her."

"Hmmph, well. I told him I didn't think his book was appropriate for a church bookstall. He wasn't best pleased. He has a bit of a temper, your Mr Lewis." Mother Joan turned to the man beside her.

"True enough. It doesn't pay to get on the wrong side of Caradoc. But we were glad to join forces with him when Mr Brown started those plans for the House of the Hare." He looked across at Jenny apologetically. "Sorry. I believe you're staying there."

"Yes. And it's lovely. Or it was until…"

"Bad business, that. You wouldn't believe that something like that could happen here. This has always been known as a place of peace and healing. But murder?"

Jenny's eyes strayed back to the detective. He had finished talking to the woman with the tweed skirt. He was watching Jenny again. He gave a lift of his eyebrows and a jerk of his head towards the door, as if to say that it was time to go.

Jenny got to her feet, unsure what it was about DS Lincoln that made her feel so troubled. Why bother to follow her to the church and here to the St Melangell Centre, as if he didn't want to let her out of his sight?

Chapter Seventeen

SERGEANT LINCOLN WALKED along the lane to the house with the Davisons. No one talked. Melangell kept looking up at the detective with a considering frown. Jenny waited for her to launch one of her devastating questions, such as, "Do you think Mummy killed Mr Brown?" But she stayed quiet.

In the foyer, flooded with light from the window on the stairs, Sergeant Lincoln turned to her. "I think we need to have that talk, Mrs Davison."

Jenny's alarm must have shown in her face as she looked at Aidan. A sudden concern leapt into his eyes. Had he really thought this was just routine questioning? Had Aidan not wondered why the detective had followed her to church and on to the Centre? But he could see now that something was wrong.

"Does it have to be straight away?" he asked the sergeant. "My wife's unwell. She needs to rest."

"I shan't keep her very long, sir. And I can assure you it's important that I talk to her."

His voice was level. Small dark eyes regarded Aidan steadily. Until now, he had been in the shadow of DCI Denbigh, taking notes. Jenny had hardly noticed him as an individual. She studied the black, receding hair, the lean, somewhat highly coloured face, the limbs that seemed too long for his casual sports jacket and trousers. About forty, she guessed. Without quite knowing why, she sensed the restrained energy of a man who would rather be physically active.

She excused herself and went to the ladies' cloakroom, to give herself a few moments to steady herself. When she came back, Aidan and Melangell had gone.

The sergeant smiled at her without warmth in his eyes. "I don't think we need to turn Miss Jenkins out of her office again. It's a fine day. Why don't we find a seat in the garden?"

As they crossed the lawn, her nervousness grew. A sense that something was not right. She looked around in a sudden realization.

"Where's Inspector Denbigh? Shouldn't he be here?"

"He's otherwise engaged."

She thought of what Aidan had told her about the larger incident room in Newtown, which must be the hub of activity. Of the house fire in Welshpool, and the woman who had died. A wife-killing, PC Watkins had confidently predicted. Most murders were committed by someone close to the victim.

Was that true of Thaddaeus?

Or for money, Constable Roberts had added.

What had that to do with Jenny?

At the far end of the lawn, paths wound away among the bushes. Jenny knew from her own explorations that there were seats in quiet corners, out of sight of the house. She looked back over her shoulder with growing unease.

Sian had found some croquet hoops and Aidan was instructing Melangell where to put them. He lifted his hand in a casual wave. There was no reason why her heart should be hammering so hard at the thought of entering one of those hidden pathways alone with this man. He was a police officer, wasn't he? Why was her alarm growing?

Lincoln led the way round a clump of bright orange azaleas. A curved stone bench had been set beside a small lily pond. He motioned her to take a seat.

The stone was cold against the backs of her legs.

It was too like the shrubbery from which Thaddaeus had stumbled to his death.

"I'm sorry for the cloak-and-dagger business. But I didn't want to say this in front of your daughter. Have you seen this morning's newspapers?"

The question startled her. "No. The nearest newsagent is miles away. And we didn't ask Sian to order one."

From an inside pocket of his jacket, Sergeant Lincoln drew a folded newspaper. He spread it out and turned it to show her.

It was one of the tabloids. The headline screamed at her.

DOES FAMOUS AUTHOR HOLD MURDER CLUE?

There was a photograph of her wide-eyed face.

She felt the blood drain from her cheeks in shock.

"That Coutts man! He got into the house almost straight after the murder. He was taking photos of all of us. Aidan was furious."

The sergeant's face was grim. "He's well known to us, Marcus Coutts. He has a sixth sense for violent crime. The slightest scent of blood, and he's there. Sometimes before we are. I'm sorry we weren't quick enough off the mark to stop him." He smiled slightly. "*Are* you a famous author?"

"Only if you're keen on Celtic saints. I've been on TV a few times. History programmes."

"It's tabloid-speak, isn't it? To them, the words 'famous' and 'author' automatically go together. They don't sell millions of copies printing articles about 'obscure historian'. I'm sorry! I didn't mean that to sound rude."

"I know what you mean."

He grew grave again. "The question is, is it true?" He read from the smaller print. "'*TV celebrity Jenny Davison was a guest at the hotel. I found her sitting only yards from where the murderer struck. Most other guests were out for the afternoon, but the famous author could hold the vital clue. Her bedroom overlooks the archery range where the body was found.*'"

Jenny gasped. "How did he know?"

"There's worse. '*She told me she may have seen something significant, but refused to say what.*'"

"That's a lie. I didn't tell him anything."

"Men like Marcus Coutts make their living by changing nothing into something sensational... The thing is, is he right?"

He caught her move of protest, and held up a placatory hand. "I don't mean you told him anything. I'm sure you didn't. But if I remember your statement correctly, you were up in your room at the crucial time."

Lincoln took his notebook out. He turned back several pages to find the record of her first interview. His dark head, with its circle of lighter scalp, bent over it.

He straightened. "You last saw Thaddaeus about two."

"It was earlier than that. I was coming out of the dining room after lunch. I saw him going off down the corridor that way." She pointed to the end of the house nearest the butts. "Then I went upstairs for a rest. I'd gone back to bed after my archery in the morning. But I was still tired. Even sitting down, it was pretty hard drawing a bow after... all this time." Her voice dropped. She did not want to go into the years of treatment that had marked off this life from the one she had known before.

"I understand." His voice was sympathetic.

"I saw the Ewarts going out and Messrs Secker and McCarthy coming in. That was from the landing. And then... nothing. I fell asleep."

"You said you saw Lorna Brown coming back to the house. Running to meet Euan Jones."

"That was later. After I woke up."

"You saw no one at the back of the house around two?"

She shook her head. "Sorry. I picked up a book, but I was asleep in no time." She frowned. "At least…"

The sergeant waited.

"No. I'm sorry. It's gone."

"What's gone?"

"I'd tell you if I knew. It's just… I have this feeling. Just as I was dropping off. I think there *was* something. Only I can't remember what." She puckered her brow in an effort at recollection. "I'm really sorry. But the harder I try, the fuzzier it gets. Like trying to remember a dream when you wake up in the morning. Perhaps it *was* a dream."

"Let's suppose it wasn't. If you were in bed, it couldn't be anything you saw. Something you heard, then?"

When she didn't answer, he tried again. "As Marcus Coutts says, your bedroom is at the back of the house. Was the window open? Could you have heard something from outside?"

"I'm sorry. I really can't remember. And anyway, how would it help? If I didn't see who it was?"

"The murderer can't be sure of that, can he, or she?"

The dark eyes were looking hard at her now. Suddenly she understood what he was trying to tell her. The hammering in her heart took on a different meaning. Detective Sergeant Lincoln was giving her a warning. Her eyes widened.

"I don't want to alarm you, Mrs Davison. As long as the murderer thought we were looking for an archer, you were even a possible suspect. That must have amused him, or her. But now we know that anyone with the opportunity could have gone into the grounds and stabbed Mr Brown, then you might be the only one who could identify that person.

And this article..." he stabbed the paper viciously, "hints that you can."

"But I was asleep!"

"You can't prove that, can you? For all Mr Brown's killer knows, you could be the only person with vital evidence of their movements. And as yet, you may not have given that evidence to the police. I don't wish to sound melodramatic, but I think you should be careful. Mr Brown was a rich man. Whoever killed him was playing for high stakes. We'll have officers on duty ourselves, of course. But it might be as well if you didn't let yourself be found alone."

The light on the lily pond dazzled her, as a fish broke the surface. The sergeant's words echoed in her mind meaninglessly. Then, gradually they fell into place, as the ripples on the pond settled.

She swallowed. "You think he... she... could kill again?"

The black eyes were steady, expressionless. "That is a possibility, yes."

Chapter Eighteen

M ELANGELL'S BALL SPUN across the lawn to knock Aidan's out of reach of the hoop for the seventh time. She burst into floods of giggles.

"You little horror! Croquet suits you, doesn't it? It brings out the mean and malicious streak in your nature. And I'd always thought you were such a nice child. Can't think where you get it from."

"You're just cross because I'm winning."

"You're not. You're just making sure *I* don't."

He would not have played well anyway. His eyes kept going up from the coloured balls at his feet to that path among the azaleas where Jenny had disappeared with DS Lincoln. His memory was haunted by the look of fear she had given him. Pain stabbed his conscience. He should never have sown that apprehension about the police suspecting her of an accidental killing. Too late, he wanted to put his arms round her and comfort her. Now that the post-mortem had concluded that the arrow which killed Thaddaeus had probably not been fired from a bow, Jenny was no longer one of a very few people who could have been guilty. The police simply needed to widen the field of their questioning, as they had with him. Jenny had been in the house all that day. She, as much as anyone, might have seen something.

"*Daddy*! It's your turn."

He grinned at Melangell and sent her blue ball spinning away from the hoop.

"That's not fair!"

"No, but it's fun."

He stiffened. They were coming back. Jenny looked sober. Aidan found the sergeant's expression difficult to read. DS Lincoln set off across the grass, away from the house, to the workshop.

As she approached, Aidan saw that Jenny was not only grave but pale. He dropped his mallet.

"You ought to be in bed. Is the pain bad?"

She nodded slightly. "That's not the worst of it." She glanced at Melangell. "I'll tell you upstairs."

They took the lift. He helped her on to the bed and took off her shoes. "There. Lie down and have a sleep. I'll get your tablets."

"Aidan." She caught his hand. "Sergeant Lincoln showed me this."

She reached into her shoulder-bag and thrust a newspaper at him. The same vulnerable face in front of him was splashed across the page of the tabloid. He read the text with growing horror.

"Marcus Coutts! For two pins, I'd take an arrow myself and run it straight through him! This is appalling."

"Sergeant Lincoln thought so too. He says they've fixed the time of the murder either side of two. Aidan, I didn't see anything. I was in bed then. But this article makes it sound as though I did."

His eyes went up to hers, not understanding.

"What if the murderer *thinks* I did?"

The bottom of his stomach seemed to fall away.

"And if it's someone here, or in the neighbourhood…"

"He told me to be careful. Not to be alone."

Aidan leapt up. "I'm going straight over to that office of theirs. I'll tell them they have to put a twenty-four hour guard on you."

"Wait!" She caught him back.

He subsided on to the bed and watched her rub her thin hands over her cheeks.

"I don't know what to think," she sighed. "It seemed so simple at first. Either Lorna had done it, because he was abusing her, or Sian took matters into her own hands to protect her. But now... We've tended to think that it had to be someone in the house. Like those old-fashioned whodunits which take place at a house party on an island. A closed community of suspects. But then this morning... I found myself looking at all those people in church. And at lunch afterwards. They seemed such nice, *good* people. But how do we know? We've only been here four days. And we've just met a few people outside the house. We've no idea of all the undercurrents that might have been going on since Thaddaeus turned up with his plans. It's horrible. I can't look at anyone now without thinking, 'Did they do it?' And now..."

He grasped her hands. "Now you're wondering, 'Do they think I saw them?' Don't worry, love. I'm not going to let you out of my sight. We can pack up and go. Harry and Debbie did."

She gave a trembling sigh. "He said something else. 'Whoever killed him was playing for high stakes.' If that's true, they could follow us, couldn't they? Here, we've got police all around us."

Aidan's mind raced over multiple possibilities. His fingers combed his beard. "I need time to get my head round this. But they must know you've given the police all the evidence you can. If you *had* seen anything, it would be out by now."

"I keep wondering. What if it wasn't anything I'd seen. What if I could have *heard* something, even lying in bed?"

"Did you?"

"I can't remember clearly. I was asleep, mostly. But I keep feeling there was *something*. Voices, a door banging, a

car engine? I can't pin it down. And I can't be sure whether
I'm just imagining it with hindsight, or if it was something I
heard earlier in the day."

"There *was* a car. It nearly mowed us down in the drive.
That Jaguar again. But that was about three. We'd just got
back."

"Those two men. I wish I knew where they fitted into
this. They look almost stereotypically sinister."

"I'm sure the police are looking into it. And they're not
here now, are they? Get some sleep."

He bent over and kissed her.

As he made his way downstairs to rejoin Melangell it
occurred to him that he had promised not to let Jenny out
of his sight. It was a manner of speaking, of course. She was
hardly going to be attacked in her bedroom. And the window
with the balcony was in sight from the lawn.

He glanced up as a new thought struck him. Should he
have told her to lock her door?

Aidan had reached the bottom of the stairs when anger overtook
him. What right had Marcus Coutts to put her in danger?
What were the police doing? If they thought that Jenny might
be at risk, why weren't they protecting her? He glanced out
of the glass panels of the front door. There were probably still
officers around, but no one was in sight outside.

The chill reality of what Jenny had told him was sinking
in. If she was in danger, it could be from anywhere. Did the
police really have no idea who had done it? Or was Chief
Inspector Denbigh keeping it close to his chest? If so, Aidan
would have to make him tell him. He and Jenny couldn't go
through the rest of this week starting at every noise, looking
over their shoulders, suspecting anyone and everyone, inside

the house or out.

The Tanat Valley, which had seemed such a peaceful, serene place when they entered it, had become a world of menace.

Would it really be any better if they left, until Thaddaeus's killer was found?

Mr Brown was a rich man. Whoever killed him was playing for high stakes.

Those sinister visitors in the Jaguar. From the world of high finance? Euan Jones the gardener, planning to marry an heiress?

He walked into the lounge and was surprised to find Sian on a stepladder, cleaning the windows.

"Is that your job?"

She threw him a rueful smile. "Life goes on, doesn't it? I ought to get Mair's mother to do more hours on the cleaning, but we're not balancing the books as it is."

He paused in front of the French windows. On the sunlit lawn beyond, Melangell was getting in some practice with the croquet mallet, aiming balls through hoops. She was getting quite good at it.

His heart turned over. This was what it should have been like. A communion service in the shrine church. A child playing in the sunshine. Young bracken springing green on the mountaintops. The silver thread of the waterfall at the head of the cwm.

Now, even these innocent things were underscored by the black line of menace. What was sacred, precious, had been tainted with murder.

Eden lost. The bitter days between the crucifixion and Easter.

On an impulse, he looked up at Sian, who was vigorously rubbing the glass with a chamois leather. The rounded arms, like a Raphael angel, showed muscle, not fat. He remembered that she had been a PE teacher. The provision of games equipment at the House of the Hare was her doing.

"Those two men who visited the house on Monday and Tuesday. Who were they?"

She had her head turned away from him. Her blonde curls obscured her face.

"Business partners of Mr Brown."

The answer was crisp. It did not invite him to enquire further. But he pressed on.

"They seemed rather impatient, from the style of their driving. Was something wrong?"

She rubbed away in silence, polishing the window with a duster. Then she sighed, and climbed down the ladder. Her blue eyes gave him a long, considering look.

"Well, I suppose it's not really confidential now. Thaddaeus's will, I mean. Now that Lorna's in the clear, it should go through probate."

But she's not in the clear, Aidan wanted to remind her. They let her go because they didn't have enough evidence to arrest her. But she must still be a suspect, along with everyone else.

"Lorna is the chief beneficiary, I take it."

"She was all the family he had left. He was apparently very fond of her mother. She died of cancer, you know."

She studied his face as she said this.

"I know," he answered quietly. "I gather that's why Lorna persuaded him to build the House of the Hare. For people like Jenny to come to Pennant Melangell. I'm very grateful to her. Or I would have been if…"

"If he hadn't been murdered while you were here. Very inconvenient of him."

"I didn't mean that. I'm not Colin Ewart. But it's not how I thought Melangell and I would remember this week after… Jenny is gone."

"You don't believe in the healing power of the shrine? Or the yew trees?"

"There are different ways of healing. I know it's helped Jenny. We shall have to wait and see how… So Lorna stands to inherit this? And the rest of Thaddaeus's business? Is that where Secker and McCarthy come in?"

"They put up the money for this house. And they're not too impressed with our bookings this first season. I told them, it's early days yet. It needs to get known. Word of mouth. People like you. Or so I hoped."

"And so we would have. We fell in love with it at first sight. I don't know that you'd have much joy out of Colin Ewart, even without the death. I bet he's the kind of person who writes stinking reviews for TripAdvisor."

"And Harry and Debbie felt it was over their budget. Well, it was always meant to be more than a youth hostel."

"So Secker and McCarthy wanted to change the game? Attract a different kind of clientèle? Outdoor types with serious money to spend, rather than people in need of healing."

"That's about it. Thaddaeus was wavering. Well, he comes from that sort of world, where everything depends on the bottom line."

"But Lorna would feel differently? She told Jenny about her mother. I got the impression this meant a lot more than money to her."

"Yes. Oh, they'll get their investment back from somewhere. But maybe not the sort of high returns they want. That's why they were putting pressure on Thaddaeus not to change his will."

"What do you mean? They wanted her to inherit?"

Sian dipped the chamois leather in a bucket and wrung it out. "Of course not. But she's only just eighteen. There was this trust fund. He put it in his will when she was younger. With them in charge, of course. They'd make the decisions and she'd get a share of the profits, at their discretion. I think it was meant to last until she was twenty-five."

"And Thaddaeus was going to change that?"

"There was a big argument on Monday. He'd decided to give her a free hand, now she's eighteen. But they must have talked him into reconsidering. They came again on Tuesday. Thaddaeus had gone to see that nutter Caradoc Lewis about something. But I heard him come back. I went to look for him, but I couldn't find him. He must already have been…" Her voice faltered. "Anyway, they weren't best pleased when they had to go away empty-handed again."

"So the codicil was never signed? The trust fund stands? Lorna doesn't get a free hand."

"That's about the size of it. Now, if you'll excuse me, I've got work to do."

She moved her cloths and cleaning liquid to the next window and set to work energetically again.

Aidan walked slowly out on to the lawn. His thoughts were somersaulting. From the moment he had seen that Jaguar forcing his own car back along the narrow lane, the men inside it had seemed like a malevolent force. It had been so easy to imagine them casting a dark shadow over the House of the Hare. Threatening Thaddaeus. Even Jenny. Yet everything had pointed to Lorna having the most to gain from her uncle's death. Now the situation had been turned upside down. If the codicil taking away their power over Thaddaeus's estate had remained unsigned, they had every reason to kill him before he could do so. And Lorna had every motive to keep him alive.

Chapter Nineteen

AIDAN'S MIND WAS WHIRLING with altered possibilities, his thoughts peopled with a shifting range of suspects. It was several moments before he registered the fact that the lawn was empty.

He looked around. The croquet hoops stood where he and Melangell had set them. His mallet lay where he had dropped it when Jenny and DS Lincoln had emerged from the path through the azaleas. There was a scatter of coloured balls. But no Melangell.

The emptiness screamed at him.

Though the sun was bright, there was a blackness crowding in over his eyes. He had not felt on the edge of fainting since he was a schoolboy in a crowded assembly hall. But now the world swam in front of him. He was deathly cold.

He made himself take deep, slow breaths. There must be a reason. He could not afford to give way to weakness now. Jenny needed him. It was Jenny who was in danger...

Melangell was missing. The possibility struck him with the force of wrecker's ball. *What if whoever DS Lincoln thought was threatening Jenny had seized Melangell to ensure her silence?*

Fool! his panicked conscience yelled at him. I should never have left her alone, even for a few moments.

A thought occurred to him on a wave of relief. He spun round. Sian was still busy cleaning the huge windows. She would have seen everything that happened on the lawn. He started to stride towards her when he heard a childish voice.

"Oh, *there* he is."

The slight, mop-headed figure of Melangell, in blue shorts and a red Shrek T-shirt, was stepping out of one of the many paths that wound among the ornamental shrubs. In her hand was the yellow croquet ball. And just behind her came a figure in mud-smeared jeans and a tartan shirt. Dark hair flopped over his head, which he hung self-consciously. Euan Jones, the gardener.

Melangell turned to look up at the young man with a radiant smile, then back at Aidan. "Euan found my ball for me. I gave it a most tremendous hit and it disappeared into those bushes. And there he was. So here *it* is." She flourished the ball at her father.

The sun was warmer now. Aidan flashed a grin of gratitude at Euan. "Thanks for that. Sorry if she's been a nuisance. I got held up, talking."

"You always do," Melangell scolded him.

"Less of that, young lady."

He raised his eyes again to find that Euan had lifted his own head and was looking directly at him. Not smiling.

Something about those dark brown eyes disturbed him. This was the first time he had come face to face with Euan Jones since the day they had discovered Thaddaeus's body. There had been venom in the young gardener's voice then: "*He deserved it.*"

Since then, Aidan had glimpsed him in the distance, about his work. He had seen him in the lounge with the other staff and guests, uncomfortably waiting his turn to be questioned.

But a memory was coming back to him of something Jenny had told him. Something that had happened while he and Melangell were out on their waterfall walk, leaving

Jenny alone at the archery butts. She had said that Euan had emerged out of the shrubbery and collected her arrows from the target.

Aidan pictured the scene now as distinctly as if it were framed in the LCD screen of his camera. But as Jenny would have seen it. Euan, walking across the grass towards her. Those earth-stained fingers gripping a fistful of red-flighted arrows. Like the one that stabbed Thaddaeus. Advancing on Jenny in her wheelchair.

The ground trembled under Aidan's feet.

He grasped Melangell's thin wrist, hardly conscious that he was doing so.

"Croquet's over. Come on. We're going."

"Where?"

"Never mind."

He hauled her indoors, nearly upsetting a surprised Sian on her stepladder. Through the foyer, pounding up the stairs. He should have gone back and told Jenny to lock the door.

"Daddy!" Melangell wailed. "You're going too fast. You're hurting me."

Conscience-stricken, he let go of her wrist. "Sorry, love. But we have to hurry."

"Why?"

He burst into the double bedroom.

Jenny lay curled up in the big bed, asleep. His heart ached to see how thin her face was, the smudges round her eyes. She had taken off her scarf. There was a sheen of tiny fair hairs just starting to cover her scalp again. Every instinct of compassion made him want to leave her there, undisturbed, wrapped in the arms of healing sleep.

But a more imperative voice was telling him he had to

snatch her up and carry her away. Now, before whoever was stalking this valley with murderous intent could realize that Jenny alone might hold the clue to the killer's identity.

He seized their suitcases from the corner where he had stacked them. He threw one on the bed.

Jenny stirred. She opened bruised-looking eyelids, then gave a cat-like yawn. She rubbed the backs of her hands over her eyes.

"Is it time to get up?"

Then she focused on Aidan, on Melangell hovering in the doorway, on the suitcase weighing down the other half of the bedclothes. She struggled to sit up.

"What's going on?"

Aidan was rapidly emptying the drawers on his side of the bed, and piling the contents into the suitcase.

"We're leaving."

"Now? But it's only Thursday."

"I know. But I'm not letting you stay here a moment longer. I should have taken you away as soon as the police had questioned us. When Harry and Debbie went."

She reached a hand towards him, but he did not stay still long enough for her to hold him. The hangers in the wardrobe rattled as he slid the clothes off.

"Love, we went over all this. Whether to go or stay. We decided it was safer here, with the police all over the place, than heading off on our own, and not knowing who might be following us."

"I was wrong. When I got downstairs, Melangell was gone. Euan Jones found her looking for a ball in the shrubbery. Where were the police then? How do either we or the police know it wasn't Euan? Or anybody else? They can't be everywhere."

Obediently, Jenny started to ease her feet out from under the duvet. She looked drawn and tired, but he must not let short-term sympathy cloud his brain.

Then she checked, her bare feet not yet on the floor. She turned her serious grey-blue eyes on him. "I can't go."

"Oh, yes, you can. I've made my mind up."

"No. I've been lying in bed, thinking about what that newspaper headline said. How I might be the only one who saw or heard something just before Thaddaeus was killed, or straight after."

"That's why we're going. And not telling anyone where."

She went on as though he had not spoken. "He was right. I just have this feeling at the edge of my mind that there *was* something. But every time I try to focus on it and remember what it was, it goes." She raised her eyes to his. "But I desperately need to remember it. Properly. The police need me to remember. Everyone here, Lorna, Sian, *they* need me to remember. I can't just run away and put it all behind me. If there's any chance of my calling that memory back, it's going to be here, where it happened. When I was lying on this bed, in this room."

Her eyes begged him to understand.

"Even the police think you're in danger."

"Haven't we talked about this before? Didn't Martin Luther King say something? '*What matters is not how long you live, but why you live, what you stand for, and what you are willing to die for.*'"

His mind was shouting at her, "But we have so little time left!"

What he said was a plea, "Jenny!"

She said nothing, just went on looking at him, willing him to acquiesce.

He knew her. That steely resolve. He would not get her to change her mind if she thought this was what she had to do.

He raised his hands in a gesture of loving helplessness. "Sorry. I shouldn't have woken you up."

He turned to Melangell, who was biting her thumb. "As you were, partner. Let's get those croquet balls rolling."

He waited until Melangell had reached the head of the stairs. Then he put his head back around the bedroom door. "Lock this behind me. Don't let anyone in. I'll give three knocks when I come back, so you'll know it's me."

Every step he took down the sunlit staircase felt like a move away from safety, into the unknown.

Chapter Twenty

WHEN THEY HAD GONE, Jenny hesitated, then locked the door, as Aidan had ordered her to.

It felt overdramatic. DS Lincoln had only told her that she *might* be in danger. Aidan was acting as though it was a real and immediate fact. She was trying to be sensible. Yet it was difficult not to let some of his fear communicate itself to her.

If only she could pinpoint just what it was she was on the verge of remembering. The shadow of apprehension grew colder as she realized that she did indeed hold crucial evidence. She must be very careful not to confirm this to anyone but Aidan and the police.

She had a sudden longing for the elderly, world-weary Chief Detective Inspector Denbigh. It would be reassuring to unburden herself to him. But it would be pointless to go to him until she had something definite to tell him.

She lay down on the bed again. But sleep would not come. Her mind replayed over and over what little she knew about the time of Thaddaeus's death. She had seen the Everts leaving after lunch, and Secker and McCarthy arriving. She had heard raised voices, which must have been the two financiers angry that Thaddaeus could not be found. But others had heard that too. Then she had lain down, here on this bed. Sometime around then, Thaddaeus had been murdered. She had not heard or seen him leave the house and walk away into the shrubbery, where Harry and Debbie had found the body.

She couldn't have seen anything. Lying in bed, she had a view of the tops of the mountains. Sunlight on the patches of young bracken and the darker shadow of the gorse. Blue sky above. Nothing of the garden below unless she went out on to the balcony.

It had been some forty minutes later when she had got up and done that. And then she had seen Lorna running back into the garden and Euan's arms. By then, according to the pathologist, Thaddaeus had been dead for at least half an hour.

She sighed and rolled over.

There was a light tap at the door.

Jenny sat up and listened. The tap came again. It was definitely not the three knocks that Aidan had arranged as a signal that it was him.

She swung her feet quietly to the floor. She wished now that she had not agreed to that overreaction of locking the door. Far from protecting her, it heightened her sense of danger. What did she think she had locked it against?

Her bare feet padded to the door. Her eyes widened as she saw the handle twist slowly. The door shuddered as someone tried to open it. The lock resisted.

Her throat was dry now, but she needed to confront whatever was happening. She had faced up to the diagnosis of cancer, and to the news that it had returned more aggressively. She would face this new threat with the same clear-eyed determination.

"Who's there?"

"It's me. Lorna," came the subdued reply.

Jenny unlocked the door with a sense of anticlimax. What had she expected? Those strange men in suits, who had driven their Jaguar so dangerously down the Welsh lanes? Euan Jones, prowling the upstairs corridor with a sharp-edged gardening implement?

She saw with concern that the teenage girl looked as tense as she had felt herself. The intense blue eyes in her heart-shaped face went past Jenny to the tall window.

"Sorry to disturb you." There was a faint Welsh lilt to her voice, which Jenny had not noticed before. "You weren't asleep, were you?"

"No," Jenny said truthfully, though she had wanted to be.

Lorna walked across the room to the balcony. "You've got a lovely view. You can see most of the garden from here, can't you? And the woods and mountains."

"Yes, it's wonderful. Doesn't your room have the same sort of view?"

"No. I'm at the end of this corridor. I look down the valley, the way you drive to get here. I can see the kitchen garden and the tennis courts. Not that anybody but Thaddaeus and I have used them yet."

"Do you miss your uncle?"

"What a strange question? Of course I do. He was all the family I've got. Since my mam died."

"It must have been a very close relationship."

"It was."

They were skirting around the subject that Jenny had dared not press her on, the last time they had spoken about Thaddaeus. This time, she felt bolder. She did not know why Lorna had come into her bedroom at a time when Jenny could be expected to be alone. But it suggested that she wanted to share a confidence. Perhaps it was something that was easier to say to a sympathetic stranger than to someone she knew well, like Sian.

Jenny sat down on the bed and wondered how to phrase it.

"Forgive me if I'm putting my foot in it, but we wondered... Your uncle seemed a very forceful personality.

Don't get me wrong. He was very warm and genial towards us. The perfect host. But it must have been difficult for you, just eighteen, and living and working so close to someone as dominant as that. Did you ever feel… under his influence? I don't just mean in business affairs. I know he was teaching you the ropes. But something more personal?"

Lorna had her back to the window now, staring at Jenny. The deep blue eyes were wide but shadowed.

"What do you mean, personal?"

"Look, I know I'm sticking my neck out. But we were worried about you, Aidan and I. The day Thaddaeus was murdered, Aidan said he and Melangell met you coming away from the waterfall. You looked upset. And your shirt was torn. Later, Aidan saw Thaddaeus not far away. We couldn't help wondering if he…"

The cupid's bow of Lorna's mouth fell open, revealing pearly teeth. Her voice rose an octave. "You think… you think Uncle Thaddaeus was making a pass at me? That he was behaving like a dirty old man? How dare you!"

She took a step towards Jenny, her eyes flashing anger now. Jenny jumped to her feet. Cancer and chemotherapy had weakened her, but she had once been a competent athlete. She balanced on the balls of her feet, wondering if Lorna was going to attack her.

She held up her hands peaceably. "I'm sorry if we got the wrong end of the stick. But you hear about it. Older male relations abusing their power over a girl in the family. And now you've no one else to turn to, I thought…"

"I've got Sian."

"So there was never anything like that with Thaddaeus?"

The door crashed open behind Jenny. She turned abruptly to find Aidan. His bearded face was blazing with rage.

"What's she doing here?"

"Aidan! I let her in."

"I told you to keep that door locked."

Lorna looked from one to the other. "Is something wrong? Why did you have to lock your door?"

Jenny scrambled to put the words back in the box from which they should never have escaped. "Aidan was worried about someone disturbing me while I was sleeping. No, it's all right. I actually wasn't asleep when you knocked. I thought perhaps you wanted to talk. I'm sorry we went off down the wrong track."

She looked back at Aidan, then at Lorna. Whatever it was that the girl had come to say, it was unlikely that she would unburden herself now in front of Aidan, or even to Jenny, since she had made that disastrous misjudgment.

"Well, I'm sorry to have disturbed you. Excuse me!" With a flash of teenage tantrum, Lorna flounced past Aidan out of the room.

Jenny sat down on the bed again, shaking. "Well, between us, we fouled that up."

"You should never have let her in, without me. I told you. We can't trust anyone."

"Oh, come on, now. It was only Lorna."

"Who was the police's prime suspect on Tuesday."

"But they let her go. And I found out something else which cuts the ground from under the scenario we'd worked out about her. Thaddaeus wasn't abusing her. Whatever happened at the waterfall that morning, it wasn't him."

"Is that what she came to tell you?"

"No. I asked her. She looked really shocked."

"So why did she knock on your door?"

"I don't know. We didn't get around to that before you burst in."

"Oh, so it's my fault now? She looked as though she was about to attack you."

"Only because I'd made an inexcusable suggestion."

"And you've really no idea why she came?"

"None. All she did was walk across the room and say what a nice view I had."

"A view! Of the grounds. Where Thaddaeus died."

"Aidan, I've told you. Thaddaeus wasn't forcing her to have sex with him. She had no motive to kill him."

He gazed at her for several moments. Then he sighed. "No. I didn't tell you, did I? About Thaddaeus's will?"

"It hasn't been made public yet, has it? I suppose Lorna will inherit most of what he had."

"Yes. But this afternoon Sian told me that there were strings, if her uncle died before he signed a codicil. Those hoodlums in the Jaguar. Thaddaeus had arranged for them to manage a trust fund for her. But he was going to change his will and put Lorna in sole charge. They had an argument about it on Monday. Lorna would only get her hands on the money if he lived to sign that codicil."

She stared back at him. Her mind struggled to make sense of what he was telling her.

A child's voice came from the corridor. "I told you, Daddy. I knew Lorna didn't stab him to get the money. She's not like that."

Chapter Twenty-one

JENNY RAN HER HANDS over her scalp in dismay. "I'm sorry, sweetie! Daddy and I weren't really quarrelling. It's just that he's worried about me."

Melangell came and hugged her. "*I'm* worried about you. But I don't shout at you."

"My fault again," Aidan said. "Look, this place is getting on top of me. I need to get out." He held up his hands in self-defence. "No, I know we agreed we're not running away before the end of the week. I just meant a change of scenery. Do you fancy a drive? Or could you manage a short walk?"

Jenny got to her feet, one arm still around Melangell. "Didn't you say something about a footpath across the fields? No, it's OK! I know I can't walk to the waterfall. But you said there was a footpath sign on the other side of the road. I wouldn't mind strolling across the fields to the river. That was the first thing that struck me when we came to Pennant Melangell before. There was a peace lying over the meadows by the Tanat that was almost tangible. I could do with discovering that again."

When they reached the point in the lane where a sign on the right pointed uphill saying "WATERFALL" Jenny looked at it with a wry regret. "That's what I'd *really* like to do. But I know I can't."

"It was tougher than I expected," Aidan said. "I'm not really sure that the sign means you can go to the foot of the waterfall. If it does, we missed the path."

"We'll settle for going left, then. Where's the path?"

They found a farm track by a cattle grid and set off over the fields. Jenny realized how much she had missed the swing of her long legs over open country.

"OK?" Aidan asked. "It's not going to be too far?"

"Watch me."

They came to a little bridge over the river. Already, the Tanat had collected the run-off from several waterfalls around the horseshoe of hills, of which Pistyll Blaen-y-cwm was the most impressive. It ran clear and lively, quite broad, even so near its source. Jenny knelt and dangled her wrists in it.

"Mmm. I can feel it washing me clean. There's been so much nastiness. Violence, suspicion. I need cleansing."

Was it really only noon when she had knelt in the church before Mother Joan, to receive her blessing and be anointed with oil? When she and Aidan had shared communion?

"Do you want to go on? According to the map, there's a smaller waterfall behind that farm."

"Yes, please."

The fall was no more than a trickle after a dry spring. Trees grew darkly over it. It slid over damp boulders in a branch-hung cleft. Ferns grew in the crevices. The water trickled over the edge in drops like a bead curtain.

Melangell started to climb among the rocks. "Careful," Aidan warned. "They're slippery when they're wet. And I've a feeling we may be on private land here."

Melangell craned her head from her vantage point above them. "*They're* here."

"Who?"

"Lorna and Mr Caradoc."

Jenny saw Aidan start. "I'd forgotten. His house is the next one along the valley. I remember now Inspector Denbigh showing me the map. He pointed out that on the day of the murder, Caradoc could actually have got to the House of the Hare ahead of us, if he'd legged it across the footpath we've just taken, while Melangell and I were walking back along the lane."

"But he didn't, did he? No one saw him at the house."

"No. But that's not to say he wasn't there. You were in bed, and everyone else seems to have been in rooms facing the front or the side. It would be easy enough for anyone to get over the wall and creep through the bushes to where Thaddaeus was killed."

Jenny shivered. "I thought we'd come out here to put all that behind us for a while."

He hugged her. "I'm sorry. That was my idea, wasn't it?… But why is Lorna with Caradoc?"

Jenny sat down on a rock, suddenly weary. "She was here on Tuesday with him and Thaddaeus, wasn't she? She must have been. You met her running away from the waterfall. And then you came across Thaddaeus and Caradoc arguing. She must have gone there with her uncle and something happened that upset her."

"And it wasn't what we thought it was."

"Apparently not."

"Then, if it wasn't Thaddaeus who upset her, it must have been Caradoc Lewis."

"So why is she back here talking to him?"

Aidan let the silence linger. Then, "So soon after she came into your room."

Jenny's head jerked up. "What are you getting at?"

He shrugged, and walked away to stand under the tree-shadowed rocks where Melangell was still climbing. "Sweetie, I'd really be grateful if you came down from there." He turned his head back to Jenny and said more quietly, "I may have done something rather foolish. When I bawled you out for letting Lorna in. It must have been pretty obvious that I was scared for you. It could have given Lorna the impression that you really did know something the murderer would rather you didn't."

The muscles of Jenny's face stiffened. "You think Caradoc...? And Lorna knows it? She'd warn him about me, rather than tell the police? But I don't *know* anything! At least, if I do, I still can't remember what it is."

"Lorna won't know that."

Jenny stood up. She tried to remember her only sight of Caradoc Lewis. She had been in the apse at St Melangell's when he came into the church. A tall, stooped man, with alarmingly quick movements. Like a large black spider that stays motionless on the wall and then makes a sudden dart. Mother Joan come in shortly afterwards, shocked by the news of Thaddaeus's murder. But when Jenny had walked out of the church she had left the two of them arguing.

Melangell hopped down from the rocks beside them. "I wish I could hear what they're saying. They had their backs to me and they were looking up the river towards the waterfall. The *big* waterfall, I mean. Where we had our picnic. He was telling her something. I know because he was waving his arms about a lot. Like this." She demonstrated how Caradoc's hands had shaped something like a ball in the air, and then had pointed towards the falls. "But that's silly, isn't it? You wouldn't play football there."

Aidan let his own hands copy her movements. "Not a ball. But something rounded? Sorry, love. I give up."

"It's important, though, isn't it? Lorna was listening, and then she started nodding. And she grabbed hold of his arm. Like so." This time Melangell seized her father's arm and looked up at him eagerly. Then she dropped it and kicked the turf. "But I don't know why."

Jenny brushed fragments of grass from her trousers. "Caradoc Lewis and the Browns have been around here longer than we have. They know each other. The fact that he had an argument with Thaddaeus doesn't make him a murderer. I think I just want to believe that he is so it won't be anyone at the house."

"You didn't see Lorna afterwards. Crying."

"I did see her. From a distance. And yes, she did look upset when she ran into Euan's arms."

"If Caradoc did that, why is she back here alone with him so soon?"

"Why don't you ask her?" Melangell broke in. "They're coming this way."

Jenny's head jerked up just in time to catch the start both man and girl gave when they saw the Davisons.

Caradoc Lewis was the first to recover. His thin lips stretched in a cadaverous smile.

"Ah, Mr Davison, and the enchantingly named Melangell. You seem to make a habit of being found on private land."

Aidan held up his hands in surrender. "It's a fair cop, guv. But we got to the end of the public path and this fall was just too temptingly near. We hadn't managed to get my wife to Pistyll Blaen-y-cwm."

The dark eyes swung round on Jenny. It was the first time she had found herself face to face with him. There was something in his tall, stooping presence which she found unnerving. His eyes held hers and would not let her go.

"Yes, Jennifer Davison. The author. Whose book is so prominently on display in the church gift shop. The Christian version of the myth of the goddess and the hare."

Jenny remembered, almost with a feeling of guilt, that Mother Joan had told her Caradoc Lewis had wanted his own book to be sold in the shop. A book which rubbished that Christian story and directed its readers to the pagan goddess who could turn herself into a hare.

"It's a balanced account," she defended herself. "I don't deny that the hare was a sacred animal to the Celts. But Melangell, or Monacella in her Latin name, was a real person. You can be pretty sure that when you get a church dedicated to a Celtic saint who isn't found anywhere else that this was someone who really lived and worked there and was remembered by local people as a holy person. The Celtic Church didn't need the pope in Rome to proclaim someone a saint."

"Pious balderdash!" He took a step closer, towering over her. "Your precious church will do anything to stamp out the worship of the true gods of this land. It's quite capable of inventing a fictitious saint."

"Melangell was genuine. The grave in the apse is almost certainly hers. It's bones from there which were disinterred and placed in the shrine."

"*Human* bones! That's not what I'm interested in. I tell you, something far more powerful would be to discover the bones of the hare. *That's* what our ancestors venerated. I've had a premonition. A dream, you might call it. But more compelling than anything that word 'dream' conveys. The sacred hare *is* in this valley. I was so convinced of it that I sold up the little museum I had in Llanfyllin and bought this land. It's *here*." His finger jabbed at the ground between them. "I can feel it in my bones. I mean to find it."

The smile that stretched his skull-like face was alarming.

Jenny longed to withdraw herself from the intensity of his gaze. There was not just the enthusiasm of his belief, but a malevolence which seemed to be directed towards her. Why? Because her book was sold in the church shop which had refused his? Or because Lorna had flown to him straight from Jenny's bedroom, to tell him that the Davisons feared Jenny was in danger? Danger that only made sense if she held a clue to Thaddaeus's murder.

Even the presence of Aidan just a few steps away could not protect her from the helplessness she felt under the shadow of this overbearing man.

She tore her eyes away from Caradoc's face with an effort, and glanced at Lorna. She was not sure how to read the expression on that sweet pale face within its cloud of black hair. Frightened? Defiant?

Might Lorna know more about her uncle's murder than she had confessed? What would have put her so much in the power of this man that she had come running to him?

Melangell was tugging at Aidan's arm. "Daddy! What's that?"

Grateful for the distraction which allowed her to turn away from Caradoc's gaze, Jenny turned to follow Melangell's eyes.

A column of smoke was rising over the hedgerow trees. For a moment, Jenny could see nothing remarkable in it. Someone having a bonfire. A smoky cottage chimney. Then the significance of the location struck home to her. She could just make out the wooden bell turret that barely rose above St Melangell's roof. Even as she gasped, a tongue of flame shot up from it.

Chapter Twenty-two

AIDAN HAD STARTED TO RUN towards the church before his mind knew what his feet were doing. He took several flying strides, then came to a sudden halt. He looked back at Jenny's horrified face. Every instinct was longing to propel him towards the fire as fast as he could go. But that would mean leaving Jenny behind with Caradoc Lewis. He had felt the animosity as the lean man stooped over her, spouting his wild theories about sacred hares. If Lewis had killed Thaddaeus, Jenny was the last person who should be left alone with him. Yet he could hardly expect her to run across several fields and down the lane. He balanced on the balls of his feet in an agony of impatience. Jenny would be devastated if the shrine they had come all this way to visit burned down.

Jenny was not the only one appalled. Beside Caradoc, Lorna's pale face was whiter still. Like Aidan, she seemed to be desperate to run back to the burning church. But Lewis had her by the arm. Long fingers, like eagle's claws, grasped her. She looked up at him in consternation, but could not pull away.

"Stay here," Caradoc commanded. "Let the fools see to it themselves."

Jenny had caught Aidan's dilemma. "Don't wait for me. I'm coming. Just not as fast as you."

She began to hurry over the grass, back along the field path. Aidan hesitated long enough to see that Caradoc and Lorna were not coming, then sped ahead. At the first gate he waited. Jenny was halfway across the field, walking fast. Melangell had opted to stay with her. No one else was following.

He plunged on, racing now. At the next field boundary she was just in sight, approaching the gate.

He sprinted across the church car park to a scene of hectic activity. Neighbours, staff from the House of the Hare, two police officers, were all hard at work firefighting. Sian was organizing a bucket chain from the nearest cottage.

Small bright flames still licked from the slatted bell turret, half lost in the sunlight. From the upper windows of the small tower, black smoke billowed. Smaller drifts of it crept from the ground floor. The frantic workers were evidently getting some sort of control over the fire in the bookshop.

He spotted the grey-haired Freda Rawlinson, who had served him tea at the St Melangell Centre. She looked distraught. "It's terrible! Terrible! How could such a thing happen?"

"Has somebody set fire to the shrine? Is it badly damaged?"

"The shrine? Oh, no, thank God. It's just the tower. But all our books and cards have gone up in flames. And I'm terribly afraid we may have lost all those newspaper cuttings and displays in the local history exhibition in the room above." She wrung her hands. "Let's pray the fire service gets here before it spreads any further."

Aidan tried to picture a large fire appliance tearing along the single track lane. What would happen if it met a vehicle coming the other way?

He grabbed a bucket from Josef and made towards the

tower. Two uniformed police officers in shirtsleeves were coming out. Their faces were red with heat and exertion, and they were coughing. But Aidan sensed that they were enjoying this physical action more than the patient gathering and sifting of information in the temporary incident room.

One pushed a hand across his soot-smeared face. "Sorry, sir. No one's to go back inside. We've got control on the ground floor, but Lord knows how it's spreading higher up. Could be in the roof beams by now. Best wait for the professionals."

Aidan stood back helplessly. How could such a fire have started? He thought of the rack of candles lit as a sign of prayer. It had been quite close to that pile of prayer cards on the base of the shrine, hadn't it? He pictured the flames crawling up the brocade that covered the stone canopy. Of, heaven forbid, the wooden screen with the carving of St Melangell's legend he had photographed only three days ago.

But no. Freda Rawlinson had said it started in the tower. The shrine was in the chancel at the other end of the church.

So, if it wasn't a carelessly placed candle, how else could the fire have begun?

A cold knowledge was creeping up on him. Someone had set this fire deliberately. But why? An arsonist who simply revelled in starting a blaze? It seemed unlikely in this remote spot. Someone with a grudge against the church? But they had left the most precious target untouched, St Melangell's shrine. He was pushing away the blackest thought of all. The fire had started in the bookshop. Where Jenny's history of St Melangell had been prominently on display. His own name was on the cover too, but it was really Jenny's creation. Had someone wanted to send her a powerful warning of what could happen if she…?

He was surprised at the relief he felt to hear the measured tones of Chief Inspector Denbigh behind him.

"Now, Mrs Rawlinson, if you could calm down and tell

me what happened?"

"I don't know any more than anyone else. I live further down the valley. Someone rang me to say the church was on fire. So of course I came as fast as I could. What a terrible thing for Mother Joan. She's only in charge this week, while our own priest is on holiday in Portugal."

"She wasn't here?"

"No. She lives over in Llanrhaeadr. She comes over when there's a service."

"So who was on duty in the shop?"

"No one. It's the same in most churches. There's a woman who orders the stock and does the accounts. She'll be devastated. But during the day people just put the money for their purchases in a box on the wall."

"So anyone can wander in and out of the church as they please?"

"Of course. It's a house of prayer. Someone locks up at night and opens it at ten in the morning. We get a lot of pilgrims to the shrine."

"Inspector," Aidan cut in. "I know of someone who might have reason to set fire to the bookshop."

He was interrupted by the blaring siren of a fire appliance. It was, Aidan noticed, one of the smaller ones. Firemen leapt out. In next to no time, it seemed, a hose was snaking from the water main to the church. Aidan and the inspector stepped clear with the others to watch.

The vehicle could not get close enough to the tower, because of the churchyard wall and the narrow lychgate. But they raised a hoist, and the fireman on top directed a surprisingly powerful jet at the blazing bell turret. Aidan felt the rush of adrenalin subside as the flames cowered under the deluge and went out. Officers wearing breathing apparatus were entering the tower.

"Now, Mr Davison," the inspector's voice said at his

elbow. "There was something you wanted to tell me."

Aidan turned away from the firefighting, trying to recapture the train of his thought.

Before he could do so, the inspector's grey eyes narrowed. "No Mrs Davison with you? I should have thought she would have been particularly anxious about the church being on fire. Having written a book about it. *Where is she?*" The final question was fired like an accusation.

Aidan felt a surge of anger. Of course he knew that DS Lincoln had warned Jenny to be careful. That she might be in danger if the murderer suspected she knew something. But Jenny had cared as much about the burning church as he had. She had *wanted* him to run and help.

"She's just behind me. We'd gone for a walk. Just a short one across the meadows. We met Caradoc Lewis and Lorna. There was a bit of an argument about Lewis's theories about St Melangell's hare and Jenny's. Then we saw the fire. She and Melangell are on their way as fast as they can." His eyes went past the inspector, searching along the lane. "I ran ahead."

"*Leaving your wife with Caradoc Lewis?*"

Aidan burst back at him, "No! I'm not an idiot! We'd left him behind. But what I meant to tell you was… The fire was in the bookshop, not the saint's shrine. Jenny's book was there. Is someone trying to send a message to her?"

But for all his protests he broke away, striding back the way he had come. He was praying for a sight of his wife and daughter.

Chapter Twenty-three

WHEN HE SAW MELANGELL standing in the road and Jenny emerging from the path, Aidan felt a sag of relief. He ran to meet them.

Jenny looked drawn and anxious. She burst out before Aidan had reached them, "The church! Is the fire bad? Can they save it?"

He tried to control his breathing.

"The fire service is here. They've got a hose on it. Most of the contents of the tower have gone, I should think. But there are no more flames coming out at the top. The fear is that the fire will have got into the roof beams and could spread up the nave."

Jenny grasped his arm to steady herself. "I shouldn't care so much. It's only a building, after all. And the tower was rebuilt in the nineteenth century. But the thought of that screen going up in flames, of the shrine being damaged again, after all that work of piecing it together... It hurts. Do they know how it started? An electrical fault? Or was it started deliberately?"

"It's too early to tell. But the general feeling seems to be that someone came in and set fire to the bookshop."

Some of the tension seemed to go out of Jenny. "That's bad enough. But at least it's the less important part. Not the shrine and the grave. Books and cards can be replaced."

"Not the local history exhibition on the staircase and the upstairs room."

"No… no, you're right. It must be terrible for the people here. Who would do such a thing?"

"The most obvious person who springs to mind is Caradoc Lewis, isn't it? After the fuss he made to Mother Joan about not stocking his book in the shop. I'm afraid yours has gone up in smoke."

He watched her thinking about this for some moments.

"You think he'd stick at the shop? He wouldn't get back at the church by striking the part that means most to them? St Melangell's shrine?"

"Maybe, whatever he says, he recognizes that as a holy place. Even though he's more interested in ancient Celtic goddesses and hares than seventh-century saints."

"Hmm. But did you notice? Lorna was just as keen as we were to rush back and see what was happening. But he stopped her."

"If he'd started it, he'd want the flames to get as good a hold as possible before anyone put them out."

She turned her tired, grey-blue eyes to his. "But why does he have such a hold over her? Why did she let him stop her?"

"I don't know. I thought it was Thaddaeus she was frightened of. Now we seem to be saying it's Caradoc who has a hold over her. How?"

"He seems a very forceful man."

"But why is Lorna important to him?"

They were walking back now, to the scene of urgent activity around the church. A police patrol car had arrived, to add to the remaining members of the murder enquiry team. The firemen seemed to be busy inside the building. That must be a good sign, thought Aidan. At least it's still safe enough, for the professionals, anyway.

Chief Inspector Denbigh was still standing, hands in pockets, observing from the edge of the crowd of spectators.

He turned his head as they came up. A smile of visible relief warmed his usually lugubrious face. "Ah, Mrs Davison. You're quite well, I hope? Your little expedition didn't prove too much?"

"I came back rather more quickly than I'd planned to do. I think I'd like to sit down."

She eased herself on to the low wall of the car park. She's in pain, he thought. But she won't tell us. She's shut it away into a compartment of her mind, because other things are more important to her.

Aidan, like the rest of the crowd, was watching the church intently. At every moment he was fearing to see the puff of smoke that would indicate that the fire had crept along the roof, under the slates, to burst out far away from the tower, at the most sacred end of the church.

But Inspector Denbigh had his back to the church. His attention was all on Jenny.

"Mr Lewis? How far away did you meet him?"

"Across the river. Near that other waterfall. Pistyll Cablyd. We were trespassing, actually. It's beyond the public footpath."

"And he was there?"

"Coming towards it. From Capel-y-Cwm, where he lives."

"Not from this side?"

"No."

"And Miss Brown was with him, coming the same way?"

"Yes."

"Mmm. That's very interesting. So we'll need the fire investigators to tell us when the blaze may have started."

"Yes. Yes, of course. If he was half a mile away, or more…"

Denbigh sighed. "My job would be a great deal easier

if there were just one clearly marked suspect with a placard saying 'GUILTY' hung round his neck. Meanwhile, I can only repeat what my detective sergeant has told you. Be careful. Keep close to your husband."

The part of Aidan's mind that was listening to their conversation winced. Had he really thought that anything he could do at the church was important enough to make him leave Jenny still close to a man who, at the very least, was jealous that she had succeeded where he had failed? But if Caradoc hadn't set the fire, was there another reason why he might be dangerous?

A whoosh of indrawn breath from all the crowd commanded his attention. He turned back to see a coil of black smoke drifting skyward from the middle of the roof. The fire officers swung their hoist away from the tower. But they still had to train their hose across the churchyard. Aidan, like everyone else, was holding his breath.

Something caught his arm. He looked down into Melangell's upturned, anxious face.

"Daddy! What's wrong? The church is on fire and you're not taking any photographs."

He stared down at her blankly, while his mind took in the significance of her words.

It was true. He felt the emptiness at his side, where his camera bag usually hung. Ever since his teens, he had picked it up and taken it with him, almost without thinking. But today he had set off across the meadows without it, and not even noticed its absence until now. Only two days ago, he had leaned over the shocking corpse of Thaddaeus Brown, mentally framing photographs, because that was what he had done all his professional life.

But Melangell was right. Another drama was happening in front of him, and it had not occurred to him to record it on his camera. He shook his head, trying to convince himself that he had had more important things to do. Helping with the bucket chain. Clearing the car park for the fire crew. But he had not even missed it.

He felt a sickening fear. Was he to lose everything now? Jenny? His instinct for photography? What would there be left to make life worth living?

Just Melangell.

He tried to shape a grin for her. "No. I'm not, am I? I've got more important things on my mind."

"*He's* taking photographs."

Aidan swung round. His muscles clenched. The remembered figure of Marcus Coutts, in his tan leather jacket and beige slacks, was busy snapping the burning church. As Aidan watched, stiffening with resentment, the photo-journalist let his camera drop on its neck strap, and turned avidly to question Jenny.

Chapter Twenty-four

JENNY WAS STARTLED by the voice beside her. "I don't believe in coincidences, do you? Two calls in one week? 'Get your backside over to Pennant Melangell.' I mean, who'd ever come out here but a bunch of religious nutters and some knobbly kneed hikers? And now a murder and arson in the same week. Coincidence? Do me a favour."

The young man must have been in his twenties, but there were still pimples on his face. Still, the leather jacket looked expensive. And she knew enough about cameras from Aidan to know that the Leica hung round his neck had cost a fair bit. She recognized, with renewed distaste, the journalist Marcus Coutts.

"Yes. It's bad luck, isn't it?"

"Luck, my granny's bedsocks." His blue eyes narrowed greedily. "You're staying at this new House of the Hare. Where someone topped the boss man. And you were there at the time. Bet that's put the kybosh on your holiday."

"I saw that disgusting article you wrote. As if I knew who the murderer was. And it was only partly a holiday. We came to visit the shrine."

"Oh, dearie me. And here it is, burning before your eyes."

Before she knew what was happening, he snapped her face, close up. She rose to her feet, frightened and furious.

"I didn't give you permission to do that! And I think the fire brigade are getting it under control."

"Do you, darling? I rather think that's smoke coming out halfway along the roof."

He swung his camera round and photographed the new drift of smoke.

"This'll be one for the nationals. *Famous church burns down. Grief-stricken author watches.*"

She wanted to protest that he was seeing Thaddaeus's tragic death and the destruction of an ancient and precious church solely in terms of the money he could get for his story. Then she remembered, with a twist of guilt, that Aidan, too, supplemented his income from the photographs he took to illustrate books like her own with better-paying news-shots when he could.

She started to move away. But there was a hand on her arm, detaining her.

"Must have been pretty spooky in that house after it happened. Everybody looking at everyone else, wondering who did it. They arrested the girl, didn't they? His niece."

"Yes, and they let her go."

"She'll come into a pretty penny, though, won't she? Is it true she's his only relative?"

"They've only just opened the House of the Hare. I think there are still some debts to pay off."

Instantly, she regretted it. Marcus Coutts seized on this scrap of information. Out whipped the notebook.

"And just who did he owe it to? Don't tell me. That creepy pair in the Jag?"

"Excuse me. I have to go."

"So there's still money owing on that fancy building? Pity whoever it was didn't set fire to that instead of the church. I bet they've got it insured…"

"Look, we don't know it's arson. Couldn't it be a fault in the wiring?"

"That's not what the guys are saying." He nodded at the

fire crew. "They seem to reckon it was probably deliberate. Now who would want to do a thing like that?"

"There are plenty of fire-raisers who think it's fun to start a blaze."

Coutts's eyes swung round the car park. They had a more intelligent look now. "They do say that an arsonist loves to come back to the scene and see the havoc he's created. The flames and the fire engines. All the excitement. And he knows it was all his doing."

Jenny didn't answer. Well, she thought, that makes pretty well the whole population of Pennant Melangell suspect. Everyone had turned out to help. Even a guest like Aidan from the House of the Hare. She made her own search of the faces around her.

Not the Ewarts. They must have gone out for the afternoon, after lunch at the Centre.

Another absence struck her for the first time. Where was Mother Joan? She had presumably driven away when her duties at the church were over.

Even as she thought that, there was a squeal of brakes. A small, pale blue Honda shot into the car park in a spray of gravel. It only just missed the fire engine. Mother Joan leapt out. She had changed her clerical garb for a floral shirt and grey trousers. But a nun-like scarf still bound her head. Jenny's hand strayed to the one covering her own bald scalp. The trousers made the dumpy figure of the priest look broader still. Her face was haggard and distraught.

"Let me through!" she demanded of the policeman guarding the plastic tape that barred the church gate. "I'm the priest in charge. At least, I'm deputizing for her. Where's the fire chief?"

The young constable looked down at the short, determined woman and quailed. "The crew commander's over there, ma'am. By the tower. But I've orders not to let anyone but fire crew through."

Mother Joan lifted the tape briskly. "He'll have to talk to me."

She strode up the path past the yew trees, like a tug boat butting out to sea in a gale. Jenny saw the senior fire officer spin round and start to order her out of the churchyard.

The stout little priest stood her ground. Jenny was not surprised to see that she was getting the audience she wanted.

She was aware of a rapid clicking at her elbow. Marcus Coutts had his zoom lens out and was busily shooting the encounter.

"Priestess in pants. I like that. Pity she's not more of a looker."

"She is not a priestess," Jenny said, through gritted teeth. "Just a priest. She does the same job as a man. In some parishes they'd even call her Father Joan."

Again the notebook whipped out. "Joan? That's her name? Joan what?"

"I don't remember." And I wouldn't tell you if I did, she thought.

"No sweat, darling. I'm sure these good people here can tell me."

He was losing interest in her now. There were new victims for his curiosity. She watched him heading for Freda Rawlinson.

Left on her own, she suddenly felt enormously tired. Her after-lunch rest had been delayed by her alarming meeting with DS Lincoln, and had then been interrupted by Lorna's visit to her room. The walk across the meadows should not have been too much for her, but the fire had brought her hurrying back faster than she had wanted. The drama of the pilgrimage church, which had meant so much to her, in flames would have been emotionally exhausting in itself. She wanted nothing more than to go back to the house and let herself sink on to the comfort of the bed.

She found Aidan, who appeared to be under interrogation from Melangell.

"I'm going back," she said. "I can hardly stay on my feet."

"I'll come with you." Aidan cast an anxious look back at the smouldering roof, where the firemen were still trying to douse the smoke.

"No. Stay if you want. I hope you've got some good pictures."

"He hasn't brought his camera," Melangell said.

Jenny looked at her husband in sudden astonishment. It was true. Why had she not noticed until now? Had he put it down somewhere while he helped fetch water? Aidan *never* set out without his camera bag.

He reddened. "It's been a strange week. It seems to have thrown me out of gear. Anyway, I'm coming with you."

She was glad, both of his supporting arm and of his presence. She wanted to tell herself that Sergeant Lincoln and Inspector Denbigh were being overly cautious. Why should the murderer fear she had a vital clue, just because her room overlooked the grounds where the crime had happened? Yet she felt a shudder in her spine. There *had* been something. It was like trying to grasp the hem of a dream on the edge of waking. Would it ever come back to her?

The house stood empty. The front door was open. But the foyer and the corridors were silent. There were no sounds from the kitchen, no voices from the lounge.

"I guess everyone ran to help with the fire," Jenny said.

Aidan went round the reception desk to fetch their room

keys from the pigeon holes. He turned to her.

"Did you take our key with you?"

"No, isn't it there?"

"Only Melangell's. I thought I'd put them both in the box on the counter for Sian to put away. When she'd finished cleaning windows." He shrugged. "Old age creeping up on me. Must have left it in the room."

"Daddy, can I have a coke from the bar?" Melangell put on a winning smile.

"Good idea. I could do with a can of beer myself, after all that running about. I'll write a chit for Sian. Anything for you, love?" he asked Jenny.

She shook her head wearily. "No, thanks. I'd just like to lie down." She made for the lift.

"We'll be right behind you."

The two of them headed for the bar in the lounge. In the hospitable manner of the House of the Hare, Sian usually left it unlocked for guests to help themselves and sign for their purchases.

Jenny leaned against the wall of the lift and let it carry her upwards. Now she just had to get herself along that short stretch of corridor and sink down upon the bed. For the moment, nothing else seemed to matter. The murder, the fire, that terrible photograph in the newspaper, the intrusion of the police into this peaceful setting... All she wanted to do was sleep.

Aidan was right. The bedroom door was unlocked. She pushed it open.

She had taken two steps across the room when a dark figure broke through the curtains partially screening the balcony. Jenny's gasp was almost a scream.

Euan Jones confronted her. A lock of black hair had fallen over one eye. The other burned at her, dark brown and belligerent.

"You saw it, didn't you? From up here?" His earthy hands seized her.

Her eyes flew past him to the balcony. *What* did he think she had seen? And now the image rushed back at her. That morning at the archery butts, when she had believed herself alone. Euan Jones appearing suddenly out of the shrubbery. Advancing on her with the arrows in his fist. A chill certainty was growing in her that this was how Thaddaeus had met his end. And his killer thought she had seen him.

His grip was painful on her arm.

She shook her head desperately. "I didn't see anything! I was on the bed over there. Asleep. I didn't go out on to the balcony until afterwards." She was aware that she was gabbling in panic. And, now that she thought about it, was it true about the balcony? Had she looked out there before she lay down? But she would have remembered if she had seen Euan or anyone else.

"It must have been half past two, twenty to three when I woke up. At least half an hour after the police think he was murdered. I saw Lorna running past the side of the house. She'd just got back. You were there."

She felt his grip relax a little. "You saw her come back after half past two? Lorna? You're sure of that?"

"Yes."

He let her go. "And you've told the police that?"

"Of course."

He drew a deep breath. Colour was coming back to his strained face. He pushed the hair back from his eyes. "Sorry, then. I didn't mean to frighten you. Only, when they took Lorna away…"

"They let her go, though. They only arrested her because they thought someone must have shot him with a bow. There weren't many people who could have done it. But if he was stabbed… it could have been anyone."

Including you, she thought, but dared not say.

No. He just wants to protect Lorna. That's all he cares about. And she's in the clear.

Jenny had a vivid picture of the girl, in her black skirt and grey sweater, running from the direction of the gate towards the sheds.

She tried to steady her breath and reassure him. "You don't need to worry, Euan. Honestly. I'm sure Inspector Denbigh will find who did it soon. They won't arrest Lorna again."

There was a sudden cry from the corridor. "*Daddy*!"

Even before she heard him, she could imagine, all too vividly, Aidan bounding up the stairs. Finding another intruder in the bedroom. She hurried to the door and met him as he came hurtling along the corridor past Melangell.

"It's all right! Really. It's just Euan. I found him on the balcony. He's still scared they'll accuse Lorna."

Aidan almost pushed her aside as he charged into the bedroom.

"What in hell do you think you're doing here?"

Euan's belligerence flared up. "I only wanted to check what you can see from your balcony. I wasn't doing any harm. Scared I'm the murderer, are you?"

"How do I know you're not?" Aidan snapped.

"What would I do a damn fool thing like that for? Lose myself a job? They're hard enough to come by in the valley as it is."

Jenny caught Aidan's arm. "He's right, love. He's just worried about Lorna. But I told him it's all right. I saw her come back after the time of the murder. It must have been someone who was already here."

"And how do we know who that is? Anyone could have been hiding in those shrubberies. Did you see anyone?" Aidan challenged Euan. "You were there."

"No," Euan protested. "Not around two o'clock, if that's when it happened. I was in the shed there." He gestured towards where Jenny had seen him meeting the distraught Lorna. "Having my sandwiches. I can't be everywhere, can I?"

Aidan's anger was cooling. But his voice was cold as he ordered the gardener, "Well, now that you've seen what you wanted to, I suggest that you leave this private room. And if you have any more questions, perhaps you would be so good as to knock on the door and ask, instead of stealing the key from reception and letting yourself in."

"Oh, yes? And just whose country do you think this is, ordering me about?"

"Let's not get into that, shall we? Right now, I'm providing you with a job by paying good money to stay here. And I expect a locked room to stay locked while I'm out. Other than the people authorized to clean it."

"Aidan!" Jenny tried. "He's upset. We all are. I don't think any one of us is behaving normally."

"There are limits. And our private space is one of them. Especially now."

Aidan stood aside from the door in a stance that clearly commanded Euan to leave. The young man's dark eyes flared, and for a moment Jenny feared he might refuse. But he walked past Aidan with what dignity he could salvage.

Jenny subsided on to the bed. Despite her efforts at reasonableness with first Euan and then Aidan, she was trembling.

There was still fire in Aidan's face, bright as his reddish hair and beard. "Five minutes! I let you go upstairs five minutes ahead of us, and I find a potential murderer in your room. First it's Lorna, then him."

"He only wanted to find out what I'd seen. What I knew. It's natural. He's in love with Lorna. And he's scared."

"If he's scared that you saw something you shouldn't

have, then we should be scared, too."

"No. What I saw was good. For Lorna, at least. We've only got Euan's word that he was in the shed on his lunch break when Thaddaeus was murdered. But Lorna definitely wasn't here."

He stroked the side of her temple. "I'm sorry about this. It wasn't what I planned when we came back here. A murder. And now a fire in the church."

She caught his wrist and kissed it. "It's not your fault. Bad things happen all the time. There's no reason why I or Pennant Melangell should be cocooned from them. I wonder if they've really got the fire under control, or whether it will break out again."

"They're leaving a skeleton crew on standby overnight, just in case. They're not sure what's happening under the roof."

"Why?" she sighed. "Why do such a vindictive thing? If it *was* arson. But I can't think about it now. All I want to do is sleep."

As she settled her head on the pillow, it was a comfort that Aidan had taken a book on to the balcony and was sitting reading just within call.

Chapter Twenty-five

T HE DINING ROOM LOOKED startlingly full, after the empty tables they had become used to. The Ewarts were back, despite Colin's threat to leave the House of the Hare early. They were talking more animatedly than usual. Even Rachel's face, normally downcast with pain, and withdrawn, seemed brighter. In view of what had happened at the church, Aidan thought that odd.

But what came as a greater surprise was to find another table occupied by Chief Inspector Denbigh and Detective Sergeant Lincoln. Aidan raised his eyebrows at Jenny as the Davisons sat down.

"Looks like they're taking the attack on the church seriously. Do you think they've booked rooms here?"

Jenny glanced sideways at the detectives. "They must think it's connected to the murder. Before, they've always driven off at the end of the day. Sian said they were talking of closing that room in the harness shed and basing everything at their main incident room in Newtown."

Aidan dropped his butter knife with a clatter. "Look behind you!"

Jenny's scarfed head turned. He saw her tense as she watched the man taking his place at the corner table furthest from the window. Marcus Coutts, in his tan jacket, began buttering a roll as he surveyed the guests around him with a satisfied grin. Even now, his camera lay on the chair beside him, not zipped away in its bag, but ready for action.

Aidan felt a sudden anger that even here, he and his family should be exposed to the prying journalist.

Professional photographer though he was, Aidan did not bring his own camera to meals. Besides… He remembered what Melangell had said. Was he losing his appetite for capturing the images around him?

Melangell, seated between them, was studying her parents' faces. "I think *he* set fire to the church," she announced in her clear voice. "So that he'd have some pictures to sell to the newspapers."

There was a convulsive sound from the table next to them, as Sergeant Lincoln choked on his roll. But his chief inspector merely lifted his deeply lined face and studied Marcus Coutts attentively.

Coutts grinned across at the Davisons, with bared teeth. Aidan had an uncomfortable feeling that they might pay for Melangell's remark.

"Hush," he told her. "What happened at the church today was serious."

"So am I," she said, in a whisper that was almost as penetrating as before. "He was here right after the murder, wasn't he? How did he get here so fast? How did he know he had to?"

"Melangell!" Jenny said. "Don't be ridiculous. He's an obnoxious man, but he's hardly going to stab poor Thaddaeus in the eye, just to sell a newspaper story."

"You don't know. He might."

Sian was serving the soup and starters. She looked flustered, Aidan thought. As she set his crab bisque in front of him and the avocado and smoked salmon for the others, he asked, "No Mair tonight? You look as if you could do with some help."

"Don't tell me! Last night we were rattling around, almost empty. And now look at it. Six rooms taken. I just wish there was a happier reason for them coming."

"The detectives are staying, then?"

"That's right. I've put them on the floor above yours. Poor Josef's running around in circles like a demented ant. He was at the fire until an hour ago. Since then, we've been working like the clappers to get enough food on the table for all of you at short notice. But I daren't turn them away. We need the business."

"If it's any comfort, you can tell Josef his soup is excellent."

Out of the corner of his eye, Aidan saw the dining room door open again. Lorna came in. She looked, if anything, smaller and paler than before. He watched her trace a path between the tables to her usual place before the tall windows. He thought, with a pang of compassion, how frail and lonely she looked without the extrovert bulk of her uncle.

He winced internally, thinking how his first impression had been that she was frightened of Thaddaeus, that she was under his thumb, perhaps even the victim of his sexual abuse.

Jenny seemed convinced that Lorna was genuine when she denied it.

But the girl had been afraid of something. She still was.

He sipped his soup. A detached part of his mind marvelled at how good it was. In contrast to the day following the murder, Josef had worked a small miracle, despite firefighting and the sudden influx of unexpected guests.

When Sian came back with the main course, perhaps he could ask her what she knew about Lorna's relations with Caradoc Lewis.

But Sian was too busy to linger. Her round cheeks, usually bright with health, were more flushed than usual. She was trying to simulate a professional poise, and not rush between tables, but heightened tension was evident in her swift movements.

Was it only because the dining room was suddenly busier than before?

"He's not wasting much time, is he?" Jenny said, as they waited for their dessert.

Marcus Coutts had moved from the corner where he had been watching the room like a pale spider. Camera in hand, though discreetly at his side, he had slipped into one of the empty chairs at the Ewarts' table. Aidan was pleased to see the typically aggressive lift of Colin's head, but Rachel, to his surprise, was smiling at the handsome young man.

He was too far away to hear what the journalist was asking. But his nerves jumped as Coutts turned to look at the Davisons' table with speculative eyes.

Aidan drummed his fingers restlessly on the leather chair arm. It was suddenly hard to talk freely in the crowded lounge. Marcus Coutts had been given the brush-off by the two detectives. When he advanced towards Lorna she had fled. Now he was eyeing the Davisons.

Aidan moved abruptly to join the Ewarts. After a moment of surprise, Jenny followed him. Melangell had found a lavishly illustrated book of tropical flowers and lay on her stomach turning the pages.

"Terrible thing, this business at the church," Colin Ewart greeted them. Yet he seemed not as angered as Aidan would have expected.

"Yes," Jenny agreed. "I do hope they haven't lost all that exhibition in the tower."

"I didn't get up those stairs myself," Rachel spoke up for once. "Still, at least it didn't touch the shrine. That's the important thing, isn't it? As long as it was just a pile of books."

Aidan flashed a glance at Jenny. Those were her books, and his, that had gone up in flames. But she nodded sympathetically.

"I really hope they've stopped it in time. I couldn't bear to think of that old screen with the carvings in the gallery being destroyed. Or what the fire might do to the stonework of the shrine."

"I'll never forget coming here. It's a holy place, isn't it?"

"It is for me," Jenny said, quietly.

"And you won't believe the difference it's made," Colin cut in. "That healing service today. We went into Llanfyllin this afternoon and Rachel was like a new woman. Weren't you, my dear?"

Aidan caught the slight wince as the little woman smiled back at him.

"Yes," Colin went on. "We had a good look round the town square. Pretty little place. And then we took a drive out to see the workhouse. It's pretty impressive. Didn't do to be poor in those days. I can't think when Rachel's walked so far."

Rachel kept her uneasy smile, but said nothing.

Aidan watched her, wondering. Had St Melangell's shrine and Mother Joan's anointing really worked a miracle for the pain-ridden Rachel Ewart? Was she trying to convince herself that it had? Or had Colin Ewart invested so much hope in this pilgrimage to Pennant Melangell that he could not bear to admit to failure? Aidan remembered the outburst of anger against Thaddaeus Brown, when Colin thought he had been misled about the healing properties of the medieval shrine.

"But then we got caught out in a shower of rain, didn't

we, love?" Rachel prodded her husband.

"Yes, and we found this quaint little museum. Not a proper council job. Somebody's private collection, I should think. Pretty old, though, the stuff they've got. Arrowheads from the Stone Age, bits of pottery, even a few items of jewellery they say are Iron Age. And a cross from the time of our saint here. You'd like that, Mrs Davison… Jenny. That sort of thing is right up your street, isn't it?"

"I'm pretty much into Dark Age history, yes. Especially if it's about the Celtic Church."

Melangell's voice spoke up from the floor. "That Caradoc man said he had a museum in Llan-thingy."

"So he did," said Aidan. "He said he'd sold it to buy Capel-y-Cwm. Well done, sweetheart."

"You should go and take a look," Colin urged them.

Aidan found himself staring at Colin Ewart in amazement. This was the first time he had heard him voice a positive sentiment all week. Now the man was glowing with enthusiasm.

He felt a pang of regret and sorrow. Colin Ewart, and perhaps Rachel herself, had believed so much that Rachel would be cured here at Pennant Melangell. Colin certainly felt he had got his wish. But Jenny? Could Aidan honestly say he had gone to the laying on of hands with the same faith for her? Could his doubts make all the difference between life and death for the woman he loved?

Abruptly, he got up. "If you'll excuse me, I think I'll take a turn around the gardens."

Jenny lifted her face to him. "Shall I come?"

"No, not unless you want to. I need some head space." He gave her a wry smile. "You should be safe with two detectives to look after you."

As he turned from the sofa to the French windows he saw that Marcus Coutts had already left the room.

Chief Inspector Denbigh looked up as Aidan passed. He did not say anything, but regarded him speculatively. Aidan felt that anything he did, whatever any of them did or said, was under scrupulous observation.

He had intended to saunter along the peaceful paths between the bushes and pools. But a persistent instinct of curiosity took him round the corner of the house to the front gate. It was only a short walk along the lane to the church car park.

As he had expected, a single fire engine was still parked there. Two firemen were perched on the stone bench in the lychgate. One of them was smoking. The other got up as Aidan approached. He lifted the police tape and walked into the churchyard to look up at the roof. The light was fading, but Aidan could see no wisp of smoke from the nave roof. Was it really over?

He was turning to greet the fireman with the cigarette when his eyes fell on another vehicle, parked in the opposite corner. Something familiar about it. A black Jaguar XF.

Immediately the growing relaxation of the quiet evening turned into a new nervousness. Mr Secker and Mr McCarthy?

But why here, and not at the House of the Hare? Had something brought them back which they didn't want Lorna or Sian to know? Who else in this tiny village could they have business with?

He strolled up to the fireman. "You're in for a long night, I hear."

"'Fraid so. Tricky things, these old buildings. Solid oak, most of the timbers. They won't go up in a burst of flame, like your modern softwood. But the fire can creep. Just sort of glows, till it gets to something it can really get its teeth into.

And then, whoosh!, you've got trouble on your hands."

"Do you think that's likely, here?"

The fireman threw his cigarette butt away and stood up. "Can't tell. That's why we're staying."

"I see there are still sightseers around." Aidan nodded at the Jaguar.

"We've had the lot. TV. Newspaper blokes. Pretty well all the local population. It's that murder, you see. Fellow with the arrow in his eye. Search me what that's got to do with setting a church on fire, but both of them, right out here, in the same week, makes you wonder."

"So where are the people with the Jag?"

"Dunno, mate. Didn't look like the usual rubberneckers you get at a fire. Smart suits. One of them looked a bit foreign to me."

"So where are they now? There isn't a pub here."

The second fireman had strolled back to the lychgate to join them. He shrugged. "They tried getting into the churchyard. But I told them, nobody crosses this police tape. It's a crime scene, or could be."

"Not that I notice the cops losing any beauty sleep over that."

"Don't be so sure. There's a WPC on that side gate over there."

Aidan followed his eyes to where a path led between the graves to a smaller gate, beyond the darkness of the yews. He wondered whether the sentinel there was PC Watkins.

Uneasy now, Aidan turned back for the gardens of the House of the Hare. He ought not to leave Jenny alone too long.

Don't be stupid, he told himself. There were two detectives in the room. They were the ones who had warned her to be careful.

He walked up the drive wondering how long it might

be before Jenny recaptured that elusive memory. What could she have heard in that crucial time when she had gone to their room to rest and Thaddaeus had been murdered?

Chapter Twenty-six

A T THE FRONT OF THE HOUSE, Aidan hesitated. He had left by a route around the side of the house nearest to the archery butts. The other side, by the kitchen and the vegetable garden, seemed more private, though there were no signs forbidding entry.

On an unexplained impulse, he turned to his right and chose that path.

There were tall wheelie bins round the corner. From a sheltered spot on the other side, a wisp of cigarette smoke traced a fragile ascent. Josef sat smoking on a bench outside the kitchen door. He was still wearing his chequered trousers and black cap.

He started when he saw Aidan. He rose and made as if to stub his cigarette out. Aidan held up placating hands.

"Peace! I'm sorry. I shouldn't be intruding on your space. I was on my way to the gardens. I've just been down to the church."

Josef regarded him through narrowed, pale-lashed eyes. Aidan wondered how good his English was, how much of Aidan's apology he had understood. He had an urge to linger and make friends with this lonely immigrant.

"You've had a hard day."

"Yes. Very busy." He was still watching Aidan nervously.

It seemed better to move on and leave him to his privacy after such a hectic day's work.

"*Ciao,*" he offered.

Josef did not reply.

Some light still lingered over the lawns, though dusk fell quickly among these steep-sided hills. The scent of azaleas perfumed the evening air. It drew Aidan closer. He did cast a guilty glance back at the lit windows of the lounge. Jenny was chatting to the detectives. Melangell still lay sprawled on a rug.

With a sigh of responsibility eased, Aidan allowed himself to stroll further along the winding paths, until the house was lost to sight behind him. He found a curved stone bench beside a lily pool. A marble nymph with an urn might once have been a fountain, though no water played from it now.

He let his limbs relax, only aware now how tense he had been. It was silly, really. The murder was terrible, but it had nothing to do with them. They had only happened to be in close proximity. It was the same with the church. A possibly heartrending loss for the priest and congregation, but he and Jenny and Melangell were only visitors.

No, more than that. Something of themselves had been invested in this sacred place from the moment Jenny had been inspired to write her book. It would be part of the memorial to her. A part of her that would live on. Could the fire in the tower bookshop really have been directed at her?

But the shrine and the grave and the carved screen were safe. Probably. And those incredibly ancient yews still guarded the site. He tried to imagine how he would have felt if that giant beside the gate, with the hollow trunk where Melangell had hid, had gone up in flames. An irreplaceable loss.

He became aware of voices in the distance. Someone else was enjoying an evening stroll among the scent of azaleas. Who? He was almost sure the Ewarts had still been in the lounge with Jenny and the police officers.

He tried to quieten the instinct that set his nerves on the alert again. Tomorrow was their last day here. On Saturday, they would go. Solved or unsolved, they would leave Thaddaeus Brown's murder behind them. For Jenny's sake, they must try to recapture some of the spiritual peace that had drawn them to this place.

Yet he was on his feet almost before he realized it. He recognized some of the journalistic impulse that had exasperated him in Marcus Coutts. His curiosity needed to be satisfied.

Soft-footed now, he eased his way closer. He could make out a man's voice. The space that followed suggested a softer tone, perhaps that of a woman, still inaudible.

The man's answer came clearer now. "You don't have time, Miss Brown. We could call in the debt and take over this place any day now."

"Why would you do that?" Lorna's voice sounded desperate. "I can pay you back as soon as I get Uncle's money. I'd sell anything else from the inheritance. Nobody else will want to buy the House of the Hare from you while it's losing money."

"Thaddaeus saw an opportunity," said another voice. "Someone might want to take that up."

"Extreme sports! In Pennant Melangell! I'll never let that happen. Not in a million years." He could hear that she was almost crying. "I wouldn't let Thaddaeus do it, and I won't let you."

Should he move in? Take her side?

There was a little silence.

The first man spoke again, softly. "Lorna? We've been wondering how Thaddaeus met such a grisly end. It isn't possible, is it?"

Lorna's voice rose high and wavering. "That's an outrageous suggestion! Get out! I should never have agreed to see you. Sian wouldn't have let you in. She knows what I want, and she'll help me see that I get it. And that means never handing over the House of the Hare to you. There are other ways of making it pay. Things you couldn't possibly understand. You haven't got a soul, have you?"

"Murder? And you talk about a soul?"

"You're saying that to frighten me. I don't have to listen to you."

"That's where you're wrong. You would be well advised to listen to our proposal."

Aidan had had enough. He walked forward round the bend in the path, taking care this time that they could hear him coming.

The argument broke off instantly. In a little clearing, shadowed by a weeping willow tree, the three of them stood alarmed, guiltily facing his approach. He could hardly make out their faces but the attitude of their tense bodies showed they were all wondering how much he had heard.

"Lovely evening," he said, cheerfully. "I gather they're forecasting rain for tomorrow. I've just been down to the church and everything seems to be under control. A good downpour would help, though."

"Oh, that's a relief." Lorna found her voice first. "I couldn't bear it if anything happened to St Melangell, after all these years."

"The shrine was destroyed once, wasn't it?" Aidan reminded her. "And put back together again."

"Not all of it. When things are broken, it's never the same."

The men stood silent.

"Mr McCarthy? Mr Secker? I think I saw your car parked outside the church. There's a perfectly good car park here."

The men looked at each other.

"The road was blocked," one of them said. "Too many people at the fire. We parked where we could."

"Drive carefully on the way back. It will soon be dark."

He stood aside, pointedly. The men walked past him. One of them turned his head to Lorna. "Think about our offer, Miss Brown. Think very hard."

There was an awkward silence when they had left.

"They were giving you trouble?" Aidan asked at last.

"They gave my uncle trouble. All they think about is money."

"It's not the most important thing," Aidan agreed. "But sometimes we need it to do the really important things we want."

"I know. I'm doing it. The House of the Hare."

"And they want you to change its character."

"That's not going to happen."

"But they hold the purse strings, don't they? The trust fund?"

She stared at him. Then she walked past him, back towards the house. Nothing in her stiff manner invited him to walk beside her and continue the conversation. He let a few moments pass, then followed her at a polite distance.

He could have kicked himself. Sian should probably not have told him about Thaddaeus's will.

A shadowy figure rose from the bench where Aidan had been sitting.

"Well, well, well. Now, what do you make of all that?" asked Marcus Coutts.

Aidan's stomach was churning as he walked back across the lawn. The encounter with Marcus Coutts had produced not only anger but fear. If the headline-chasing journalist had overheard that conversation too, what meaning would he give to it? McCarthy and Secker had practically accused Lorna of murder. But she had every reason to keep Thaddaeus alive until he had changed his will in her favour.

Of course she had denied the charge with outrage. But then, if she was guilty, she would, wouldn't she?

Lorna's words came back to him. "*I wouldn't let Thaddaeus do it.*" What had she meant?

Had there been an argument at the waterfall? That would explain the tears and the torn shirt. But Jenny had seen her running back at least half an hour after the time of the murder.

Wasn't it more likely that the two financiers were themselves guilty? They had been at the house. They had argued with Thaddaeus about changing his will. It was in their interests for him to die before he did. Did the police know that?

He sighed. There were so many other people who hadn't liked what Thaddaeus was planning. There was even Josef's wild theory about Debbie French.

He wondered what information the detectives were gathering which was barred to him.

DCI Denbigh and DS Lincoln had never stayed at the house before. They evidently saw the fire at the church as a significant leap forward in the case. How?

He was almost at the French windows to the lounge when he looked up at its lit interior. The room was empty.

He bounded upstairs and was relieved to find Jenny supervising Melangell's bathtime. She didn't need to, but it was good to hear the two of them laughing in the bathroom, with rather more splashing than might be expected for a seven-year-old.

He settled himself into a chair beside the bed and picked up a copy of *The Lion, the Witch and the Wardrobe*. It was a delight that Melangell had reached the age when he could share the Chronicles of Narnia with her. She could probably read it herself now. Her reading age was way ahead of her years.

But there was a special pleasure for both of them in a bedtime story. He hoped she would not grow out of it just yet.

It was only when he had kissed her sweet-smelling face on the pillow, and Jenny too had settled herself in bed, that his dark mood returned. He wished he didn't have to burden Jenny with it, but what had happened in the garden was too important to keep to himself.

"Do you think I should tell the police? I mean, it wasn't really evidence, was it? Two men accusing her, who could easily have done it themselves. *More* easily. We know she wasn't here then. They were."

Jenny pleated the sheet between her fingers. She had taken off the scarf. The hair was growing back over her scalp in a pale gold fuzz. The tiny hairs were even beginning to curl.

"I think you should tell them. That those men were here again. And they left their car at the church and arranged to meet her in secret outside the house."

"You don't think that was genuine? About not being able to get their car through because of the emergency vehicles and the crowd?"

"What time did they arrive? We didn't see them at the fire, did we?"

"No, you're right. Most people went home hours ago. And Lorna said something about not letting Sian know they were here. In case Sian stopped them from seeing her."

"I think she might have. She's very protective of Lorna, isn't she?"

"Well, I really hope Lorna doesn't give in to them. They're the kind of men who only think about the bottom line. Lorna really cares about Pennant Melangell. She wants to keep it as the sort of holy place that struck us when we first came here, and made us want to come back. Men like that wouldn't begin to understand the importance of that."

Jenny's thoughts were pursuing another track. "Just how much would Sian do to protect Lorna?" She raised her troubled eyes to Aidan.

"I've thought about that, too. She seemed loyal to Thaddaeus when we first arrived, though a bit nervous of him. But if it came to a choice, I think she'd back Lorna. And she's the sort of physical person who might have the strength of will and body to do it."

Jenny sighed. "I'm sure the chief inspector's thought of that. I had the feeling this evening that we were all under close observation."

"It doesn't have to be someone from the house. Anybody could have got into the grounds."

"Sian says Lorna is talking of burying Thaddaeus here at St Melangell's, when they release the body. If it was someone from round here, that will be a strange experience, won't it? Walking past his grave every time they visit the church."

"It may not have been a churchgoer."

"They had the most to lose from his plans."

"I wonder what other tragedies those yews have seen in 2,000 years. What else is buried here."

Chapter Twenty-seven

THE FORECAST WAS RIGHT. They woke to find a light rain falling. Fronds of mist lingered under the trees, and raindrops beaded the branches. The tops of the hills were blotted out by rain.

"It may clear." Aidan sounded not entirely hopeful at breakfast.

"I'll tell you what I fancy. Do you remember the Ewarts telling us about that little museum in Llanfyllin? With bits of ancient history that had been discovered around here? It might be worth a look."

Jenny glanced over at the Ewarts' table. Colin still looked in an ebullient mood, but Jenny thought that Rachel looked more strained than the night before. Was her husband, desperate for a cure, overestimating her new capability?

"He said it was right up your street," Melangell observed over her toast.

Jenny turned her attention back to her own family. "He was probably right. I might even feel the stirrings of a story."

Jenny's first love was history, making the buildings and landscapes, and the people who had lived there, come alive for her readers as they once were. But her enthusiasm sometimes spilled over into children's stories.

She saw Aidan's eyes go up to hers, sharp, worried. I know what you're thinking, she told him internally. That anything I start now may never be finished. But I can't stop living, can I, just because I'm dying?

May be dying, she corrected herself. Nothing is certain. There was that laying on of hands yesterday. The oil on her forehead.

"Is it one of those museums that lets you do things?" Melangell asked. "Like grinding corn or making mosaics?"

"I shouldn't think so, honey," Aidan said. "Not if Caradoc Lewis used to run it as a one-man show. I don't see him as an educational archaeologist. Unless he was trying to promote his Goddess-as-Hare theory."

"He said he'd sold it to somebody else. It might be different now."

"We'll see."

"You're not wearing your scarf," Melangell said, as Jenny came down the stairs.

"My hair's starting to grow again. And I thought, if it's raining, I might as well have a wet scalp as a wet scarf."

She didn't say how much she had missed the breeze in her hair, the sense of freedom in going bareheaded. It was probably vanity to have been so self-conscious about her nude scalp.

Curiously, this small return to normality made her feel she was getting better, rather than an admission that her treatment had reached the end of the line.

Aidan stopped the car beside the church. A fire-service car was already there. He peered past Jenny out of the side window. "I wonder if the fire's well and truly out. This rain will have helped, but I doubt if it's been as heavy as they would have liked."

"Water can sometimes do as much damage as the fire. Why don't we ask?"

She stepped out, slipping her arms through her anorak.

A senior fire officer was talking to one of the bleary-eyed crewmen who had been on duty overnight. Detective Sergeant Lincoln was with them.

As she approached, she heard the fire chief say, "We'll get our forensic guys on to it straight away. But from what I've seen, I'd say there wasn't much doubt about it. I'm betting the seat of the fire was that table in the middle of the ground floor room. No wiring there. It has to be deliberate. And some sort of accelerant, to get a hold of the tower so quickly."

"So somebody with a grudge against books about churches and maps of local walks?" Lincoln's voice held a smile of weary cynicism.

"Is the fire out?" Jenny asked.

"Yes, love. We managed to keep it to the tower and a few roof timbers," the fire chief assured her.

"Is it all right to go inside now?"

"I'd rather you didn't just yet."

The rangy detective turned to her. "It's still a crime scene."

Jenny looked past them at the plastic tape barring her way. She should be grateful that the church was saved. But she felt a sense of loss that she was shut out from it.

Aidan spoke from behind her. "Do you think this had a connection with the murder? I see you and Inspector Denbigh have taken up residence."

Lincoln opened his mouth, hesitated, then shut it again. "I can't discuss it, sir," he said, after a moment.

"Just so you know, we're going over to Llanfyllin this morning. We'll probably be back this afternoon."

"Thank you, sir. Have a good day."

Jenny got back into the car, disconsolately. "I would have liked to have gone into the church to pray. I know I can pray anywhere, but it seemed particularly important this morning. To feel part of all those tens of thousands of people who have come on pilgrimage and worshipped here over the centuries."

"Perhaps they'll have taken the tape down by the time we get back. The fire officer seemed pretty positive about what started it."

"But Sergeant Lincoln is a lot less positive about why."

She hoped Aidan would not see her shudder as he steered into the lane. Could it really be something to do with me? she thought. My books?

The rain had turned to drizzle by the time they had left Cwm Pennant and driven the ten miles to Llanfyllin. Aidan parked the car and they got out to explore. A mix of centuries-old buildings, some half-timbered, some red brick, surrounded the square with its memorial cross. They found a black-beamed coffee shop. Melangell fell on a strawberry milkshake and a fruit-studded slice of bara brith with enthusiasm.

Jenny asked the teenage waitress about the museum. The girl looked blank. But the woman Jenny took to be the manager called across from the till.

"Across the square. Do you see that side street almost opposite? It's down there. Chap who owned it used to be a bit of a character. But he's gone now."

"Caradoc Lewis? We've met him," Jenny said. "He lives in Pennant Melangell now. Yes, he does seem a bit eccentric."

Eccentric enough to set fire to a Christian church?

Melangell skipped across the square beside them. She really is such an easy child to be with, Jenny thought. Any other seven-year-old would be complaining she was bored, as we drag her round yet another site of Dark Age history.

She was glad to see that Aidan had brought his camera this time. Like the absence of her scarf, it restored a semblance of normality.

The museum looked little more remarkable than any of the other houses in the street. The buildings here were smaller than those in the square, domestic in scale. There was a bow-fronted window to one side of the door.

"Looks more like a gift shop than a museum," Aidan said.

He was right. The window was filled with boxes of fudge, flowered notelets, rather crudely fashioned china animals. Jenny noticed several rabbits, which might have been meant as hares. The signs were not encouraging.

Over the window a sign read: "THE LEWIS COLLECTION". A small metal stand by the door said "OPEN".

They stepped indoors to a jangling bell. A youngish man, perhaps in his thirties, came hurrying to greet them, smiling broadly. He wore a red T-shirt with the same words, "THE LEWIS COLLECTION", arranged in a circle around the figure of a hare. Jenny checked its long ears and rangy legs. This one was definitely not a rabbit.

"You've come for a look round, have you? It's a shame about the weather, isn't it? But we need the rain. Still, you'll be snug and dry in here. There's lots to see."

Jenny glanced around her. It still looked like a gift shop.

Aidan had his wallet out, eyeing the curator expectantly.

"Oh, yes! Silly of me. That'll be £3 each and £1.50 for the young lady."

Melangell beamed up at him.

"Just take your time," he went on. "There are more rooms at the back and upstairs. If you have any questions, I'll do my best to answer them."

Jenny studied the gifts on sale. They were not of a high quality. Mostly tourist tat.

But I suppose he'd have to take a lot of £3s to make it pay, she thought. And people seem to buy this sort of stuff.

Had it been like this in Caradoc's time? She couldn't imagine him selling merchandise like this. A teddy bear with a T-shirt saying "*A Present from Powys*"; plastic dolls in an approximation of traditional Welsh dress, which bounced on springs; a dragon key ring that said "*I Love Wales*".

She would try to find something not too awful to take away afterwards, as a souvenir.

The room at the back of the house was a complete contrast. It had been given over to the Stone Age. The impression was instantly serious. The artefacts were laid out in glass cases on tables around the walls. Each was carefully labelled with descriptive title, an approximate date and a note of where it was found.

Scraper. c. 8000 BC Pengwern

She noticed two from the Pennant Melangell area.

What she missed, especially with a child, were the explanatory boards that she now took for granted in a modern museum. Those scenes of our early ancestors working in their encampments, fishing, hunting. A vivid picture of how these items in the cases would be used, and by whom. She felt for Melangell. She was sure that to a seven-year-old, one knapped flint must look much like another.

Aidan had found a case of arrowheads. They, at least, were more interestingly recognizable.

Melangell turned her face up to Jenny. "Could *you* shoot an arrow with a flint head like this?"

The question jolted Jenny. The fire at the church had pushed the shocking nature of Thaddaeus's death to the back of her mind.

"I've never tried," she said. "But I suppose I could, yes. It would take a bit of getting used to. They would be heavier than the arrows we use now."

Not necessarily, an inner voice told her. There are enthusiasts who go out into the wildernesses of North America to hunt with bows and arrows. It would take a powerful missile to bring down an elk or a bear.

She found a tray of beads, fashioned from coloured stones and shells, and called Melangell over to admire them.

But the things that really interested her, if they existed, would be upstairs, in the room set aside for the Celtic kingdoms after the Romans left Britain. The time of the real St Melangell.

To get to the display on Celtic Christianity, they had to go back to the gift shop, and take the staircase. The curator, Kevin, gave them a cheery wave. Apart from him, the shop was empty. The way led them through rooms devoted to the Bronze Age and the Iron Age. Jenny lingered over a 3,000-year-old pottery urn, reddish clay, stained with black.

"They were cremating their dead then, and burying the remains in these."

There was a badly damaged bronze knife, some bone pins, rings from a horse harness. It was a poor display compared with the glories of the British Museum, or the local treasures you would expect to find in a county museum. This time, it was enlivened by photographs of the remains of hut circles. The ruined walls of boulders were half lost among heather and tall grass.

"Still, if it's all stuff he's found himself, you've got to give the guy credit," Aidan said, with grudging respect. "It may not be much by professional archaeology standards, but it's a lot for one man."

They moved on to the Iron Age. Jenny felt a ripple of excitement, and knew that Aidan's interest was quickened too. These were the centuries immediately before Christ, and before the Roman invasion. Here there were indeed echoes of a dying glory.

"Gold!" exclaimed Jenny. "That's the finial of a torque." She turned eagerly to show Melangell. "A torque was like a metal collar you wore round your neck. At least, you did if you were rich and important. The two ends didn't quite meet, so that you could open it up to put it on. And each end had a knob called a finial. Do you see? It's been shaped to look like an animal's head."

"A cat. No, a lion. I didn't think they had lions in Wales."

"It could be a bear. They had them."

Aidan had joined them. "If he found gold, he'd have to report it, wouldn't he? It would be treasure trove. Property of the Crown."

"They might have decided a broken bit like that wasn't important enough to interest the big museums. Do you remember the National Museum in Dublin? They had a whole room full of dazzling Iron Age gold. The authorities could have let him keep this."

"Always supposing he told them."

There was a recognizable spear head, part of an amber necklace, a battered coin.

"This is more like it," Aidan said.

"They've got a hare," Melangell's voice came suddenly high from the other side of the room.

Jenny started, and hurried to join her. A collection of bones was laid out in a glass case. They were small and slender. There was a skull with a sharp-toothed snout. A card behind them announced:

Skeleton of a hare.

Ritual sacrifice. c. 150 BC.

**The Celts in Powys worshipped the
goddess in the form of a hare.**

**Found by Caradoc Lewis in the
Tanat Valley 1983.**

"So he was barking up that tree thirty years ago," Aidan said.

"How did he know they were a hare's bones?" Melangell asked. "I've seen a rabbit with big teeth like that."

"Good question. Longer legs? But how did he date them to 150 BC?"

"Do you think he sent them away to a lab and paid to have them expertly analyzed?" Jenny wondered. "Or did he just convince himself they were what he always believed he would find in the Tanat Valley? Because of the story about St Melangell."

"You could always ask him," Aidan grinned. "Though I don't fancy putting the question myself."

"It's the last room I'm really looking forward to. The Celtic Christian one."

"I'll be interested to see how he copes with the things he doesn't believe in."

They stepped down into the third room on the upper floor. The first thing that met their eyes was a vertical shaft of granite mounted in the centre of the floor. It bore the faint trace of interlacing knotwork carved on its face.

"Don't tell me!" exclaimed Jenny. "That's the shaft of a Celtic cross."

There were floor tiles from a vanished abbey. A silver cloak pin with some more Celtic interlace and a dragon's head. A pewter goblet that might have served as a chalice.

A larger notice was attached to the far wall.

**The Tanat Valley retained its memory of
former holiness even after worship of the
goddess was suppressed by the Christian
church. It survived in disguise in the
cult of the Virgin Mary. The legend of St
Melangell and her hare in Cwm Pennant
clearly points to the fact that the animal
was still a sacred hare.**

Below it was a piece of slate with a modern etching of a hare.
Melangell stroked it.

"He's here again, isn't he?"

Jenny thought she was referring to the animal her small
fingers caressed. But then she heard the irascible Welsh accent
coming up the stairs on the far side of the Bronze Age gallery.
The young curator was remonstrating with him.

"Mr Lewis! This really isn't on, you know. You sold me
the museum, house and stock. I paid you a fair price for it,
considering you weren't exactly making a profit from it. You
just can't…"

Jenny felt her face whiten. She pulled Aidan's arm.

"It's Caradoc Lewis again. I don't think I can face him."

He drew her back into the corner of the room, out of
sight of the door.

"No, Mr Lewis!" came the anguished voice from the Iron
Age room next door. "You had no right to keep a set of keys.
These things don't belong to you now."

"I did the excavations, year after year." Caradoc Lewis's
tones were savage now with passion. "I found these things. Do
you think I'd have sold my collection if there was any other
way I could have raised the money to buy that land? Capel-
y-Cwm. My bank manager had the nerve to call it 'just a pile

of stones at the back of beyond'. But I bought everything that goes with it. A sacred place, if ever there was one. Forget the church. Christian mumbo-jumbo. Well, no, the yews mark it out as an ancient place of worship. Still…"

There was the sound of a door slamming open. Things shuffled and rattled.

"Please be careful! I haven't catalogued what's in these cupboards yet. I don't want anything damaged."

Caradoc's voice became more muffled, as if he might have had his head inside one of the cupboards beneath the displays. "I know what I'm doing, boy. No need to wet your trousers. There are just two things I want. And they wouldn't mean anything to you unless I told you what they were. Ignoramus!"

"If there was anything you wanted to keep, you should have said so at the time of the sale."

"There! These boxes will do." The voice rose clearer now, triumphant. "Want to take a look? No, I can see it in your foolish face. You wouldn't have a clue what you'd be looking at, would you? Not gold. No Iron Age sword. Not the Holy Grail. Not how you'd think of it as, anyway. What's in these boxes would be boring to someone like you."

"I thought the stuff you kept there was just duplicates of what we've got on display."

"Then you won't miss these, will you? Good day to you."

"It's the principle of the thing," the young man's voice faltered.

With relief, Jenny heard footsteps cross the bare boards as they moved to leave.

The steps halted. Caradoc Lewis's rich voice rose high with surprise.

"Well, well! The curiously named Melangell. What are *you* doing here?"

Jenny looked round in alarm. Melangell stood, a slight figure with a mop of pale brown curls, in front of the slate carving of the hare, directly opposite the door into the Iron Age room.

Caradoc Lewis's steps came slowly closer. Jenny clutched Aidan more tightly. He was starting to move protectively towards Melangell.

One step down into the room where the Davisons stood. He turned savagely to find Jenny and Aidan against the wall behind the door.

Aidan he ignored. His dark eyes went straight to Jenny. Their malevolent gaze seemed to bore into her skull. His tall, stooped form was poised like a snake about to strike. He was clutching two cardboard boxes to his chest.

"*You!*" he hissed. "Always you, isn't it? Well, you won't stop me this time."

He wheeled about and almost bounded up the step to the Iron Age room. He clattered across it and they heard him going down the stairs.

The curator in the red T-shirt came into the Christian Era gallery.

"I'm sorry. That man's quite mad. I wish I'd never had anything to do with him. People did warn me."

He was shaking, and so was Jenny. But she hardly heeded him, because her memory still burned with the malevolence of Caradoc Lewis's gaze. She knew with certainty now that the fire in the tower bookshop *had* been directed at her, *had* been the work of this eccentric amateur archaeologist. That to him, she was the enemy to his passion for the goddess and the sacred hare.

And if he had lit that fire to punish her, had endangered that precious church, what else might he have done? Certainly Chief Inspector Denbigh believed there was an intimate connection between the arson and the murder. It might have been Caradoc Lewis's ferocious enmity towards those who stood in his way that drove him to kill Thaddaeus Brown.

What did that mean for her?

Chapter Twenty-eight

"I T MUST BE HIM, mustn't it?" Jenny said, as they drove back to Pennant Melangell.

They had followed the Ewarts' advice and made a visit to Llanfyllin's historic workhouse. But not even Melangell's delight at the horrors of being a pauper could dim the memory of Caradoc Lewis's malevolence.

"The police seem fairly sure the fire is directly related to … the other." She glanced briefly back at Melangell, but the girl's pointed face seemed to be studying the slate quarries on the steep sides of the valley .

"It seems the only conclusion that makes sense. There are hardly likely to be two violent maniacs on the loose in such a small population." Aidan looked sideways at her in concern. "We need to tell them about this latest encounter. The police."

"I know. It probably won't sound like anything much, just in words. But when you were face to face with him, it was."

"Home tomorrow," he said. He grinned back at Melangell. "How do you fancy stopping off at Warwick Castle? They've got some great realistic scenes of what life was like if you lived there. People, horses, food, weapons. You can dress up as a princess."

Melangell's face came to life.

"Have they got a dungeon?"

"Definitely. With bodies."

"Aidan! I don't think that's appropriate."

"They're only giving kids what they like. Little ghouls."

"Mm. If you want to."

The brief enthusiasm had faded. Melangell seemed subdued now. She was sucking her thumb and clutching the velvety hare Jenny's conscience had persuaded her to buy from the museum's tawdry gift shop.

Aidan swung into the laurel-fringed car park in front of the House of the Hare. The rain had stopped, but the leaves still glistened wetly.

"I thought they were closing that little incident room. But things look busy."

The number of cars indicated a renewed police activity. Jenny wished she knew which way the detectives' minds were tending.

Her legs felt strangely like cotton wool as she stepped out of the car. She steadied herself against the bonnet.

"Are you all right?" Aidan was suddenly at her side. "No, of course you're not. Silly question. It would have been quite an energetic day, even without that upset. Go and lie down."

"No. I have to see Inspector Denbigh first. He needs to know."

"I can tell him."

"It wasn't you he was looking at, as if he was skewering a chicken."

They threaded their way through the side path that led to the row of sheds where the police had set up their outpost. PC Watkins came to greet them. She seemed to have established herself as an essential part of the team, among the plain clothes detectives.

"Can we speak to Chief Inspector Denbigh, please?"

Aidan asked. "We've got some new information."

"You're out of luck. Will DS Lincoln do?"

They told their story to the lanky sergeant. He seemed as interested in Lewis's reason for visiting his former museum as in his encounter with the Davisons.

"And you've no idea what was in those boxes he took away?"

"That side of the room was mostly pottery. A few remains from burial urns. Shells and bones from middens that show what people ate in those days," Jenny recalled.

"The really interesting stuff was on the other wall," Aidan said. "Such as it was. Bits of weapons, jewellery, metalwork."

"But it's not really that we came to tell you about," Jenny broke in. "It was… I don't know… the *hatred*. He looked at me as though he really loathed me." She looked over her shoulder. PC Watkins was showing Melangell a big map hung on the wall, with pins to mark where key things had happened.

"There's the waterfall!" Melangell cried. "Our waterfall."

Jenny lowered her voice to DS Lincoln. "As if he wanted to kill me."

The sergeant's eyes were suddenly grave as he looked down at her. "I warned you to be careful. We weren't sure at the time who might be in the frame. At least, if it's Caradoc Lewis, he's not inside this house. You're leaving tomorrow, aren't you?"

"Yes," Aidan said. "We'll meander back. Spend the night at Warwick, perhaps."

"That's probably best. But if you have any cause for concern, ring the police straight away."

A prickle of unease caught Jenny as they walked back to the house. Should Aidan have told anyone they were going to Warwick – even the police?

"Not particularly reassuring, was it?" he said.

"It's my fault. If only I could remember what's been tantalizing me at the back of my mind. About Tuesday. Around the time of the murder, when I was upstairs, and you and Melangell were out at the waterfall. Sometimes I think I've got it, but just as I start to remember it, it slips away."

"Something about Caradoc Lewis?"

"I don't see how it could be."

Melangell had run ahead. They caught up with her in the foyer. She was talking to Sian, who had her arms full of a pile of bed linen.

"And they had arrows *thousands* of years old. And you could see the bones of the animals they shot. Deer and *hares*. And then that Caradoc man came, and the man in the museum was scared of him. He took some boxes, even though the other man told him not to."

"Steady on!" laughed Sian. "You've lost me. I've no idea what you're talking about."

Jenny, coming through the front door with Aidan, was about to explain.

A voice interrupted them. "Would you like to learn to shoot arrows like that?"

The question came from the other side of the foyer, through the door to the lounge. Lorna stood there, not smiling like Sian, but looking seriously at Melangell.

A protest rose in Jenny's throat. It was still too close. Thaddaeus, killed by one those red-and-white fletched arrows from the sports shed. One of the arrows she herself might have shot. Only three days ago.

With shame she remembered her own brash return to the archery butts. Wanting to prove to a sceptical Inspector

Denbigh that she was not yet so physically weak that she couldn't draw a bow. Wanting to show that Lorna was not the only archer on whom suspicion might fall.

Before she could find the words to prevent it, Melangell had swung round with shining eyes.

"Could I?" Then eagerly to Aidan: "Can I, Daddy? Please!"

"All right. I suppose so."

"We can find you a bow with a light draw weight," Sian said. "We've got all sorts."

Jenny questioned Aidan with her eyes. But he seemed merely amused at the idea.

I'm being oversensitive, she thought. And tired. And in pain. Thaddaeus was Lorna's uncle, after all. If it's all right with her, why should I object?

It was only a few steps to the lift. Soon she would be upstairs. All she needed now was a good rest and the world would be all right again.

No. There was more than sleep could cure. There were darker things she had to fear.

Aidan came with her, attentive, concerned.

He closed the bedroom door behind them. She turned, and buried herself in his arms.

"I'm frightened."

He held her close. "It's OK. He can be a very unpleasant man, but he's not here now. You don't have to see him ever again. We're heading for home tomorrow."

"I didn't mean just Caradoc Lewis." Her voice fell to a whisper. "It's what he showed me when he looked as though he wanted to kill me. Aidan, I'm afraid of dying. I've tried not to be, but I am."

She felt the little start he gave. He had not expected this. She had tried so hard to go serenely towards the death the oncologist had showed her was imminent. With faith.

Making it as easy as she could for Aidan and Melangell. They must not know that it was a bereavement for her as well, to know that she was losing them both, very soon.

Is this a betrayal of my faith, to think that I won't still be with them, unseen?

But the blackness came over her that would no longer let her be strong for those she loved.

Aidan stroked her back, her hair. "Ssh. You've been fantastic. I couldn't have been as brave as you have. But it's OK to let go and say how you feel. It's only to be expected. Anyone would be scared of dying. It's absolutely normal. Would you like us to pray about it?"

She sniffed back tears. "I'm not sure I can. I really wish I could have gone into the church today. I know I should be able to pray anywhere, but it feels like a special place. In the apse, beside her grave. There was... peace. He's even taken that away from me."

He kissed her head. "It may be open again by now. We didn't stop and look, did we? Lie down and rest, and perhaps we'll go and see later. They don't lock it up till six."

She allowed him to lead her to the bed and take off her shoes. He found her tablets for her, then tucked her under the duvet and held her hand. His voice came low, faltering.

"Dear Lord, you know better than any of us how Jenny feels. Give her the peace and strength she needs. Beyond loss, beyond pain, take her in your loving arms and hold her."

She closed her eyes. Blessed sleep was drifting over her. At last her overstrained body was beginning to relax. Reality was slipping away from her. The frightening images of the day were changing into insubstantial dreams.

Suddenly she jolted awake. Her head snapped up from the pillow. Aidan rose in alarm.

"What's wrong? Is the pain worse? Shall I call someone?"

"No. It's not that. Aidan, I've remembered. What it was that's been bothering me since that day. I didn't *see* something. I *heard* it."

"What? What are you talking about?"

"The day of the murder. I'd come up here to rest after lunch. I lay down on the bed, like this, and started to drift off to sleep. It must have been round about two. And then just now, as I was falling asleep, I dreamed I heard it again. But I don't think it *was* a dream. I was remembering what I'd heard before."

"What? What could you have heard up here? Did Thaddaeus cry out?"

"No. It was *inside* the house. Running footsteps in the corridor outside this room. And a door shutting. Aidan, the Ewarts were out. The other rooms on this floor were empty. It could only have been the room at the end of the corridor." She looked up, her eyes widening. "Lorna's room."

He looked back at her, puzzled. The import of what she had heard had still not dawned on him.

"Don't you see? It was soon after two. About the time Thaddaeus died. So when I saw her from the balcony later, she wasn't coming back from the waterfall as I thought. She must have been here nearly an hour before."

His mind was racing now to catch up with hers. "So she could have killed him and come running upstairs. Yes, that makes sense. If she had blood on her clothes… Jenny! You remember I told you that when she passed us, running away from the waterfall, her clothes were dishevelled. She had on black jeans and a white shirt. Some of the buttons were torn and it was hanging open. She looked too upset to care. Do you remember what she was wearing when you saw her from the balcony, around twenty to three?"

"Yes." Jenny frowned. "Not trousers. A black skirt and a grey sweater, I think."

"Exactly what she was wearing when she and Euan came and saw the body. You're right. She'd already been back long enough to change when you saw her after your sleep."

"Long enough to kill her uncle." Jenny stared at the rumpled duvet. "I didn't want to believe it. Even when they arrested her. I felt sorry for her. That she was a victim, too."

"This turns everything on its head. We have to tell Denbigh."

"He isn't here."

"Well, Sergeant Lincoln. He'll get through to him…" Aidan drew a whistling breath of shock. "And meanwhile, Lorna is on the archery butts with Melangell." He made for the door.

Jenny swung her legs out of bed. "She wouldn't do anything to her, would she? Melangell's got nothing to do with this. If it's true, Lorna wouldn't want to draw attention to herself."

But she was scared as never before.

Aidan was already halfway down the stairs.

Chapter Twenty-nine

AIDAN SHOT PAST a startled Sian.

"Where's Lorna? Is Melangell with her? Are they on the archery butts?"

"Yes. You were here when she offered to teach Melangell. What's wrong?"

"Only that Jenny's remembered something that may mean Lorna is the murderer."

He was out of the French windows now and haring across the patio to the bank of bushes that separated the lawn from the butts. He carried in his mind the image of the shock in Sian's face.

He burst out of the shrubbery by the path that brought him almost to the sports equipment hut. He was willing the scene he longed to see. The two of them on the green. The older girl leaning over the younger one, black wavy hair brushing the mop of light brown curls. The practised archer showing a beginner how to hold and draw the bow. Friendly, innocent.

Why should Lorna see Melangell as a threat?

It would be all right. It had to be.

The archery range was empty. The hut had been opened, but no one was about.

With thudding heart, he raced over to check the shed. Bows, croquet mallets, tennis racquets. The equipment Sian and Thaddaeus had provided for their guests. Even the red-and-white fletched arrows. He shuddered.

Had they taken anything? He couldn't tell.

He had told himself that Melangell's shots might have gone wildly astray, and that the girls were in the shrubbery near the butts, retrieving them.

"Melangell!" he called, running into the bushes nearest the target.

The laurel leaves dripped from a recent shower. He pushed through the low branches. Already the silence told him what he feared. There was no one here.

He looked wildly back towards the house. Had Sian been lying? Did she know where Lorna really was?

He felt ill with panic. His racing brain would give him no sensible information about what to do next.

Like a man overboard clutching at a lifebuoy, he thought suddenly of the police incident room, with its detectives and uniformed officers still collecting information. Detective Sergeant Lincoln.

He would have preferred the more experienced, if mournful, Chief Inspector Denbigh. But it could not be helped. Anything to share the nightmare with other people, men and women who dealt with emergencies day in, day out. Officers trained to be calm and decisive. He knew he was neither.

He pounded up the step to the first in the line of sheds. He burst into the incident room without bothering to knock.

PC Watkins sprang to her feet. Others, whose names he did not know, turned and stared. DS Lincoln, his tall form outlined against a whiteboard, turned his head and then came hurrying across to meet him.

"Where's the fire? Sorry. Bad joke, under the circumstances."

"It's Melangell," Aidan panted. "We left her with Lorna Brown while I took Jenny upstairs. Lorna offered to show her how to use a bow and arrow. They've gone! And Jenny remembered something she's been trying to recall for days. She didn't see Lorna coming back from the waterfall. She'd already been back more than half an hour. She was here when Thaddaeus was stabbed."

"Sit down," ordered Lincoln, pulling out a desk chair. "Now, let's get this straight. Jenny thinks Lorna may have killed her uncle. Is that what you're saying?"

"Yes! Jenny remembers hearing someone running along the upstairs corridor, around two. A door shutting. It could only have been Lorna's bedroom. And we discovered that the clothes Jenny saw her in later were not the same as the ones she was wearing when Melangell and I saw her. So she wasn't just coming back from the waterfall, as Jenny thought. She'd been back here easily long enough to change. And to kill Thaddaeus. And now Melangell's missing. With Lorna."

"Steady. There's probably a simple explanation. They changed their minds about archery and went off to do something else."

But Aidan read the alarm in the sergeant's eyes.

"Why? Why Melangell? We thought Jenny might be in danger, if Thaddaeus's killer thought she'd seen something. Though it was really *hearing* something. But why should Melangell be a threat to her?"

"Unless she's getting at the two of you through the kid. But it hardly makes sense. If you're right, she was getting away with it. We hadn't taken her off the suspect list, but we'd swung round to looking elsewhere. Especially since the fire."

"Caradoc Lewis?" Aidan groaned. "That was our fault. We came straight over to tell you about him when we got back. We led you up the garden path. We ought never, for a moment, have left Melangell with her." He beat his fist on the nearest desk.

The policeman's hand descended on his shoulder. "Get a grip, man. Like we said, there's no good reason why Lorna should harm Melangell. Just the opposite. She'll want to keep her slate clean so we don't arrest her again."

All the same, he turned decisively to the listening officers. "Right, all of you! Get this place searched for Lorna Brown and the girl. Inside and out. Watkins, the house. You two, sheds, bushes. Parkinson, check if anyone in the cottages has seen them leaving. Go!"

"What can I do?"

"I'm ringing the chief inspector. Then, unless someone finds them pretty quick, I'm driving over to confront Caradoc Lewis. You saw those two together yesterday. Him and the girl. I thought at the time it was an odd combination. They may be there."

Aidan swallowed the lump that was choking him, at the thought of those eyes burning in that cadaverous face.

He followed the fast-moving officers out of the incident room. As the others scattered, Aidan saw Jenny and Sian coming across the grass towards him.

The women stopped in shock. Then Jenny ran forward. He saw the tragedy written on her thin face.

"Aidan! What's going on? Where is she?"

He put his arms around her, gently. The newly growing hair made her head look heartbreakingly vulnerable. "They're taking the place apart until they find her."

Her hand went to her mouth. "Is it because of me? Does Lorna know I heard her? Is that why she's taken Melangell?"

"We don't know that she has. It may be something perfectly innocent."

But that was not what he thought.

Lincoln was trying to phone his inspector. "Damn!" he said, thrusting the mobile back into his pocket. "I keep forgetting you can't get a signal out here."

He dived back into the incident room and grabbed one of the landlines.

Waves of sickness shook Aidan. It was foolish to think that the world-weary presence of Chief Inspector Denbigh could put things right, but it would be some comfort.

"I'll rouse Josef," Sian volunteered. "We'll help you search the grounds. They can't be far."

Images haunted Aidan's imagination. Those lily ponds, screened by flowering shrubs. A child's body, face down in the water.

Jenny's face looked grey with exhaustion and terror. He wanted to tell her to go and lie down, but he knew it was useless. She could no more rest until Melangell was found than he could. She seemed bewildered, as though she should not think where to begin to search.

"PC Watkins is doing the house," he said. "That nice WPC who was first on the scene when Thaddaeus was killed. Help her."

He watched her hurry indoors. For a moment he was tempted to follow her. What might she find in Lorna's room? Or the protective Sian's? Even Josef's? But Lincoln was heading for Caradoc Lewis's house further up the valley. Remembering that explosive meeting with him this morning, Aidan knew that he had to be there.

He started to run after the detective sergeant as Lincoln strode towards the car park. But the detective's car drove off before Aidan could reach it. He jumped into his own and followed.

To his surprise, Lincoln turned left towards the church, not right towards the head of the valley.

A rather younger version of DS Lincoln was talking urgently to a man outside the cottage in front of the church. He was tall, big-boned, with sandy hair paler than Aidan's.

From his sports jacket and brown trousers, Aidan guessed he must be a detective constable.

Even as Lincoln stopped his car, Freda Rawlinson and Mother Joan came from the church and were beckoned over. Aidan was not near enough to hear what they said, but he saw them shake their heads. Melangell and Lorna must not have been seen coming this way.

Did Lorna have a car? Would she use Thaddaeus's? How far might they have got if they had sped past here unseen?

"Parkinson!" DS Lincoln called, sharply. "I take it there's nothing doing here?"

"No, sir. Nobody's seen them."

"I want you to come with me. DCI Denbigh is on his way, but I'm heading out for Caradoc Lewis's patch. I've a hunch that's where they are."

"I hope to God nothing's happened to the kid." The constable's eyes went past his sergeant and met Aidan's.

"Let's go."

As the constable leapt into Lincoln's car, the detective sergeant called back to Aidan, "I should stay where you are, sir. We'll handle this. Hopefully, we'll have your daughter back to you pronto."

The car whirled away, back up the lane and on past the House of the Hare.

Aidan cast an anguished glance at the smoke-blackened church tower. First a murder at the House of the Hare, which had seemed such a place of welcome and refreshment. Then the fire at this much-loved pilgrimage church. What else? What new and terrible desecration might he find at the ancient stones of Capel-y-Cwm, which Caradoc Lewis had sold his museum to buy?

He wished he knew more of the rites of the goddess Lewis worshipped. Did he believe they sacrificed more than hares?

He did not remember getting back into his car. But he found he was already driving past the St Melangell Centre, with the weathervane of the hare on its slate-roofed garage.

The walls of the valley closed in around him. Dark conifer forests swept down on one side. The day was still overcast.

He had not told Jenny where he was going.

He came to the place where signs warned that the road ahead was private. The gate stood open. He drove through and saw farmhouses on either side of the river. Capel-y-Cwm lay beyond the left-hand one. The last house before the waterfall of Pistyll Blaen-y-cwm.

Beyond the farmhouse, the metalled drive ran out into a rutted track. Grass grew down the middle, between the tyre marks. The detectives' car lurched ahead of Aidan's. He had wondered if Lincoln would order him back, but the sergeant seemed to be ignoring him.

The neat fields gave way to rougher meadow. No sheep had grazed here. Tall stems of hedge parsley were spreading umbrellas of lacy white flowers. Thistles spiked through the long grass.

There was a belt of trees ahead he remembered. That was where a stone wall had barred their way, when he and Melangell were seeking an easy route back from the waterfall. Where they had heard Thaddaeus arguing with Caradoc. Capel-y-Cym lay on this side of the trees.

The car ahead stopped suddenly. Aidan was jolted into the present as his foot stamped on the brake. He had failed to notice a nearer stone wall crossing the track. This gate was closed.

The rangy Parkinson unfolded his limbs from the car and got out to open it. Lincoln drove through. Aidan followed.

Only now could he see the low grey house which Caradoc had reconstructed from scattered stones. Aidan was quickly out of the car.

Immediately he felt the silence. The floor of his stomach dropped as his instinct told him Melangell was not here.

All the same, the men moved towards the house.

"Some sort of church, is it?" Parkinson asked.

"He says it used to be. That nutter Lewis. Locals say it was a Methodist chapel. He swears it's older. Did a lot of the restoration work himself, apparently. Dan Pritchard the builder says he was a pain to work with. He had some weird ideas."

"There *was* something older here," Aidan raised his voice behind the detectives. "Look at that tall stone in the door frame. That's prehistoric. And the stone carving over it is at least medieval."

The two men turned. Their faces registered no more than polite acknowledgment. They were not really interested in architectural history. He should be glad of that. None of this was important now.

All the same, he could not have spent so many years accompanying Jenny round ancient churches, standing stones, medieval castles, photographing the places she wanted to write about, to miss the signs here. He felt a flash of anger that Caradoc's "reconstruction" could so cavalierly have mixed together features from different centuries. The nineteenth-century arched window of the Methodists, timbers that might have supported a Tudor farmstead, and that stone over the door with its interlace of Celtic knotwork, eroded enough to take them back before Norman times, at least. As old as St Melangell's monastery? Older? And where had that standing stone by the door come from?

DS Lincoln was hammering on the stout oak door. Aidan had not expected an answer. His mind was running ahead to think where else Melangell and Lorna could be.

DC Parkinson placed an enormous foot against the lock and pushed. It did not give. He shoulder-charged the door, and withdrew rubbing the bruise.

"That's not the sort of door you buy down the DIY store," Lincoln told him. "And that lock's solid iron."

"Window, guv?" his constable asked.

"Try not to make more mess than you have to. I didn't waste time on a warrant."

The small-paned window was meant to look in period, but it was almost certainly modern. Parkinson carefully broke a pane of glass and reached inside for the catch. He thrust a long leg over the sill. Lincoln followed him.

Aidan hesitated. At first he had been sure that Melangell wasn't here. But a chill thought crept up on him. What if he was wrong? What if he had failed to sense her living presence because only her body was here?

He had to overcome an enormous reluctance to climb over the windowsill into the small dark room on the other side.

The detectives had already moved on. He could hear one in the downstairs room beyond this. Another was going up the wooden stairs.

Aidan looked around at the signs of their swift search. A battered sofa, with a crimson loose cover, had been pulled out from the wall. The lid of an oak chest stood open. In other circumstances, Aidan would have thrilled to explore the stash of documents it held. Knowing Caradoc Lewis's interests, there might be gems of historical importance. But he delved through them only far enough to satisfy himself there was nothing hidden underneath. A sideboard door hung ajar. There was nowhere else to hide the body of a seven-year-old girl.

By the time he reached the inner door, Lincoln had

already finished examining the kitchen. He shook his head.

They could hear Parkinson overhead.

"Any joy?" the sergeant called.

"Nothing so far," came the muffled reply.

Lincoln mounted the narrow stairs, Aidan behind him. There were two rooms upstairs. One was a rather Spartan bedroom. There were rag rugs on the bare floorboards. Parkinson had clearly examined the old-fashioned walnut wardrobe and the brass-framed bed.

They turned to the second room.

There was a jolt of surprise. It was unexpectedly modern. A large desk stood in front of the window, with its view of the mountains opposite. It was equipped with computer, monitor, printer. Aidan's eye was briefly caught by an etching on the desktop. It seemed to show the waterfall, with a man in Victorian costume posed before an upright stone.

He turned to search for other clues. Metal-bracketed shelves on one side bore neatly labelled box files. On the other wall they supported row upon row of books. Aidan raked his eyes over the titles. Ranks of well-regarded authors on ancient and medieval history. Celtic myths and poetry, in the original and in translation. The lower shelves carried more esoteric material. *The Goddess Way. A Magic Primer. Pentangles and Power.*

His eye ranged further along the line. Darker covers. Darker material.

Black fear began to crawl along Aidan's spine. He tried to tell himself that the presence of the books did not mean that Caradoc Lewis believed in them. Jenny's own bookshelves contained a range of esoteric material.

But this was his daughter. It was impossible to remain coolly rational.

He pointed out the books to DS Lincoln. His constricted throat would hardly let him speak.

"You don't think… You hear sometimes… I thought he was just an amateur archaeologist with a thing about Celtic religion. Most modern paganism is pretty harmless. But what if he…?"

Lincoln scanned the shelves. His face showed the same fearful understanding. "You're thinking a Satanic cult?" Their eyes met.

"Do they do child sacrifice?" Parkinson's voice blurted out what the other two dared not.

Chapter Thirty

"WE'RE RUNNING AHEAD of ourselves." Lincoln made a visible effort to take charge of the situation again. "She's not here. We don't even know that she's with him, let alone that he's done her any harm."

He had his mobile in his hand, toying with it regretfully. Aidan could see he was wanting to contact his chief inspector. It was not reassuring to Aidan that the detective sergeant was wondering what to do next.

"I've got my radio, guv," Parkinson offered.

Lincoln snatched it from him and bounded downstairs. Aidan and Parkinson followed at a respectful distance. The sergeant was under a rowan tree, head bent in conversation with his senior officer.

"Sarge! Have a look at this." Parkinson's shout made both of them swing round. The detective constable was waving from the corner of the house. They ran to join him.

A crude car shelter had been made from wooden poles and a corrugated iron roof. A car was parked under it. A metallic red BMW. There was an expression of triumph on Parkinson's freckled face.

"That's it, isn't it, Sarge? That's Brown's car."

Lincoln ran his hand over it, as if to confirm the evidence of his eyes. "That's Mr Brown's, yes. We handed it back to Lorna Brown. Well done, boy."

Aidan felt the rush of adrenalin that might be either joy

or fear. That could only mean that Lorna was close. And if Lorna was here, then Melangell…

His stomach sickened as Lincoln raised the unlocked lid of the boot. He relaxed in relief as it showed the space to be empty, except for two pairs of walking boots, a groundsheet and a coil of rope.

Lincoln studied these. "At least we know what she didn't think necessary," he said, enigmatically. "That's probably good news." He turned to Aidan with a sudden intensity of expression. "Denbigh reminded me that you saw Lorna Brown around here shortly before the murder. Where, exactly?"

Images of that day leapt back into Aidan's mind. Two figures glimpsed from high above, on the path along the stream to the foot of the waterfall. Then Lorna dashing past them. The torn white shirt, her tear-stained face. Later, coming upon Caradoc Lewis and Thaddaeus Brown in a shouting match.

"It was almost at the waterfall." He nodded along the narrowing valley to where Pistyll Blaen-y-cwm came tumbling down the wall of rock that barred their view. "We'd seen two of them earlier, from much higher up. Lorna was one. I couldn't say who the other was. Something had happened then. When she rushed past us she was in tears. I asked her what was wrong, but she wouldn't stop. It was after that that Jenny… Jenny heard her come back. Thaddaeus must have already driven back to the house by then."

"To be killed. So we don't know what those two were doing there?"

"I've always assumed it had something to do with land. Who owned what, and what they could do with it. But the waterfall is public access land."

A thought struck him. The memory of an etching laid out prominently on Caradoc Lewis's desk. A standing stone, very like the one which now formed part of Lewis's doorway.

A figure standing beside it.

"That's it! I don't know what Caradoc Lewis is up to, but there was a picture of the foot of the waterfall on his desk. And his raid on the museum has to have something to do with it, too. That's where they are. I'm sure of it!"

"Right. It may be a long shot, but that's where we need to go. Let's move it."

For all his desperation to find his daughter, Aidan's shorter legs found it hard to keep up with the two tall detectives.

They sped through the gate in the wall under the trees, where Aidan and Melangell had stumbled upon the men arguing. It was open moorland beyond. But a trodden path that seemed to be more than a sheep track converged on the crystal stream that was the young River Tanat.

Aidan's eyes were racing ahead to the shadows under the horseshoe of hills that enclosed the foot of the falls. The ground was hillocky, with unexpected mounds and boulders. The river had split into a confusion of streams. He stumbled. He needed to watch where he was going.

Parkinson had taken the lead.

"They're here!" He stopped dead on the path and held out a long arm to stop Lincoln and Aidan from going further. They rushed to join him.

The constable was standing on a raised bank some thirty metres from the base of the waterfall. Out of the corner of his eye, Aidan caught the flash of its triple streams glancing down the rocks. But all his attention was directed to the figures frozen at the foot of the tumbling water.

There were two of them. Lorna and Melangell.

A wave of indescribable gratitude surged over him. Melangell was still alive. Apparently unhurt.

He tore his gaze from her small pointed face under the mop of unruly curls, to the figure beside her.

He knew than why Parkinson had warned them to halt.

Lorna Brown had, after all, taken something from the boot of her car. In her hands she gripped a spade. Even as she turned her startled gaze on them, she raised the blade.

The images were framed in Aidan's mind. The silvery steel of the lifted blade. The darker green of the handle. Lorna's black hair falling around her heart-shaped face. The eager surprise of Melangell's expression. Even the golden stars of gorse behind them. All frozen in a moment of shock. Digitally recorded on his memory.

DS Lincoln raised his voice. "Put the spade down, Miss Brown. Now!"

Lorna stared at him, unmoving. Every nerve in Aidan's body was urging him to dash forward and wrench it from her hands. But the gap was too wide, Melangell too close to her.

Then Melangell's high voice called across the distance. "I want to see the hare."

Lincoln turned to Aidan, his face puzzled. Aidan's own mind was blank. He gazed back at his daughter.

"Daddy! She's going to show me. She promised."

Sergeant Lincoln shrugged slightly in incomprehension and nodded to Aidan. The detective stood back from the path to let him past.

Aidan walked slowly towards the two girls. Lorna said nothing, but she lowered the spade. The blade rested on the peaty earth.

Melangell was bouncing with excitement now. As soon as Aidan got near she shouted, "Lorna knows it's here. Mr Caradoc told her where to look. She said if I came with her, we could find it together."

Aidan tore his eyes away from the eager face with its dusting of freckles. He turned to look at Lorna. His hostile stare interrogated her.

"You promised to show Melangell how to shoot a bow. We left her with you in the garden. How dare you take her away without telling us?"

"We've got half the police force in Wales out looking for her," put in DS Lincoln.

Lorna's usually pale face flushed. "You were all busy looking for Uncle Thad's killer. There's not one of you understands what this is all about." She looked almost as small and defiant as Melangell.

"Perhaps you'd tell us just what it *is* about," Lincoln answered, coming closer.

"This." Lorna's spade jabbed the ground at her feet. "At least… I think it's here… Yes! I know it is. Caradoc explained to me. He had a picture. I'll show you!"

She began to dig, swiftly, convulsively. The men watched her. Melangell's head was bent over, so close that Aidan was afraid she was in danger from the jabbing, lifting blade.

He went and put an arm around Melangell and drew her gently back. She twisted her head to look up at him. Her light grey-blue eyes were shining under pale gold lashes.

Small clods of black earth were flying through the air. Lorna did not dig the spade far. She was deepening her hole inch by inch. Sometimes the steel struck sparks from a stone.

"Do you need any help, love?" Parkinson offered.

She glanced around her, past the watching men, and then down at the rectangle of soil she had cleared of turf. She might, Aidan thought, be checking for landmarks, to judge whether she was digging in the right place.

She smiled, a little secretive smile.

The spade struck something. It was not the screech of steel on stone, but a more hollow sound. At once, Lorna dropped her tool. She was down on her knees, hands scrabbling away at the dark soil.

Melangell darted forward to kneel opposite her.

Between their two heads, one black, one mousey brown, Aidan saw a glimpse of reddish pottery.

From the pocket of her anorak, Lorna drew a small trowel and a brush. She was carefully uncovering more of her find.

"Is this it?" Melangell cried. "Is this what we're looking for?"

Still Lorna said nothing. Her breathing had quickened.

Aidan was beginning to know what he was seeing. The rough earthenware, red streaked with black. The band of chevrons incised around the shoulder. There had been urns like that in the Lewis Collection in Llanfyllin. He was already starting to suspect what they would find inside.

Lorna sat back on her heels. She looked up defiantly at Aidan and the policemen. "I told you. I knew it was here. Uncle Thaddaeus thought I was talking nonsense."

"Is that what you were arguing about on Tuesday?" Aidan asked. "When you were here?"

She stared back at him, her vivid blue eyes unreadable. "That, and other things."

"Come on, now," Lincoln said reasonably. "How could you know it was exactly here? And what is it, anyway?"

"Caradoc knew. There used to be a stone to mark the spot. *You* wouldn't understand. And it's a burial urn. Of course." There was an edge of hostility in her voice.

Aidan waited. He knew there was more to come.

Lorna bent and scraped away the deeper soil that still held the urn trapped. The full curve was starting to emerge. At last it lay below them in full view, free of its hiding place.

Lorna put down the trowel and brush. She reached down her pale, peat-smeared hands, and cupped them to lift her find. Her eyes darted across at Melangell.

"Help me."

Almost too excited to breathe, Melangell leaned over, so that their hair brushed and mingled. Two small hands, and two even smaller, lifted the urn out of the hole and set it reverently on the turf.

Aidan saw a lid of crumbling metal. There was the faintest rattle of something inside.

"What is it?" Melangell begged. "Is it the hare? It is, isn't it?"

"Try and see," Lorna said.

Melangell's hand removed the lid reverently. She gave a cry of dismay as it fell into two.

Aidan fought back the alarm that said they should not be doing this. They should leave it to the experts.

But Melangell set the fragments aside and reached in. Dirt trickled through her fingers as she drew out a tiny bone. She laid it in her palm and looked down at it in wonder.

Lorna's hand followed hers, and lifted out a small, blunt skull.

Even Aidan felt the magic of that moment.

Now Lorna looked up, challenging them. "You saw it, didn't you? You saw me dig it out of the ground. The first time for thousands of years. You can witness that I'm not making it up."

"Of course," murmured Parkinson, "we don't know how it got *in* the ground. You seemed to knew exactly where to dig."

She threw him a withering glance. "I told you you wouldn't understand."

Aidan's mind was a mass of confusion. He was still trying to get over the shock of believing that Lorna had abducted Melangell to do her harm. That she was Thaddaeus's killer. But was she mad? Or had she deliberately tricked them here to provide just the independent witnesses she needed for her discovery?

And did this have anything to do with Caradoc Lewis's bizarre visit to the museum he had sold? Was this what had been in the boxes he had snatched from under the nose of the unfortunate curator? Had he planted this find? Or... could it be genuine?

But first and foremost, there was the overwhelming joy that Melangell was safe.

Lincoln turned to him. "Sorry, sir. I'm not really into archaeology."

"If it's what it seems to be, it's the burial of the remains of a hare. Two or three thousand years old. Probably a sacrifice. Hares were always sacred in this valley."

"I'll leave that to the experts. This young lady has a lot to answer for, taking your kid away like that. If it was one of mine, I'd have been having kittens. But she doesn't seem to have come to any harm. And Caradoc Lewis isn't here. He's the one I thought we were after. I was banking on finding all three of them together..." His voice trailed off. Aidan saw his colour pale. Already he had started to stride back along the path, almost running.

Aidan darted after him. "What's wrong?"

"Nothing, I hope. But I'm asking myself where Caradoc Lewis *is* now." He threw an angry glance over his shoulder. "Did *she* have orders to get us away from the house? Is that what all this performance is about?" He was actually running now. "Meanwhile, I'm afraid we've left your wife alone at the house. Just what we warned you never to do."

Aidan nearly lost his balance. He looked back in dismay.

Parkinson had swept up Melangell in his long arms and was running after them.

The small figure of Lorna Brown stood at the foot of the falls, the urn of hare bones in her arms.

They were back at Caradoc Lewis's house and their cars. Lincoln was just opening the driver's door when he smote the heel of his hand against his head.

"Idiot! We came haring out here because your wife remembered something that meant Lorna *could* have murdered Thaddaeus. And she'd got Melangell. But we were so keen to get the kid back that we've left Lorna behind. And she's back in our sights as prime suspect now."

"Beg pardon, Sarge," Parkinson panted as he set Melangell down. "She doesn't know we're on to her. She thinks this is all about snatching the kid. No reason for her not to come back to the house in her own good time. Thank God the kid's not hurt."

"You don't think Jenny's in danger from Caradoc Lewis, then?" Aidan was bundling Melangell into his car.

"It's all *right*, Daddy. I can do it myself." She snatched back the safety belt.

"Whatever it is they're up to, they're in this together. I'm sure of it. I haven't a clue about this hare bones stuff, but it has to be connected. Get back to the falls," Lincoln ordered Parkinson. "Don't alarm her. Just say we'd like her to come in for questioning. Make her think it's just about Melangell."

"Will do." Parkinson set off at a loping run.

Lincoln and Aidan's cars sped away towards the road.

Not far down the track, Aidan saw a black car racing towards them. There was no room to pass. Yet still the other car came on at speed. Aidan peered past the blue flank of Lincoln's vehicle. With a sense of inevitability he recognized the Jaguar.

One hand on the wheel, Lincoln's other hand shot out of the window and clamped a blue light to the roof of his unmarked car. He sounded the siren. It seemed an age that the cars hurtled towards each other, before the Jaguar reluctantly stopped. Lincoln was forced to slam on his brakes to avoid colliding with it. Conscious of the precious burden of Melangell in the passenger seat, Aidan had already slowed.

DS Lincoln was flashing his warrant card and shouting, "Police! Back up! I want you off this track in two seconds."

The window of the Jaguar was wound down. Aidan could neither see the men inside or hear what they said. He inched closer.

It was the purplish, spectacled face of Mr Secker at the driver's window.

"We need to see Mr Lewis urgently. About Mr Brown's estate."

"He's not there. And God knows what he's doing while our backs are turned. Back off, or I'll have you on a charge."

To Aidan's relief, the Jaguar gave way, as it had not done for the Davisons on Monday. At speed, and accurately, the black car reversed along the way it had come. Presently it reached an indentation by a field gate and drew over. Lincoln and Aidan sped past.

Through the lowered driver's window, past Secker, Aidan had a glimpse of Mr McCarthy's slick blond hair. The pair were staring curiously at him.

What are *they* doing here, he wondered, heading for Caradoc Lewis's house?

With a jolt of unease, he looked up at the Jaguar again, now a small black dot in his rear-view mirror.

Thaddaeus had not had time to change his will. Secker and McCarthy now had their hands on Lorna's trust fund. Whatever feud there had been between Thaddaeus and Caradoc Lewis about the use of land in this valley, the two financiers would continue it. So what could have made Lorna kill her uncle before he signed the codicil that would give her freedom?

But the nearer he got to the House of the Hare, the greater his fear was growing for what might be happening to Jenny. How far might Caradoc go to protect Lorna? The pain of the thought of losing Jenny was all the more intense because there was so little time left. In a few months, he really would lose her, finally. It was no use telling himself that death was not a permanent loss. That was not how it felt now.

The police were with her, weren't they? PC Watkins was searching the house. Others were combing the grounds. He tried not to let himself think that by now they would have checked every hiding place. They would not have found Melangell. How long before the search moved on beyond the grounds, leaving Jenny alone in the House of the Hare?

Chapter Thirty-one

JENNY WAS FILLED WITH overwhelming anger. How dare Lorna do this to her? Wasn't it bad enough that she was dying, facing the premature loss of everything she held dear on earth? Did Lorna have to snatch away the last few precious months that Jenny could have with Melangell?

Dismay struck her. How could she be thinking of herself when Melangell's life was in danger?

She ran into the house, pushing aside the pain and weariness that had been threatening to engulf her. It took only a second to decide where she needed to go.

Running up the shallow golden stairs, surprising herself that she had not thought about using the lift. Down the corridor, the way she remembered hearing those running footsteps.

Lorna's bedroom door stood open. PC Watkins was just coming out.

"No luck, I'm afraid."

Jenny pushed past her. The room was light and airy, even at the end of an overcast afternoon. Unlike Jenny and Aidan's, it faced east, down the valley of the Tanat, to where the sky opened out between two walls of hills. The white candlewick bedspread had been pulled aside in PC Watkins' search. Jenny knew she would have checked the wardrobes. All the same, she rifled through the hangers and the chest of drawers. Even pulled out Lorna's suitcase and opened that. No sign of the white shirt with torn buttons that Aidan had seen Lorna wearing as she ran from the waterfall. The shirt she must have been wearing when she killed Thaddaeus.

Had she buried it? Burned it? Thrown it out with the rubbish?

The fact that it was missing chilled the heat of Jenny's anger. That she had destroyed it made it all the more certain it had carried evidence of her uncle's blood.

And Lorna had Melangell.

A tiny voice of common sense asked why Lorna should want to keep a torn shirt. She was surely not a girl who needed to mend her clothes.

It didn't cancel the fear Jenny felt.

The awful tiredness was creeping up on her again. She was not sure how much longer she could keep going. The room was beginning to swim. But she had to find Melangell.

The Ewarts' room was empty, stripped. Other unused bedrooms stood ready for guests. Should she search the floor above, where Chief Inspector Denbigh and his sergeant Lincoln had their rooms? And which was Sian's room, and Josef's? She did not know.

PC Watkins seemed to be doing a thorough job of checking the house. If Melangell was here, she would have found her.

Jenny was tempted to go into her own room, close the door, lie down on the bed and sleep. Shut out this violent world in the hope that when she woke up everything would be normal again. Melangell would be back.

She would be well.

She made herself walk past and down the stairs.

Marcus Coutts was waiting in the foyer. His eyes lit up when he saw her.

"It's the little girl this time, is it? How old was she? Seven?"

Jenny stared at him in horror and grasped the banister

to steady herself.

"You! Who told you?"

The knowledge hit her. There could only be one way the headline-seeking reporter could have been on the scene of Thaddaeus's murder so quickly. And now, less than an hour after they realized Melangell was missing.

"Josef! Josef's been telling you, hasn't he? For money. You've been paying him for information about everything that's been going on here."

"I couldn't possibly say, darling. My sources are confidential. We journalists have our standards."

She wanted to strike him across the face.

"Do you have a photograph of her?" He held up his hands to restrain her anger. "Could be helping yourself, you know. Picture of her on all the front pages. Anyone seen this girl? Last seen in company of murder suspect. Grieving parents appeal for help."

The camera was on her in close-up before she could stop him.

She stormed past him, willing herself to stay upright. The kitchen door was at the end of the ground-floor corridor. She threw it open.

Josef had evidently been startled in the middle of preparing supper. Chopped vegetables on the central work table made a shout of brilliant colour. Orange carrots, green courgettes, red beetroot. A wickedly sharp knife lay dropped on the chopping board.

Did that mean Josef had fled?

She gripped the table for support.

Of course not. He would be out searching for Melangell, like everyone else. As she should be.

She could not help herself. She needed to sit down.

There was a kitchen stool, higher and less comfortable than she wanted. She subsided on to it.

She heard some distant calls from the search party, now some distance from the house. They did not have the urgency of something discovered.

The house was silent now. She could not hear PC Watkins. Where had Marcus Coutts gone?

There were footsteps approaching the door. She looked up in apprehension. Was he following her?

It was Sian who came into the kitchen, brisk and purposeful. When she saw Jenny, her rounded features lit up in a strangely satisfied smile.

"So that's where you're hiding."

Jenny jumped to her feet with hope. "Have you found her? Is she safe?"

"I think there's something you need to come and see."

Immediately, Jenny's emotions tipped the other way, making her sway. She could hardly speak. "What do you mean? What have they found?" Her eyes begged Sian for reassurance.

The other woman's face looked businesslike, neither soothing nor confirming Jenny's worst fears. "See for yourself."

As if in a dream, Jenny accompanied her down the long corridor. Sian led her past the dining room and the lounge, across the foyer, and on into the corridor on the western side of the house, where Jenny had not been before.

At the end was a side door. It opened on to a path overhung by a tall laurel hedge. The glossy leaves were wet, though the rain had stopped some time ago. There was a smell of damp earth.

As Sian turned right, there was a glimpse of bright green grass. For a moment, Jenny thought it was the lawn outside the lounge, where Aidan and Melangell had played croquet. But as they came nearer, she saw with a small shock that it was the archery range. The lawn was hidden from them by another bank of shrubs.

This, she thought with sudden awareness, must have been the way that Lorna came in pursuit of Thaddaeus.

The sick tension was growing. In the bushes at the other end of the range was the spot where Thaddaeus had been found stabbed with an arrow. "Please, God!" she prayed. "Let it not be Melangell this time."

The door of the sports equipment hut hung open. Lorna had indeed started to give Melangell an archery lesson. The golden yew bow lay dropped on the grass. Beside it were three arrows, fletched with two red feathers and one white.

Jenny was feeling dizzy now. Everything had a sense of unreality. When Sian motioned to her, she followed obediently into the hut. A distant part of her brain was warning her of what she might see inside. She could no longer believe this was happening to her, here, now, in the real world.

"Have you told the police?" she managed to whisper.

Something was stirring in her brain, calling her back to awareness. She looked around the hut. Bows, croquet mallets, tennis and badminton racquets. She had seen them all before. Her eyes raked the shadows for something new and sinister, and found nothing.

Baffled, she turned to Sian and found the manager staring at her with a strange smile on her face. In her hands she held a coil of bowstring.

"Appropriate, don't you think?"

In a second, the string was round Jenny's throat.

Jenny fought then, using what little strength she had left. She tried to claw the string loose.

Sian whipped her arms behind her in a painful lock. Jenny was gasping for breath. The noose was tight, but Sian had let go of it for a moment. Jenny found herself manhandled backwards and lifted on to a box. Sian's strength matched the bushranger outfit she wore.

Jenny looked up, and found to her horror that the other end of the cord was already slung over a beam above her head.

"What are you doing? Where's Melangell?" she choked.

"Oh, don't worry. Melangell's safe. It's you who's the problem. You're the only witness to the time Lorna got back."

"Aidan's… told… Sergeant Lincoln." She could barely gasp the words through the increasing pain. Sian was hauling on the cord, drawing it tighter. Black spots were swimming in front of Jenny's eyes.

"Hearsay, once you're dead. And your mind was unbalanced. Who's going to believe you?"

Gathering all her strength, Jenny kicked out. Sian stumbled sideways. For a moment, the pressure on Jenny's neck lightened. Her hands were freed, but Sian was now behind her. The cord was in her grip again.

"You can't get away. I could have killed you already with the pressure point in your neck. No trace. I'd have murdered Thaddaeus for her, if that little fool Lorna had told me straight away what he did to her. He thought he could buy her, body and soul. I'd have got rid of him without resorting to an arrow in his eye."

Lorna? Jenny groaned. She really *had* killed her uncle. And it sounded as if Thaddaeus had abused her. The confirmation came too late.

"But that way, the post-mortem would find out you were dead before you hung. This way is better."

Sian grunted and stepped back. Jenny knew the cord was secure now. She could feel the tension round her choking throat almost lifting her off the box. All that it would need would be for Sian to kick the box away. Jenny would be left hanging, fighting for breath, strangling on a length of the same bowstring she had pulled so confidently three days ago.

A shaft of hope. The police outpost was less than a bowshot away. Someone from there would come by.

Then bitter disappointment. The officers were all out searching for Melangell. They had moved beyond the grounds of the house. No one would stop this.

Her hands were straining for her constricted throat. She could not move them. She had not been aware of the moment when Sian had tied them behind her back. Something soft, that would not leave marks on her wrists. She saw the scenario moments before Sian told her, in that brisk, capable voice of a former PE teacher.

"It will be understandable, if painful, for your family. You saw the end coming. More pain. More weakness. You were a fit woman before the cancer. You couldn't face the thought of a slow decline. Once they were out of the way, you decided to end it quickly. Probably the shock of Melangell's disappearance upset the balance of your mind. Your testimony will be worthless. I've sworn I saw Lorna arriving back forty minutes later."

Jenny wanted to scream that it wasn't like that. That she had accepted the fact of her death and had been going towards it as serenely as she could. That she trusted in God to accompany her through the last shadows. That she had already had talks with Hospicecare, who had promised her a peaceful and painless final journey. That she would never have taken her own life.

But she could not speak. In a few moments, she would not be able to breathe.

"Aidan!" her heart screamed out. "Where are you? I need you!"

There was a brilliant flash of light in her face.

Chapter Thirty-two

THEY HIT THE ROAD below Blaen-y-cwm farm. As the gateposts of the House of the Hare swung into view, Aidan felt a release of tension that they were back at last, and yet a growing anxiety about what he might find. He slowed the car, expecting Lincoln ahead of him to swing into the drive.

"Daddy! What are you doing?" Melangell demanded. "I wanted to stay with Lorna and the hare. I found it, didn't I? It's *important*. Wait till I tell Mummy. She's going to be so jealous."

"Yes, sweetheart," Aidan said, preoccupied.

Further down the lane, a tall figure was crossing the road from the church. Caradoc Lewis.

Lincoln's car accelerated forward, and stopped abruptly just short of running him down. Aidan followed. The man turned in shock and fury.

Aidan was out of the car only seconds after DS Lincoln. "Where's Jenny?"

Lewis looked at him with withering contempt. "Your wife? I haven't the faintest idea."

Was he bluffing? Could this whole bizarre thing about the hare and Melangell's abduction really have nothing to do with the fact that Jenny had vital evidence about the identity of Thaddaeus's murderer? Was she safely back at the House of the Hare? Should Aidan be getting Melangell back to her as soon as possible, instead of standing here?

He had not seen the other car approaching from the opposite direction. Now Caradoc Lewis stood hemmed in between the bonnets of the two detectives' vehicles. Chief Inspector Denbigh got out more heavily than his younger sergeant had.

"Caradoc Lewis, I am arresting you on suspicion of arson. You do not have to say anything…"

The words of the caution faded in Aidan's ears. Surely this was about one murder and the fear of another? He had followed Lincoln because he believed that where Caradoc Lewis was, Jenny would be. Or had been. It was a thought so chill that he dared not pursue it. Caradoc Lewis had come from the church and its graveyard.

But arson? Did it really matter that the tower of St Melangell's had been engulfed in flames?

For the first time he noticed that Mother Joan and Freda Rawlinson were standing at the entrance to the church car park. From the shocked expressions on their faces, he guessed they had had an uncomfortable encounter with Caradoc. The fire investigation officer joined them.

"No doubt about it, I'm afraid. Accelerant, probably paraffin. Your chap targeted the table in the middle of the room. Didn't even have the sense to make it look like faulty wiring."

Caradoc tossed his long black hair contemptuously. "Idiots! Christian saints! Pretty little stories about a beautiful woman hiding a cuddly bunny under her skirt. Do you think *that's* what the Hare and the Lady is all about? Sentimental piffle!"

He rounded on Aidan and Melangell, his face eager. "She found it, didn't she? *You* saw it. You took the bait. You were there when she unearthed it? *That's* what the world needs to know about. Not *this*!" He waved a scornful hand at the church.

The crowd was growing. Police officers were coming down from the hill fields and up from the meadows by the river. Euan's worried face was among them. Josef was looking shiftily at the police on either side of him.

"You've got the kid. Thank God for that!" The uniformed Sergeant Morris, who had been so dismissive of PC Watkins, raised himself in Aidan's eyes with his heartfelt joy at the sight of Melangell.

It was hard not to be caught up in the sudden explosion of cheering and clapping. Melangell looked suddenly confused and startled. But when she saw them all smiling at her, she beamed.

"Sergeant," Denbigh addressed the local man. "Take one of your constables and get this character back to your station. He's wanted for setting fire to this church. I'll be along later."

He got back into his car. "Lincoln, if we could sort out what happened to this young lady… Maybe we could go back to the house. I'm sure her mother's dying to see her."

"Parkinson's bringing Lorna Brown in," his detective sergeant told him. "She doesn't know yet she's back on a murder charge. She thinks it's about making off with this young lady." He nodded at the smiling Melangell.

The smile vanished from the child's face. She looked up at the men around her in sudden alarm. Aidan could only bundle her back into the car. Explanations must wait.

Lincoln and Aidan turned their vehicles in the car park and followed the inspector's Rover back to the house.

Was it all over? Caradoc Lewis under arrest for arson. Lorna soon to be charged with murder. Was Jenny really safe now to give her evidence in court? How long did it take a murder case to come to trial? Would Jenny still be fit to testify? Might she be in the hospice by then? Or…? Aidan pushed the worst thought away.

After all, it was only circumstantial evidence. Footsteps of someone unseen running along the corridor. The fact that Lorna Brown had had time to change her clothes before she met Euan. All it proved was that Lorna *could* have killed her uncle.

His mind was churning with conflicting emotions. At least he was bringing Melangell back safe. Surely that was the most important thing.

Caradoc and Lorna were under arrest. There was no one now to threaten Jenny.

He jumped out of his own car, without waiting for Lincoln to park.

The House of the Hare had a feeling of emptiness. The sky was clearing at last. A shaft of sunlight fell on the landing above him.

The silence was not surprising. Everyone had been out searching for Melangell. He stood with her at the foot of the stairs. She was unnaturally quiet.

Would Jenny be in the bedroom? She ought to be resting, but he knew that she would not have been able to stay still while everyone else hunted for her daughter. Still, he doubted that she would have had the strength left to go far.

"Jenny!" he called.

Silence.

"Run into the lounge and see if she's there," he told Melangell.

She darted off.

He climbed the stairs. His footsteps echoed on the polished wood.

Through the patch of sunlight, past the vase of dried flowers on the windowsill, into the darker corridor. The bedroom door was half open. He stepped through it softly, just in case she was asleep on the bed.

The bedding was rumpled. There was no sign of Jenny.

He went out on to the balcony and scanned the garden. Nothing moved.

Faintly, he heard Melangell's voice call, "Mummy? I'm back."

No answering cry of joy.

He went downstairs more quickly. PC Watkins came through the front door and stood in the foyer, looking up at him.

"Have you seen Jenny? My wife?"

"Yes, she was here. I was searching the house and she came and joined me. I last saw her in Lorna Brown's bedroom, though I'd already been through it with a fine-tooth comb."

Aidan ran back up. Lorna's bedroom was unlocked. And empty.

His feet clattered down the stairs again. He caught up with Watkins outside the French windows of the lounge as she greeted Melangell enthusiastically.

"We found the hare!" Melangell was telling her, her face bright with excitement again. "Lorna says it's thousands and thousands of years old. It was in the ground by the waterfall. We dug it up. Lorna knew where it was because Mr Caradoc has a picture of a special stone that used to stand there. And she let me help her. It was in this..."

"Was anyone else in the house?" Aidan interrupted.

PC Watkins turned her kindly face, trying to switch from Melangell's enthusiastic account to Aidan's urgency. "No. They'd all been detailed to search the grounds, or check the village. As soon as they heard Melangell was missing, everyone offered to join in. The staff here, people from the houses by the church. I was told to do a thorough search of the house."

Sergeant Lincoln emerged from the corridor beyond the reception desk that led to rooms not used by guests. He shook his head.

"Then where *is* she?"

Watkins' face creased with concern. "She wasn't well, was she? And then all this upset. You don't think she had a fainting fit? She could by lying somewhere."

Aidan was suddenly conscious of time racing past, when anything could be happening to Jenny. He seemed to hear her voice calling inside his head. *"Aidan! Where are you?"*

"Wait a minute!" Watkins exclaimed. "There *was* someone. I didn't see her, but I heard her voice. I'd just finished checking the house and I was crossing the foyer on my way to join the boys outside. It was down that way." She nodded towards the corridor leading to the kitchen.

"*Whose* voice?"

"Sian. The manager. I thought she must be talking to Mrs Davison."

Sian. The former PE teacher in her bushranger's outfit. Sian, folding Lorna in her arms, fiercely protective of her. Sian in the kitchen talking to Jenny.

Aidan flew down the corridor and threw the door open.

The kitchen was empty. His eye immediately registered the wickedly pointed knife on the table. Its blade was smeared with red.

Beetroot, he told his thudding heart. It's only beetroot.

He turned a pleading gaze on Lincoln. A distant part of his mind told him that Denbigh was no longer with them.

"Where can she be?"

He saw the sergeant struggling with the unanswerable question.

His own mind was racing through the possibilities. And horror was growing all the time. Why was Sian in the house, when everyone else was outside looking for Melangell? Even

PC Watkins had finished searching the rooms and had gone to join them. Until she had passed the foyer and heard voices, she thought she had left only Jenny in the house.

What possible reason could have brought Sian to the kitchen, except that Jenny was here? Alone.

He cursed himself for the time he had spent chasing up the valley to the waterfall in pursuit of Melangell. For the delay while they searched Caradoc's house. For waiting while Lorna unearthed that stupid urn, which must be either a plant or a fake. For the nerve-wracking moments it took for Secker and McCarthy to reverse down the track to let them pass. For believing that the arrest of Caradoc Lewis for arson was all that it needed to ensure Jenny's safety. And all that time…

He was nearly sick.

But the more he concentrated on that smiling picture of the muscular Sian Jenkins, the more other images were falling into place. Sian, showing Melangell where to find the croquet mallets. Sian, eager to introduce Jenny to the archery range, helping her to choose the most appropriate bow.

All the images coalesced in sudden sharp focus. The small sports hut at the start of the archery range. Its shadowed interior crowded with bows, arrows, mallets, spikes. Any one of them could be an instrument of death.

He almost threw Melangell back to Watkins. "Look after her."

He was out of the side door into the gleam of late sunshine. He almost expected to find Josef sitting smoking on his bench. But there was no one.

He raced round the corner of the house and along the patio that fronted the lounge. Wicker chairs went flying.

Lincoln was pounding alongside him. "Where are we going?"

"The hut," was all Aidan could gasp.

They were past the house now, and bursting through the

wall of laurels and camellias that screened the lawn from the archery range.

A sudden surprise of space. Grass gleaming brilliantly green after the rain. The multicoloured circles of the butts. And at the nearer end, the dark-stained timbers of the hut.

There was someone already outside.

Chief Inspector Denbigh.

Aidan flew towards him. He could not bear to imagine what he might find inside.

Chapter Thirty-three

SIAN STAGGERED BACKWARDS as the camera flash exploded in front of her face.

"Luvverly!"

"Aidan...!" The joy of recognition died on Jenny's lips as her dazzled eyes realized the true identity of the photographer.

Marcus Coutts stepped forward and felled Sian with a right hook.

Darkness claimed Jenny. She fell forward against the tightening bowstring.

A voice came from a long way away.

"You realize that I'm not in a million years going to let you use that photograph. I'm impounding your camera now as key evidence."

"But, guv! You can not be serious! That's the shot of a lifetime! Jenny in the noose. The killer alongside. It's worth a fortune!"

"Are you going to let Mrs Davison down, or stand there and let her strangle to death?" Inspector Denbigh ordered.

The unbearable tension suddenly went slack. Jenny tumbled off the box. The freed cord was still close around her neck, but it had not tightened fatally. Hands were prising it loose. She was going to be sick. Marcus Coutts was holding her steady.

When she could speak she gasped, "Sian's not the killer. It was Lorna all along. And she's got Melangell."

The chief inspector straightened from the prostrate form of Sian. The manager was struggling against the handcuffs he had snapped on her wrists. Sudden surprise rearranged the creases of Denbigh's face.

"Lorna?" He stepped forward to release Jenny from the reporter's hold. "Don't upset yourself, Mrs Davison. Melangell's safe and well. But what makes you blame Miss Brown?"

"Sian told me." It was cruelly painful to speak. "She said she would have done it for Lorna, if she'd asked. But now she... she was covering up."

"By silencing you? So you couldn't testify to what?"

"That I heard Lorna come back to the house. It wasn't more than half an hour after the murder, as I thought. It must have been straight after. I heard her run to the bedroom to change her clothes."

"And what would make Miss Jenkins think you'd remembered this?"

Even as he spoke, he swung round to Coutts.

The journalist flared. "Have a heart! I've got to get a story, haven't I? It's my living."

"You told Sian Jenkins information that could have cost Mrs Davison her life? You followed them here so that you could get your 'shot of a lifetime', as you call it? What kind of reptile does that make you?"

"I got it, though, didn't I? All the proof you need to put her away."

"And Mrs Davison?"

"I wouldn't have let her swing. That's God's truth. Give us a break, guv! I stopped Sian, didn't I?"

Jenny's appalled imagination showed her the front page of a tabloid. Her own contorted face struggling against the noose.

A figure catapulted past Denbigh and snatched the

expensive Leica from Coutts. Aidan hurled the camera across the grass. It shattered against the stone boundary wall.

Coutts let out a scream of rage, but Lincoln had him in an armlock.

Jenny stumbled into Aidan's embrace. "Don't be too hard on him," she whispered. "He did rescue me."

Denbigh went to retrieve the shards of the journalist's camera.

"It would have been helpful to remove the disc first, before you gave vent to your understandable feelings. But I dare say the lab will be able to get what they want from this." Sian snarled from the floor beside him. "Charge her with attempted murder, will you?" Chief Inspector Denbigh told DS Lincoln.

Aidan had his arm firmly around Jenny as he guided her back across the lawn to the house. She felt the most precious burden in the world. He could hardly believe that she was here, alive, even though she was still breathing painfully. From now on, every moment he had her was doubly miraculous.

Melangell came running across the grass to meet them. Her springy curls bounced with her enthusiasm.

"Mummy! You should have been there! Lorna took a spade and Mr Caradoc had a picture which showed her where to dig. And he was right! I helped her lift it out and *it was the hare*! Wasn't it, Daddy?"

"It looked like it," he said, cautiously.

Jenny leaned against his shoulder, smiling weakly. "I haven't the faintest idea what you're talking about, but it sounds very exciting. Can it wait till I sit down?"

He helped her across the patio, into the lounge. She was just sinking into one of the leather sofas when there were fresh sounds from the foyer. Aidan looked round to see Parkinson escorting Lorna in through the front door. Lorna was still holding the pottery urn cradled in her arms like a baby.

"That's it!" squealed Melangell. "Look!"

Lorna's exquisite face looked defiant.

Does she know? Aidan thought. No, she can't. She doesn't know Sian identified her to Jenny as the murderer. She thinks she's just being brought in for questioning because she took Melangell away without permission. And Melangell's safe, so she assumes it's no big deal. She's got what she wanted. Lincoln and Parkinson and I were all there to witness her unearth her precious urn of bones.

Caradoc must have planted them, mustn't he? He wasn't there himself to arouse suspicion. He stole the urn and bones from the museum and buried them there for her to find. He told her where to dig.

A niggle of suspicion gnawed at his mind. That old engraving laid out on Caradoc's desk. A carved stone pillar set at the foot of Pistyll Blaen-y-cwm. It wasn't there now. It had been embedded in the motley of masonry that was Capel-y-Cwm. But once it must have marked a significant spot. Why? Was that how he knew that Lorna had to dig for the urn there? Was it even possible that her find was genuine?

He looked at Melangell with renewed admiration, and even jealousy.

Then a voice he had never wanted to hear again came from behind him.

"Don't tell them anything, Lorna!"

Sian had just been ushered into the house in the custody of DS Lincoln.

Lorna looked, startled, across the lounge crowded with the Davisons and the police. When she saw Sian in handcuffs her mouth fell open in dismay. The earthenware urn started to slip from her protective arms.

Aidan dived forward to catch it.

He stood, cradling it as she had. He was half afraid his shielding arms would crush the fragile pottery. Hairs prickled on the back of his neck. This might really be what Caradoc Lewis believed it was, or wished others to believe. A sacred object from thousands of years ago. The ancient hare of Pennant Melangell.

But a very twenty-first-century drama was crackling across the space between the black-haired girl so close to him now and the woman who had very nearly killed Jenny to protect her.

Inspector Denbigh looked from one to the other. He was taking his time. Aidan sensed his dilemma. All the proof he had that Lorna had stabbed Thaddaeus was the fact that Sian had boasted to Jenny that she could have killed her employer more discreetly if Lorna had asked her to. And that Jenny had heard someone running to Lorna's bedroom just after the time of the murder. Hearsay. Circumstantial evidence.

In all probability, Sian would confess to the murder to save Lorna.

A new voice broke into the tension. Euan Jones's deep Welsh accent.

"It wasn't her. I did it."

Chapter Thirty-four

THE YOUNG GARDENER'S FACE looked yellow, which was as pale as his weathered skin would allow. His dark brown eyes were wide and fearful.

Aidan glanced swiftly round at Lorna. Her white, proud face showed no change of emotion. There was none of the shock she had shown when she saw Sian in handcuffs. Could it be true? Had Lorna known all along that it was Euan who had murdered her uncle?

But what had Jenny meant about Sian's admission of Lorna's guilt?

His eyes went back to the handcuffed Sian. At once he registered the change in her. Her head was up. Her eyes had brightened. He knew she was seeing a way out for Lorna.

Neither woman said anything. They let Euan's confession stand.

Could he really have done it?

Chief Inspector Denbigh walked slowly across the lounge. He rested his hand on the teenager's shoulder.

"Now, boy. Why exactly would you do a thing like that?"

There was something of the hunted hare in Euan's face.

"H-he bullied her. I couldn't stand it." It came out as an uncertain croak.

Denbigh turned to address Lorna. "Is that true?"

The muscles of her face hardly moved as she answered. "That he bullied me? Yes. I had a quarrel with him that morning. Mr Davison knows about it." Her eyes met Aidan's. "At least, he saw me running away from him. He asked me why I was upset."

"And you told Euan?"

"Yes."

True or not, Euan's doing this because he loves her, Aidan thought. But she doesn't care about him. He's offering her a way out and she's taking it.

But the chief inspector had not finished with Euan. There was still that air of the weary schoolmaster that had impressed itself upon Aidan when they first met.

"So, boy. You decided to get rid of Mr Brown. You're the gardener. You have a shed full of tools, any one of which could serve as a murder weapon. Would you mind explaining to me just why you chose an arrow to kill him with? You must have known that suspicion would fall immediately on the young woman who stood to gain by his death and who was one of the few people here who could use a bow. The very person you say you wanted to protect. Lorna Brown."

Euan gulped. His eyes darted round the room full of intently listening faces. They came to rest on the sofa where Jenny sat. He pointed.

"You're wrong. It was her. Mrs Davison. She'd been shooting at the butts that morning. I hoped they'd think it was her."

"I se-ee. A guest who had just arrived at the House of the Hare the previous day. Who had never met Thaddaeus Brown in her life before. What possible motive could we find to charge her?"

Aidan shuddered, remembering Jenny's defiant display of her archery before the chief inspector. Of the nightmare in which he had feared that Jenny really might have shot Thaddaeus. He was glad that the inspector had never got to hear that.

Denbigh shook his head sorrowfully. "Nice try, boy. But it doesn't add up. I could charge you with wasting police time, or trying to subvert the course of justice. But we'll let that pass."

He moved across the lounge to the foyer, to stand in front of Lorna.

"Lorna Brown, I am arresting you on a charge of murder."

Sian Jenkins let out a yowl like an injured cat.

Euan's face crumpled in grief.

Lorna's sapphire eyes looked back at the inspector in stony silence.

After a paralyzed moment, Aidan's eyes suddenly sought Melangell. In his ears there rang her glad confidence of a few days ago. "*I don't think she did it. She's nice.*"

Melangell had gone trustingly to the waterfall with Lorna.

The child's eyes, a paler blue than Lorna's, were wide with shock. She turned imploringly to her mother. Jenny took her hand.

Aidan knew a burst of anger then that almost made him hurl the Iron Age pot at Lorna's head. Wasn't it enough that she had murdered her uncle, whether for money, or to escape from his pressure on her, or to save the valley? Did she have to shatter Melangell's trust in humankind too?

He strode across the lounge to his daughter.

Jenny was stroking her hand. "I'm sorry, sweetheart. We thought the same. That Lorna was innocent and someone else was trying to blame it on her."

"You've hurt your neck," Melangell said suddenly to her. "Did Lorna do that too?"

"No, sweetheart. That was something else. I'm all right now."

"Aidan Davison, I could kill you!" Marcus Coutts's voice broke across them. "The perfect shot! Mother and daughter, back from the brink of death. Reunited. *And you smashed my camera!*"

Aidan set the urn down very carefully on a coffee table.

"Unless you remove yourself from this house in the next ten seconds, I might just conceivably smash your head in as well. And I don't care if half the police in Powys are listening."

"Aidan," said Jenny, quietly. "Peace. It's over."

Chapter Thirty-five

A S THE DAVISONS CAME DOWN the stairs, a sense of the emptiness of the house struck Jenny.

"It doesn't look as if the Ewarts have come back. Do we know there's even going to be any supper?" she exclaimed. "Who's in charge now?"

Aidan laughed at the alarmed face Melangell turned up to them. "Don't worry, kid. It's only two miles to the pub."

Jenny pushed open the dining room door. She half expected to find the tables bare.

She hardly had time to glimpse the linen tablecloths, the fluted napkins and the gleaming glasses when the half-forgotten figure of the teenage waitress came bouncing to greet them.

"Mair! I thought you were back at college."

"Well, you've got to help out in an emergency, haven't you? And it's Friday. Shocking, isn't it? Who'd have thought it? First Mr Brown. Now Lorna and Sian up for murder. Josef's in a right state. Lucky it's just the two tables. And you're off tomorrow morning, aren't you?"

As they took their seats, Aidan looked round at the other table laid for the evening meal. There were two places set.

"Guess the detectives must be coming back after they've taken Lorna and Sian to the police station. Though I can't think why."

Mair was back with the menus. "The police have cleared out that barn they were using. Most of them have gone. What would you like? Josef says he can do you a chicken consommé or a grilled goat's cheese for starters."

When the main course came, Jenny looked down at the medley of courgettes, carrots and beetroot. Into her mind came the vision of the chopping board in the kitchen. The crimson-stained knife. The door opening behind her as Sian came in. She put down her knife and fork.

Aidan's hand covered hers.

They took their coffee on the patio in the padded wicker chairs. Mair brought a little plate piled with squares of fudge.

"Go on." Her eyes twinkled at Melangell. She appeared to be revelling in the excitement. "Spoil yourselves."

Melangell fell on the fudge with glee.

It was quiet when Mair had gone.

"It's strange having the place to ourselves," Jenny said. "Almost as if it were our own house."

"I wonder what will happen to it now?" Aidan said. "Those guys Secker and McCarthy were supposed to be holding a trust fund for Lorna, since her uncle didn't change his will. But I don't suppose she can inherit if she's... If they find her guilty."

"I don't know the law on that. I don't imagine they allow you to profit from murder."

There were voices barely audible in the dining room. Two men.

"Sounds like Denbigh and Lincoln are back," Aidan said.

"Good. I wanted to say goodbye to them, and thank them. Especially the inspector. He has that wonderfully lugubrious face, like a bloodhound, but he's a sweetie."

They let the stillness of the evening lengthen. There was a faint scent of azaleas. Jenny had positioned her chair so that her back was to the bank of shrubs that masked the archery butts. She focused resolutely on the bed of pink tulips and misty blue forget-me-nots that brightened the space before Euan's vegetable garden.

"I wonder what will happen to them now? Josef, Euan. And Mair's mother does the cleaning. There can't be much employment around here."

There were sounds approaching from the lounge. The two men who had been dining came out on to the patio to join them.

Mr Secker and Mr McCarthy.

Jenny started, making the coffee cups rattle. She laughed in embarrassment.

"Sorry! We thought it was Chief Inspector Denbigh and Sergeant Lincoln in the dining room."

Aidan was looking at the men with barely disguised dislike.

Mr Secker, the smaller of the two, with the round purplish face and wiry curls, rubbed his hands together.

"No. The good gentlemen of the constabulary – and the delightful WPC Watkins – have folded their tents and departed."

"So why are you here?" Aidan asked, brusquely.

Secker's thick eyebrows rose. Behind him, the taller figure of McCarthy, with his sleek blond hair, stiffened.

"A fair question, I suppose." Secker smiled, thinly. "If Thaddaeus had lived a little longer we should have been in charge of the trust fund he intended to put in his will, to manage his estate until Lorna is twenty-five. But as it is…" He shrugged. "We are still his executors. And as you can imagine, there is quite a legal tangle to sort out. In the meantime, it is in everyone's interests to keep the House of the Hare as a going concern. Thaddaeus owed us a considerable amount of money for it."

"We'll arrange for one of our staff to come over and

manage the house, until we can put it back on a proper footing," came McCarthy's deeper voice.

Aidan was staring at them in incomprehension. "But… you said the trust fund would only have kicked in if Thaddaeus changed his will."

"That's right. Unfortunately. Recent events aside, Lorna was too young for the responsibility he was going to give her."

"She had some strange ideas," McCarthy added.

"But surely it was the other way round? You had a row with Thaddaeus before he died because he wanted to add a codicil rescinding the trust fund and giving Lorna sole charge of the money."

"Who told you that?"

"Sian…"

Jenny watched Aidan's features rearrange themselves as the realization struck him.

"Did she, now?" Secker settled himself into a wicker armchair at the adjacent coffee table. His eyes behind their spectacles were oddly bright. "And you thought that we stood to gain, and Lorna to lose, by the death of her uncle before this codicil was signed?"

Aidan's colour rose.

McCarthy seated himself beside Secker. "No doubt Miss Jenkins wanted to divert your suspicions from Lorna. That might explain why your manner towards us was a little, shall we say, hostile?"

Jenny thought about the Jaguar speeding down the lane towards them, forcing their own car back. No, she thought, maybe you're not quite the bad guys we once thought you were. But you could still learn some manners.

"So what are you going to do now?" she asked. She heard an edge of hostility in her own voice. "I suppose, if Lorna is out of the picture, you'll go ahead with your plans to turn this into some sort of executive playground. Hang-gliding and bungee jumping from the cliffs by the waterfall."

"Sadly, no," McCarthy put in. He steepled his fingertips and looked at her over them with his pale blue eyes. "We are only Thaddaeus's executors. And we may not be able to prove his will until we know the result of Lorna's trial. Until then, we shall look after his affairs. It was unlikely we'd have got planning permission anyway, given the fuss there was over just building this delightful house. And now, with Mr Lewis's discovery of a collection of bones…"

"You mean the hare?" Melangell cried. "He didn't find it. Lorna and I did."

"Exactly," Secker smiled at her. "Well done." He turned a more businesslike stare back at Jenny and Aidan. "It's hardly a money-making proposition, I fear. But the man is determined to make something of it. With a newly discovered pagan sacred site, as well as the medieval shrine church…" He shrugged. "Well, you can imagine, anything more commercially viable is going to be on the losing side."

"But there's still the House of the Hare," Jenny said. "More people will want to come to it now, won't they?"

"I rather think we may have the remarkable Mr Coutts to thank for that. He seems determined to get his murder story all over the pages of the tabloids. But the upmarket press will pick up on this hare thing too. Plenty of free publicity." Secker swung round to Aidan. "You're a photographer, too, I gather. I take it you had your camera out when the urn with the hare bones was found. If you have a young woman charged with murder digging it up, think what a photograph like that would be worth."

Aidan stared at him, speechless. Then he managed to choke out the words.

"No! I… did… not… take… photographs! I was looking for my kidnapped daughter, for heaven's sake!"

Mair appeared with another tray of coffee.

"There! So you'll tell Josef he's still got a job, will you? And Euan?"

She winked as she offered the second plate of fudge to Melangell.

Chapter Thirty-six

AIDAN WATCHED JENNY putting clothes in a suitcase. Even in the few days they had been here, he thought the light fuzz of new-grown hair was more visible, sleeker. His breath caught. It made her look just a little less vulnerable than before. But it was an illusion. He must not waste time counting the weeks, the days.

Today was all that mattered. Jenny knew that. The day they might not have had together.

"There's something you'll want to do before we go," he said quietly.

"Yes, but they won't be open yet." She turned and smiled. "Breakfast?"

As they descended the stairs, they met a small plump woman in a flowered nylon overall. She beamed at their look of surprise.

"I'm Mair's mum. Well, somebody's got to do your bedrooms, haven't they?"

In the dining room, Aidan nodded curtly to the two financiers who were already finishing their breakfast.

Afterwards he caught Mr Secker in Sian's office behind the reception counter.

"We prepaid the accommodation, but I've got a bar bill to settle. Who do I pay?"

He wondered if the man might waive the small account, considering the circumstances. But the florid face beamed back at him.

"Me."

He went to fetch the notepad from the bar, in which Sian had recorded their purchases, and produced a credit card machine.

"Thank you," said Aidan, at a loss for the right words. "It's been an interesting stay."

Secker's face darkened, as though he was not sure of Aidan's sincerity. He did not apologize.

With an effort, Aidan made himself smile. "I hope you can keep this place open. In spite of everything, it's a lovely house. This is somewhere people ought to visit."

"We'll try."

Jenny and Melangell were already loading Jenny's suitcase and Melangell's flowered holdall into the boot.

"You should have waited for me," he scolded.

"We took the lift." Jenny smiled at him. "We can manage, can't we, love?"

"Of *course*," Melangell said.

"Do you want to walk round to the church, or stop the car on the way out?"

"It's on our way. We've nothing to come back for." She straightened up and looked at the façade of the House of the Hare. Morning sun was creeping over the hilltops, gilding the floor-to-ceiling windows and lighting the dramatic angles of its slate roof.

"Such a shame," she said. "It's beautiful. But it will still be here after we've gone, for other people to enjoy."

She would not be coming back.

Aidan stopped the car outside the church. He let Jenny walk ahead up the churchyard path. He reached out to restrain Melangell, but she had already darted away to the giant yew tree with the cave-like hollow in its trunk.

He followed Jenny at a discreet distance. The familiar weight of the camera round his neck felt like an old friend rediscovered. But he was in no hurry to use it. He had all the photos he needed of St Melangell's Church.

The interior was not the haven of peace he had anticipated. A small army of helpers was already at work with cloths and buckets and scrubbing brushes. They were busy scouring the smoke-blackened walls and floors of the tower rooms. He recognized Mother Joan and Freda Rawlinson among them and lifted a hand in acknowledgment.

Mother Joan came bustling out of the tower room. She wore a large oatmeal-coloured apron over her clothes. It was splashed with sooty water.

"My dears! I'm so very sorry. This can't have been what you imagined when you planned to come back here."

Jenny held up her hand. "It's all right, really. At least, it is for us."

Mother Joan seemed to have more immediate concerns than a murder and an attempted murder.

"The Priest-Guardian gets back today. I don't know how I'm going to face her. She leaves me in charge for just one week, and look at it!"

"It's not your fault. If anything, it's mine. Caradoc Lewis did it to spite me. Because of my book."

"And because he hates the fact that the Christian story takes precedence here over his own fancies. Oh, I blame myself. I'm a professional counsellor, yet I got on the wrong side of him. I should have handled it better."

"I doubt if you stood a chance," Aidan told her. "He's not a listening man."

The nave was quieter. Jenny went to sit in one of the pews, her head bent in prayer. He joined her in the pew opposite.

When he lifted his head, he was looking straight up at the woodwork of the rood loft separating the nave from the chancel. The carved figures of the hare and the hunters stood out in bold relief.

Melangell was sitting next to him. "Is it the same hare?" she asked in a loud whisper.

"Sort of," he said. "They're hundreds of years apart, the hare you found and St Melangell's. But stories live on. We'll never know what really happened when Prince Brochwel came hunting in this valley. But St Melangell is real. She truly did live here."

"So did my hare," Melangell said, firmly. "I know it did."

Jenny had moved from the pew to walk up the aisle to the chancel. She passed St Melangell's canopied shrine, with its freight of prayer cards, with only a brief downward look. Through the archway behind the altar was the cobbled apse, the Cell-y-bedd, the Room of the Grave. There was just enough space on the bench inside for one person to sit in prayer, opposite the coffin-shaped grave-slab set in the floor.

Aidan drew Melangell aside to look at the row of differently sculptured hares along the north wall of the nave.

Presently, Jenny came walking slowly towards them. He saw the light in her face, the calm joy.

"All right?" he asked.

She nodded and smiled.

Mother Joan met them at the door.

"Deep peace of the running wave to you. Deep peace of the flowing air to you. Deep peace of the quiet earth to you. Deep peace of the shining stars to you. Deep peace of the infinite peace to you. Go with God."

They stepped out into the morning sunshine.

Caradoc Lewis stood between them and the gate.

He was standing with his back to them. Like Melangell,

he had laid his hand on the deeply rutted bark of the ancient yew. He seemed to be saying something to himself, or to some deity.

They walked quietly over the grass, hoping to pass him unobserved.

As they drew level, he swung around. His dark eyes burned in his skull-like face. The greying black hair fell forward over one eyebrow.

"You!" he almost hissed at Jenny.

"I thought you were under arrest for arson," Aidan exclaimed. He drew protectively close to Jenny.

"I was taken in for questioning. Idiots! Of course I did it. The fire, I mean. Not the other. But they've allowed me out on police bail. I'm forbidden to go anywhere near the church."

"And yet you're here," Jenny said.

"Of course I'm here. What do I care about their poxy conditions? Or their church? These are what matter." He caressed the yew lovingly. "It's all coming back. I'll re-erect the standing stone where it always used to be. At the foot of the waterfall. The classic place for a Celtic sacred site. We'll have the urn and the hare bones on display…"

"Did you steal them from the museum?"

Caradoc turned pitying eyes on Aidan. "You don't begin to understand, do you? You think it's all moonshine. The product of my fevered imagination. I got them out to show her what she was looking for. Lorna understood. She knew we couldn't let anything stand in our way."

"Are you saying *that's* why she killed her uncle? Not because he abused her?"

Caradoc's face closed up. "You'll have to wait for the trial. Yes, there were other issues between them. But she found the hare. That's all I care about. Ask *her*."

He swung round on Melangell.

The girl gulped.

Jenny's arm was round her shoulders. "Melangell knows what she and Lorna found. She doesn't know how it got there. Just as I don't know what really happened when Prince Brochwel Ysgithrog went hunting and found the other Melangell. But I know this. I went into the Cell-y-bedd today and knelt beside Melangell's grave. And I felt what the hare must have felt when it hid from the hounds under her skirt. Suddenly, I wasn't afraid."

Caradoc's eyes narrowed. He seemed to be taking in for the first time her recently bald head, her thin face. He swallowed.

Then he broke off a fragment of yew bark and solemnly presented it to her.

"Take this. Let it remind you that we live in the presence of the sacred."

He stepped back to let them pass.

"Well!" Jenny whispered when they were through the gate. "I didn't expect that." She stroked the ancient wood. "It's vandalism. But I shall keep it." She raised her eyes to Aidan's. "Will they really convict Lorna? They haven't much to go on, have they?"

"Your testimony. About Lorna's movements. Sian's admission."

"How long will it take to bring her case to trial? Months? I'm not going to be there to give evidence, am I? Just my statement. And Sian will deny it."

Her eyes were steady. He squeezed her hand.

They turned for a last look at the little church with its squat tower, now streaked with soot. At its screening ring of ancient yews, older than the church itself.

Jenny said quietly, "There are thin places, where heaven and earth are only a gossamer curtain apart. Pennant Melangell will always be like that. No matter what happens to us." She touched Aidan's face. "Thank you for bringing me. In spite of everything."

Aidan could not trust himself to answer.

He lifted his other hand and rumpled Melangell's hair. "I know I promised you those dungeons in Warwick. But I think we've got a more important call to make."

Carefully, he lifted a cardboard box out of the boot. The contents were swathed in bubble wrap. He lifted a flap aside.

"I rang the county archaeologist. We're going to see him this morning. He wants you to tell him exactly where and how you found this."

"My hare?" Melangell's eyes shone.

She looked up at Jenny with a wicked grin. "Do you think I'll get into a book, too?"

Here follows the first chapter from *Death on Lindisfarne*, the sequel to *The Hunted Hare*.

DEATH ON LINDISFARNE

Chapter One

"DADDY, ARE YOU *sure* this is a good idea?" Melangell tilted her pointed face towards her father. Her eight-year-old voice had the patient reproach of one used to dealing with a wayward parent.

Aidan looked ahead at the line of slender poles which led the way across the glistening sands towards the southern tip of Lindisfarne. He glanced to his left. Now the tide was falling there was steady traffic of cars crossing the modern causeway to the island. But even that would be submerged at high water. Lindisfarne – Holy Island – was only intermittently linked to the mainland.

"Of course I am. Walking across the sands is the only proper way to come to Lindisfarne. That's how the pilgrims always came in the past. And the monks who lived here back in the time of St Aidan and Cuthbert. You wouldn't rather drive here in a *car*, would you?"

He was pleased to hear the cheerful confidence in his own voice. He had got his calculations right, hadn't he? He had parked the car for a week on the Northumbrian coast. He had helped Melangell pack a small rucksack with spare clothes. He had shouldered a larger one himself and his all-important camera bag. And he had consulted the tide tables with considerable care.

The sea channel that separated the island from the

coast had been falling for a while, uncovering pink-tinged sand. It was jewelled with shells and pebbles. He must try to resist the temptation to take dozens of photographs of the miraculous and unique patterns the shells and quartz revealed at every step. He needed to time this journey right, so that the channel in the middle would be low enough to cross when they got there, but not leave it so late that the tide turned and swept back in over the sands before they could complete their pilgrim crossing.

He gave a grin of delight and drew a deep breath of anticipation.

"Come on, then. To Holy Island."

The wet sand oozed slightly round his boots and Melangell's trainers, but held firm.

Aidan had abandoned his modern walking pole for a wooden staff. It seemed more appropriate.

"Mummy said the king used to come and talk to St Aidan on Lindisfarne. But he only brought a few men and he never stayed to dinner, because he knew the monks were poor and didn't have much to eat. It's in her book."

Aidan stopped short. He couldn't help himself. The loss was still too new, too raw. He glanced down at his daughter with her mop of light brown curls and her freckled elfin face. He had feared for Melangell. Seven had been terribly young to lose her mother. But she had seemed to accept the bereavement better than he had. She could talk of Jenny easily and fondly, as if her mother were still a real presence, someone she could turn to whenever she wanted.

Perhaps she is, Aidan thought. I ought to believe that, oughtn't I? That Jenny is here, now, watching over us. But the pain was real. They had come to Lindisfarne together, researching the first of Jenny's books about Celtic saints and kings. There was a row of these small books in Melangell's bedroom, her constant companions. All of them were illustrated with Aidan's photographs. The Lindisfarne book had been a special joy for Jenny and Aidan, because the saint who founded the monastery here had shared his own name.

The camera case hung heavy on Aidan's shoulder. He still carried it dutifully with him wherever he went. He still took photographs. If he was lucky, he sold some of them. But the chief purpose of his photography had been taken away from him. Without Jenny's enthusiasm, her pursuit of Celtic history and visions, he no longer knew with any certainty what he was taking photographs for.

Just now, his attention should be concentrated on following the line of poles to mid-channel.

When they came in sight of running water, it was Melangell's turn to stop.

"You told me we could walk across."

The seawater channel was still a few metres wide. The Easter sunlight had drifted behind a bank of high cloud. The sand looked more brown than pink, the rippling water grey and cold.

"Memory's a funny thing. I thought you could. But there has to be somewhere where the water drains away. We can wait and see if it runs dry. But if we want to get to the other side before the tide catches us, it might be better to get our boots off."

He unlaced his own and slung them round his neck. Melangell picked up her trainers and held them in her hand. He took her other hand and they stepped down into the shock of the tide race.

"Ow, it's *cold*!"

"It's the authentic experience, though, isn't it? You have to imagine all the other visitors who came this way. Northumbrians, Scots, Irish, missionaries from Rome. All paddling across this little bit of the North Sea. Like us."

"Did they have nuns on Holy Island?"

"Sadly, no. St Aidan was a great friend of Hilda. She would have loved to go to his school here. But she had to go and set up her own monastery at Whitby. Only hers had men as well as women."

The water swirled almost to his knees. With the coming of spring he had seized the opportunity to put on shorts for walking. Melangell was having to roll her jeans higher.

"OK? Do you want a lift?"

"I can *manage*," she retorted.

A few steps later, they climbed the shelving bank of wet sand on the far side. Lindisfarne looked suddenly much closer. All the same, Aidan turned his eyes seaward. The North Sea was a grey line along the horizon. It was hard to judge distances with no vertical features to mark perspective. How long before the tide turned? Had it done so already? How fast would that line of sea come sweeping in across the sands where they stood?

They would be leaving behind the only refuge on this route. That was little more than a wooden box on stilts.

The wood of the pole beside him was still dark and dank from the previous tide. There were only a few hours a day when it was possible to ford the channel safely and reach the island.

Yet now they had crossed the mid-point, he felt sufficiently confident to unfasten his camera bag and take out his Nikon. His hand hesitated over which lens to use, rejected a wide-angle and settled on the f2.8 telephoto one.

The outskirts of the village on the tip of Lindisfarne sprang into instant life. No longer a smudge of buildings against the grey background. He could see now how the line of poles would lead them safely up the shore.

He moved the camera, trying to find how best to frame the shot that would capture that sense of arrival. The end of pilgrimage. As yet, the ruined abbey and the statue of St

Aidan were still out of sight. But this view was not unlike the one which would have greeted King Oswald, or St Cuthbert, or all the other famous names of the past whose histories had led them to this island.

He steadied the lens, then gave a sudden start. He had not intended to photograph people. This was all about the sense of sacred place. Yet there were two people framed in his shot. A man and a woman, perhaps? Or a girl. She looked quite slight. Even with the lens's magnification, it was not possible to be sure of their faces or ages, or even their gender. The one he thought was a girl wore a red sweater or fleece, the larger figure something brown.

They seemed to be holding each other. A couple of lovers? Or was the man holding on to the girl? As he watched through his viewfinder she broke away from him. Instinctively, Aidan snapped the shutter.

She was not exactly running away from him, now. More floundering, as if through softer sand than the damp ridge he and Melangell stood on.

He lowered the camera, and suddenly the pair were distant specks. The island shore was further away than the zoom lens of his camera had made it seem for those few moments.

He took a few more shots, focusing this time on the composition of poles and shoreline. Then he slung the camera back on his shoulder.

"Come on," he said. "This is not the place to stand about wasting time."

"You're a fine one to talk." It sounded an adult phrase. Had she picked it up from Jenny?

That pain again.

Melangell started forward. Then she paused. "Are those people over there? If they want to walk across to the mainland, they'll have to hurry, won't they?"

He looked round at her in surprise. "You've got sharper eyes than I have. I didn't notice them until I used the zoom lens."

"I can see a little red dot and a darker one."

"I don't expect they're coming across. They've just come down to the beach for a walk. Perhaps they're waiting to see if *we* make it across before the sea gets us."

"It won't, will it?" The upturned pointed face was momentarily anxious.

"No." He put a reassuring hand on her shoulder. "Not if we don't hang about."

They toiled up the gently shelving sands. He took Melangell's hand. When at last they passed the line of sea wrack that marked the high tide point, he lifted her up and swung her round in celebration.

"Told you! We did it. Now, wasn't that much more fun than driving across the causeway?"

She tumbled down into softer sand, and let handfuls of it fall through her fingers. She sat up to see what she had found. A blue-black mussel shell, the white-ridged fan of a cockle, a scrap of amber seaweed. Suddenly she dived to capture something that had fallen into the sand by her leg. She lifted it up triumphantly.

"She must have dropped it. One of those people we saw when we were halfway across."

She held out her hand, palm upward. Nestled in it was a single earring. A little golden beast with a scarlet tongue. Its tail twisted into Celtic knotwork that twined around to form a ring.

"Interesting," said Aidan. "It looks like something from the pages of the Lindisfarne Gospels."

He looked around. He hadn't been watching the shoreline since he took that photograph. The couple he had seen briefly grappling on the beach were nowhere to be seen.